STARTING OVER AT PRIMROSE WOODS

JILL STEEPLES

Boldwood

First published in Great Britain in 2021 by Boldwood Books Ltd.

Copyright © Jill Steeples, 2021

Cover Design by Debbie Clement Design

Cover Photography: Shutterstock

A CIP catalogue record for this book is available from the British Library.

Paperback ISBN 978-1-80280-694-6

Large Print ISBN 978-1-80280-690-8

Hardback ISBN 978-1-80280-689-2

Ebook ISBN 978-1-80280-687-8

Kindle ISBN 978-1-80280-688-5

Audio CD ISBN 978-1-80280-695-3

MP3 CD ISBN 978-1-80280-692-2

Digital audio download ISBN 978-1-80280-686-1

Boldwood Books Ltd
23 Bowerdean Street
London SW6 3TN
www.boldwoodbooks.com

For Stella and Reg, with love xx

1

Abbey Carter pulled the front door shut behind her and took a welcome breath of the fresh spring air. As much as she loved her little cottage in the heart of Wishwell, a pretty little village in the depths of the countryside, with its stone flint houses, a beautiful Norman church and a duck pond with a resident family, today she needed an escape.

Luckily, within ten minutes of walking out of the front gate to her cosy cottage she could be stepping through the kissing gate at Long Acre Lane and into the hundreds of acres of woodland, meadows and heathland that made up Primrose Woods Country Park. There she could lose herself in the landscape, marvelling at the ever-changing scenery around her, giving herself permission to forget any worries or concerns. There were several marked trails to follow, but Abbey preferred to go her own way, off the beaten track, scrambling up muddy banks to see what she might find on the other side, exploring the outer reaches of the park. Today, the wind whistled against her cheeks as she strode out amongst the trees as though she didn't have a care in the world.

It was funny to think she'd only recently discovered the

delights of Primrose Woods. She'd driven past it for many years, every day on her way to work, but it was only lately that she'd experienced first hand what a haven of peace and beauty it was. It had quickly become her happy place. Now it was part of her daily routine, time she carved out for herself when she would head to the park for either a gentle leisurely walk or a more demanding hike, depending on her schedule for that particular day. She tried to persuade Jason of its charms but he always complained that he was too tired to go hiking through the countryside on his weekends off, preferring to spend his spare time playing rugby or watching sport on the TV. Fair enough. He did work hard, she supposed. Just then her phone beeped in her back pocket and she pulled it out to take a look. *Talk of the devil.*

Sorry, babe. Another late one tonight. Have this report to finish. Don't worry about food. I'll grab something on the way home.

She swiped the message away. This was a regular enough occurrence these days; Jason was working all hours, but she couldn't really complain. He was doing it for her, he told her. Striving for a promotion to provide the sort of lifestyle they'd always hankered after – a bigger house with a large garden for the children they would have one day. Once they were married things would need to change. Work was important, but it wasn't the be-all and end-all. They barely saw each other these days so they would definitely need to find more time for their relationship if their wedding day was to herald a new beginning.

Taking a deep breath, she momentarily closed her eyes, bringing herself back to the present and banishing the negative thoughts. She wouldn't dwell on it. Being outside, next to nature, was the cure-all she needed right now. A little later, after walking several miles and feeling suitably invigorated and re-energised from her exertions, she headed home. Her heart lifted, as it always did, when her little house with its white panelled wooden door and oak porch came into view. The camellia, a gift from her dad a couple of years ago, had sprung into full bloom for the first time this year, its glossy leaves and deep pink, showy flowers heralding the arrival of spring. She put her key in the lock with a smile. The cottage was her sanctuary even if she had a whole host of jobs waiting for her behind the idyllic facade.

Indoors, she turned off the slow cooker. She would freeze the chilli con carne later. It would keep for some other time and she would make do with a sandwich tonight, which was becoming something of a habit these days. Taking a moment at the table, she opened up her notebook, running a pencil down her to-do list, the top item, *Sort dress*, highlighted with asterisks and underlined in thick red pen, filling her with dread.

Honestly, what had possessed her? Perhaps if she took another look, it might not be as bad as she remembered. Ha! Who was she kidding? She jumped up and dashed upstairs into her bedroom, her heart in her mouth. She whisked out the bridal gown from her wardrobe, unzipping the fabric protector, her fingers reaching out and caressing the ivory lace fabric. Carefully, she scooped up the folds of the dress into her arms and held it up against her body in front of the mirror. *Damn.* She swallowed hard, that same unnerving sensation of nausea returning as her gaze swept over her reflection.

When she had first set eyes on the dress she'd fallen in love with it. It was the one that jumped off the rails and screamed *pick me* at her. There were other more sophisticated, elegant dresses on the rails, but she reckoned you only got married once – if you were lucky – so why not go the whole hog and opt for the fairy princess look that she'd dreamt of when she was a little girl.

The gown was a concoction of organza and tulle decorated

with appliqué daisies, sequins and beading, with a scalloped lace sweetheart neckline. She gulped. More Sugar Plum Fairy than anything else, now she came to think of it. She hoped it was pre-wedding nerves. The dress no longer fitted as well as it had when she first tried it on. Then she'd been some ten pounds heavier and her soft curves had filled out the flowing design, accentuating her fulsome cleavage. She thought Jason might appreciate the effect and she'd spent far too long imagining his face lighting up when he saw her in it for the first time as he waited at the end of the aisle.

She undid the mother-of-pearl buttons at the back of the dress and stepped into the gown, pulling it up over her body and shoulders. She sighed heavily. If anything, the dress was even more ill-fitting now. It fell off her shoulders and swamped her lithe figure. She grabbed a handful of fabric and pulled it tight around the back. It didn't really help because it wasn't only the bad fit making her wonder if she'd made a very bad decision. What on earth had possessed her to choose this floating meringue with all its flounces, frills and frou-frou-ness? She would need to get it altered or find another dress entirely, but that was unlikely when her wedding fund was seriously depleted. She shrugged off the gown and hastily zipped it up in its cover, hiding it away in the wardrobe again.

No wonder she'd lost so much weight. Organising a wedding had to be one of the most stressful experiences she'd ever had. It was at times like these when she missed her mum's caring, sensible presence in her life. If she were still here, her mum would be settling Abbey down, reassuring her that everything would turn out all right and helping her with the practical jobs that needed doing. Her dad was lovely and supportive in his own way, but a girl really needed her mum at her side when she was planning her wedding, and on pretty much every other occasion too, Abbey realised, quickly brushing the thought aside, determined not to wobble. One thing was for sure, her mum would certainly have put her straight regarding that dress, telling her just how ridiculous it was and steering her towards something eminently more suitable. Whether or not she would have taken her mum's advice was another matter, but it would have been lovely to have the opportunity to ignore her mum's words.

She'd reached the stage where she would be glad when the wedding was over. She was looking forward to finally being Jason's wife, of course, but she was eager for all the fuss to subside and to simply get on with living their lives together and starting a family.

It was definitely last-minute nerves. Perfectly natural for a bride-to-be. Just because she hated her dress didn't mean it was a bad omen. Her marriage to Jason would herald a new chapter in her life, absolutely, and she couldn't wait for the big day to arrive.

2

Lizzie Baker ran a cloth over the last of the tables and was just upturning the remaining chairs, always one of her final jobs of the day in the Treetops Cafe, when she spotted Sam pull up outside in his jeep. He leapt out and his distinctive figure in the uniform of bottle-green cargos and sweatshirt came bowling along the path, a wide smile on his face.

'Are you all done, Lizzie?' He stood in the doorway, his hands held on his hips as though ready for action, which seemed to be his default mode. 'Fancy a lift home?'

'No, it's fine.' She batted away his offer with the cloth in her hand. 'There's no need for you to do that. I can take the bus.'

'It's no trouble. I'm going your way. Grab your stuff and I'll see you outside.'

She smiled to herself. This was a small ritual they went through at least a couple of times each week. She was always grateful, but never wanted to take his kind-heartedness for granted.

'I've got something for you,' she said, as she climbed into the cab of the jeep. She handed over the brown paper bag she'd picked up from the chiller cabinet and Sam peered inside, his eyes lighting up at the sight of the sticky bun inside. His hand reached for its plump, gooey deliciousness and he took a big bite, his lips smacking as it hit the right spot.

'You spoil me, do you know that?' he said, after quickly demolishing the bun.

'Well, you're worth it.' She laughed.

He grinned, brushing his hands together to clear the crumbs, before starting up the engine and beginning the drive along the windy, narrow road back towards the main entrance of the country park.

Lizzie's gaze drifted out of the window as they passed through the row of magnificent monkey puzzle trees, her head craning to see the tops of the exotic, spiky structures. There were definitely worse places to spend your days. Having worked at the Treetops Cafe in Primrose Woods for over ten years now, she was as familiar with the landscape as if it was her own back garden, but still it never ceased to amaze her with its wild, natural beauty. She loved to witness the arrival and departure of the seasons, the sometimes subtle, sometimes sweeping changes in the landscape, which she found both invigorating and reassuring. She'd made so many good friends at the park too, especially in the rangers who would pop in on their breaks for a natter and a cuppa. She would never admit to anyone to having favourites, but Sam Finnegan was definitely hers.

'How was your day, Lizzie?' he asked as the jeep trundled slowly along the track.

'Good.' To be fair, most of her days were enjoyable at work. She loved her job running the cafe, preparing the food orders and dealing with the customers. It got her out of the house and gave her the opportunity to meet a wide range of different people. Most of the visitors were day trippers, dog walkers or rambler groups who met up at the cafe before embarking on their treks. She had her regulars too. Those who came in a couple of times each week, meeting up with their friends, or coming specifically for lunch. Their selection of quiches served with a choice of specialist salads was renowned and drew people in from all around the local area. One thing was for certain, no two days were the same at Treetops.

'We had a mother and toddler group in this morning. You should have seen the little ones in their wellies, clutching leaves and trailing sticks behind them. It really made me smile. Listening to the mums swapping stories about their kids took me back to when Katy was small. Honestly, it doesn't seem that long ago.'

'Time's a funny thing, isn't it?' As he pulled up at the exit to Primrose Woods, he leant forward in his seat, checking for traffic each way before pulling out onto the main road.

'I should say so,' she said wistfully.

It was five years since her husband, David, had died suddenly. In some ways it seemed like only the other day, the shock of his sudden passing still retaining the power to poleaxe her with pain when she least expected it. At other times it felt like a lifetime ago when she tried to conjure up the sound of his voice or his laughter ringing out around the house.

'Anyway,' she breezed, eager to change the subject, 'tell me how it's going with that new young lady of yours?'

Sam turned to look at her, his brow furrowed and his mouth curling with a touch of mischievousness, being deliberately obtuse.

'You mean, the... Lady?' He gestured with his head behind him where his faithful companion, Lady, a liver and white springer spaniel, had her snout stuck out of the back window, her ears flapping in the breeze, her nose twitching in the air.

'No, I don't, as you well know. I'm talking about that date you went on with... what was her name, Stephanie?'

'Hmmm, yes. I've seen her a couple of times now. She's...' He paused, running a hand through his chestnut, floppy hair, considering how best to describe her. '... very pleasant.'

'Really?' Lizzie shook her head indulgently. 'Is that the best you can come up with? I'm sure she'd be delighted to hear herself described that way.'

'Don't get me wrong. She's a lovely girl, but she's not right for me. She's a bit full-on, you know, high maintenance and, to be honest, a bit... scary too.'

'Scary?' Lizzie did a double-take at Sam, unable to hide her disbelief. 'How come?'

From what Sam had told her, Stephanie sounded ideally suited to him. She was a primary school teacher who worked in one of the nearby villages and who loved the great outdoors just as much as Sam did. What could possibly be scary about that?

'She's a woman on a mission to find a husband and have babies.' Sam grimaced exaggeratedly, making Lizzie laugh. 'She's already chosen their names. And I think I might be in her line of sight as daddy material!'

'And would that be such a bad thing?'

'Yes, Lizzie, it would.' Sam's words were loaded with serious intent. 'I mean, I'm not opposed to the idea in principle, sometime in the future, but only when I meet someone that I can imagine spending the rest of my life with. Sadly, Stephanie isn't that person. You've reminded me, actually. We're supposed to be meeting again this weekend. I will need to cancel that. I don't want to give her any false hope.'

'Aw, she'll be ever so disappointed,' said Lizzie, feeling a pang of sympathy for Stephanie. 'You never know, you might grow to like her as you get to know her a bit better.'

Sam shook his head, giving Lizzie a fierce look. 'You can't conjure up that special chemistry if it isn't there in the first place.'

Sam Finnegan was a catch in anyone's book and it was easy to understand why Stephanie might be so enamoured, but dating was way down on Sam's list of priorities. It wasn't that he didn't have girlfriends. He'd seen several woman in the time Lizzie had known him, but none of them lasted longer than a few months and he was always the one to bring those relationships to an end. Was he looking for someone or something that didn't even exist? With his unwillingness to commit to a long-term partnership, Lizzie had to wonder if he might ever find that special someone he spoke of, the one to spend the rest of his life with, or if it was something he even really wanted in his life, after all.

Lizzie looked across at Sam, shaking her head ruefully.

'Don't look at me like that!' scolded Sam. 'She'll get over it. And much better to do it sooner rather than later. Like ripping off a plaster. That way there can be no misunderstandings. Besides, I'm perfectly content with the women I have in my life at the moment.' He grinned, looking from Lizzie to Lady, who rewarded Sam with a damp nose in the crook of his neck. 'What more could I want?'

It was such a shame, thought Lizzie, but she was mindful that it really wasn't her place to say anything.

'Thanks for the lift,' she said brightly as they pulled up outside her house. She climbed out of the jeep and Lady took the opportunity to quickly jump into the now vacant front seat, looking very pleased with herself.

'No problem. See you tomorrow.' Sam waved, watching as she made her way up the front path. He always waited until she was safely inside the front door. Such a gentleman. She waved back, closing the door behind her, her heart sinking as she was greeted by the crushing loneliness she always felt within the walls of her own home. She took a deep breath, quickly turning the lights and the radio on, filling the cool silence with voices. Never mind, in less than twenty-four hours she'd be back at the Treetops Cafe, ready for her next shift. With all her colleagues, friends and customers there, she almost considered it her second home these days.

3

As soon as Abbey finished her shift at the care home, she rushed back to the cottage, changed into her jeans and sweatshirt, and headed straight outside again, embracing the sensation of the cool air upon her skin. In the ten minutes it took to walk along the country paths to Primrose Woods, she was able to process everything that had happened that day at work and clear her head. She loved her job managing the office at Rushgrove Lodge for the Elderly, but it could be intense and emotionally demanding making sure the residents' needs were met, organising their social calendar and arranging the carers' shifts and workloads.

At home a different sort of stress awaited her. The dining table was covered with draft seating plans, sample table favours and a to-do list that stared at her reproachfully. She groaned inwardly, ignoring the mischievous thought that had popped into her head telling her to swipe the whole lot onto the floor with a flourish. No, she would deal with it all later, but for now she needed her fix of the great outdoors.

When she reached the park she took the sandy path to Kings

Wood, which was an ancient woodland, according to the information board she stopped to read, with a variety of species including ash, birch and sessile oak. It was the sight of the pretty, creamy yellow primroses growing in clusters around the woods that always brought a smile to her face, though.

Striding out among the towering trees, she felt like a tiny specimen, a small part of something much, much bigger. Occasionally she would pass a dog walker and exchange a friendly greeting, but most of the time she was alone in the wilderness. Not that she was bothered by that. She felt totally safe and protected in the environment and, being in the depths of the countryside, she could leave all the niggles and hassles of her daily life behind. All she concentrated on was how she felt and how her body reacted to the elements. The wind picked up and buffeted her cheeks, her hair flapped around her face. The only sounds were those of bushes and shrubs rustling around her, the chattering of birds and squirrels hidden in the greenery, and her boots pounding against the ground.

She marched on, at a greater pace now, her breath audible too. On a normal day, she would cover between three and five miles. Some days it could be double that. No wonder the wedding dress swamped her now. She'd become so much fitter and leaner in recent weeks through all this physical activity. But much more important than that was the effect it had on her general well-being. She'd discovered a new-found enthusiasm for life, a positivity that had been missing in recent months, and she felt enlivened and excited for her future.

She took a detour and headed for the centre of the park where the Treetops Cafe and the visitors' centre were located. It was where everyone congregated as it was close to the car parks and the picnic area. Although it was the busiest area of the park, you were still able to find a quiet spot on one of the oak benches or the many overturned tree trunks used for seating. On a previous visit, Abbey had found a bench that gave a panoramic view of the whole area and she'd spent a pleasant hour or so there, just watching the world go by. She loved a bit of people-watching and was relieved today to see that the same bench was empty. A group of young men were having a game of frisbee in the distance and some young mums were meeting their friends, pushing toddlers in their buggies at a snail's pace, chatting animatedly as though they had all the time in the world.

A couple in their sixties walked past, hand in hand, and Abbey liked to imagine what their lives might be like at home. Had they been happily married for years and were now enjoying a quiet retirement together, or had they only recently found each other, experiencing all the joys of a second-time-around love? Either way, they looked a picture of happiness. Abbey tried to imagine herself and Jason in thirty years' time and how their lives might have panned out. Would they still be walking through a park holding hands? Not that they shared those kind of moments now, she realised with a pang. They were too wrapped up in their own busy lives for those kind of spontaneous moments. These days she couldn't see beyond their wedding, when she hoped everything would fall miraculously into place. She sighed, pushing the thoughts creeping into her head about ill-fitting dresses and table plans to one side, and brought her focus back to the present. The sun was trying its best to break through the clouds and she closed her eyes, holding her face up to the sky, attempting to catch its rays. When she opened them again, her gaze fell upon a couple chatting outside the Treetops Cafe. She shuffled to one side of the bench to get a better view. She recognised the man as someone she'd seen before around the park. In his early thirties, he was tall and broad-shouldered with thick chestnut-brown hair and a friendly expression. He cut a striking figure in the uniform of the park rangers, bottle green cargo trousers and sweat top, with a walkie talkie slung into his belt. He was good-looking, she immediately decided, her gaze lingering on his physique for far longer than was strictly necessary, but there was something entirely compelling about his self-assured and imposing presence. Abbey switched her attention to the woman who was of a similar age, slim and attractive, with blonde hair tied up in a neat bun, but she couldn't help thinking the woman looked out of place in the rural landscape in her pencil skirt, high-heeled court shoes and smart rain mac. Not the sort of get-up for walking in this kind of terrain. Their interaction seemed intense, the woman dominating the conversation and gesturing animatedly while the man seemed to be placating her, nodding his responses and shifting his body weight backwards, subtly putting some distance between them. Perhaps she was a customer complaining about poor service or she might even be his boss, giving him a dressing-down over a job poorly done. Abbey wished she was a little closer so that she could tune in to their conversation, but all she had to go on was their body language. The man definitely seemed uncomfortable, looking over his shoulder and surreptitiously glancing at his watch, as though he couldn't wait to get away.

On one of the occasions when he looked up and around him, as though searching for a means of escape, his gaze fell on Abbey and stopped there for an excruciating moment too long. She quickly looked away, embarrassed to be caught staring at them, fishing inside her jacket pocket to find her phone, pulling it out and fixing her attention on the screen. When she dared to look up again – she was invested now and couldn't stop herself from taking another peek – the woman leant across and kissed the man on the lips. A kiss that couldn't be misconstrued as anything other than a display of deep affection between a man and a woman. It solved the mystery. A girlfriend visiting her boyfriend at work, turning up unexpectedly, catching him unawares. He was embarrassed, that was it, and obviously relieved when their meeting was over and he could get back to doing his job. No doubt having made promises that he would give her all the attention she deserved, later, after work. *Relatable.* Abbey watched him hold his hand up as a farewell to his girlfriend and then he turned and marched off, without so much as a backwards glance.

It took only the briefest moment for Abbey to realise that the man was actually marching straight towards her, a look of determination on his face. She gulped, fearing that she hadn't been quite as discreet as she'd intended. She'd obviously been gawping at the man and his girlfriend the entire time they were talking. He must have known that she couldn't have heard a word of what they were saying, but now he was marching over demanding to know what she thought she was doing and to mind her own business in the future. *Oh dear God!* She crouched over her phone, hoping she might be able to blend into the background.

'Lady!'

'Yes? Sorry?' She glanced up guiltily, feeling a heat throbbing in her cheeks.

'Hi!' The man looked directly into her eyes, the slightest of smiles hovering at the corner of his mouth. 'Lady... my dog?' he ventured, softening his tone. 'She's supposed to be well-trained, but honestly, once she gets the whiff of a scent there's no stopping her. Would you come here?' He bent down on his haunches and addressed the dog who was burrowing beneath the bench in search of goodness knows what. He pulled a leash from his pocket and quickly secured the dog, pulling her away from the pile of whatever delightful deliciousness she'd discovered.

'Oh, she's gorgeous.' Abbey laughed, hiding her relief and embarrassment.

'Don't let those deep brown, soulful eyes inveigle you. She can be a menace.' He chuckled, dropping a hand down to ruffle the dog's chin. 'Do you mind?' The man gestured to the empty space beside her on the bench.

'Sure.' She shuffled up a bit, making some room. The dog sat down obediently in front of them, surveying the activity around her, indulging in her own bit of people and, perhaps more pertinently, squirrel watching.

'This is such a beautiful spot, isn't it?' she said, grateful that she had someone to share the moment with, although more grateful that the man was now sitting beside her, so that she didn't have to look him directly in what, she'd quickly discovered, were very magnetic eyes.

'Ah, it's the best. Is it your first time visiting the park?'

'No, I try to get here most days. I only live ten minutes away so all of this is literally on my doorstep, although I've only recently discovered its vast beauty. I'm definitely making up for lost time.'

'That's good to hear. I count myself very lucky to work in such a beautiful environment.'

The lapel badge on the man's sweatshirt told Abbey that his name was Sam Finnegan. Up close, he was as attractive, probably more so than she'd imagined at a distance. From her vantage point, she noticed his strongly defined jawline covered with a dark shadow of stubble, golden tanned skin, no doubt from all the time he spent outdoors, and what was that he'd been saying about deep brown eyes? She wriggled away slightly, unsure why his innate masculine presence beside her felt so imposing and potent.

She gave a passing thought to his partner, wondering what their relationship was like. She was doing a lot of wondering about other people's relationships at the moment. Her gaze drifted to Sam's left hand. There was no ring in place, but that didn't mean anything. A lot of men, especially those practical outdoorsy types who used their hands in their line of work, didn't like to wear jewellery. Perhaps the pair of them were planning on getting married soon as well. She could just imagine how amazing those wedding photos might be. Was that why Sam's girlfriend had been giving him such a hard time, because she'd been left to sort out all the arrangements and was trying to pin down Sam on some very important issue? *Very relatable.*

She smiled to herself, realising she was giving far too much thought to Sam and what he might get up to away from the country park.

'What a great job you must have.'

'There's nothing in this world I'd rather do, that's for sure. And I have a great working companion.' He indicated to Lady, who was looking up at him eagerly. 'And of course I get to meet a whole range of interesting people, which is great.' Did she imagine his gaze flittering over her features as though talking specifically about her? Yes, of course she did. Sam was just doing his job by being friendly, approachable and accommodating. He wasn't singling her out for special attention. The romance of her upcoming wedding was clearly rubbing off on her in all sorts of odd ways. A beep came from Sam's phone.

'Ah, I'm afraid duty calls, Lady.' Abbey had to remind herself again that he was talking to the dog and not to her. 'We're needed over by the boathouse, although I think both of us could sit here all day if we had the choice. Anyway, nice meeting you. I'm Sam, by the way.' He stood up, smiling down at her.

'Yes, it's been lovely meeting you... Sam, and Lady too.'

'Well, we might see you again...?' He held open the unasked question, tilting his head to one side before she realised.

'Oh, Abbey. My name's Abbey.'

'Abbey.' He smiled as he said her name slowly, as though trying it out for size, the sound of her name on his lips sending a delightful ripple of goosebumps along her arms. He strode off, Lady following obediently behind, before stopping abruptly. 'Goodbye, Abbey,' he called, turning to look at her again, as though remembering something important he ought to tell her. Instead, he simply smiled and said, 'Yes, well, hopefully we will see you again sometime.'

4

Rhianna West slowed the car down as she approached the main entrance to Primrose Woods Country Park, indicated and turned off, following the windy road that led to the car park. At this time of evening, the last of the visitors were leaving for home, which was probably why Jay had suggested meeting here in the first place. It was quiet, secluded and the tall redwood trees lent a protective romantic atmosphere. It had become their special spot, and at the beginning Rhianna had felt a delicious buzz of anticipation arriving at the park knowing she would be spending precious time with Jay. Now, her emotions were all over the place. Her nerves were on edge and the more her thoughts whirled around her head, the more upset and angry she felt. Tonight she was determined to get some answers from Jay. She'd given him enough time already.

The trouble was, as soon as she spotted his car waiting for her, her body went into overdrive, those feelings of hope, excitement and, yes, lust too, running riot around her system. Her heartbeat picked up apace and a heat prickled beneath her skin. *Get a grip*, she told herself. Turning off the ignition, she stepped outside the car, took a deep breath of the cool evening air and walked round to the passenger door of Jay's car. He was watching her the whole time, she knew, his gaze appreciative and longing.

'Hello, gorgeous,' he said as she slipped into the seat next to him, deliberately turning her body towards the door, keeping some distance from him. Not that it did her any good. Immediately he leant over and the scent of his familiar citrus aftershave taunted her nostrils as he kissed her enthusiastically on the lips, his touch sending shots of desire to every part of her body. He came up for breath.

'God, Rhi, I can't tell you how much I've been dreaming of doing that all day. Seeing you walking along the corridor at work does nothing for my blood pressure. Honestly, I need a cold shower every time I look at you.'

A heat filled her veins, her body reacting involuntarily. She couldn't help herself. She liked the way Jay made her feel, the power she held over him. His hand reached for her bare skin, untucking her blouse from her skirt, causing her to gasp. It felt so good, but she knew there was only one place this was going to end. Where it always ended. And then how would she feel? Frustrated and powerless, back to square one. Mustering all the willpower she possessed, she extracted herself from his embrace.

'No, Jay, stop it! We need to talk.'

'Oh sweetheart, do we have to? I can think of much better ways of spending our time.' He ran a finger down her cheek, looking intently into her eyes. There was a seductive smile on his face and Rhianna knew how easy it would be to succumb to his charms, like she had on so many other occasions before, but not this time.

'Yes, we do. This is important.' She did up the buttons on her blouse and got her breathing under control, sitting up primly in her seat. 'I'm fed up with all of this, Jay. Meeting in car parks, not being able to come clean about our relationship and never having any proper time together. It makes me feel...' She searched for the right word. '... cheap. All of this, it's very tacky, isn't it?'

'No, Christ no. I don't see it like that at all. I'm sorry if you feel that way, babe. I've told you, this won't be forever, it's just the way it has to be at the moment. You know the situation at work. If the top management find out we're seeing each other then we'll both be hauled in and I really don't want that to happen. We'll probably get official warnings, and while I'm at this stage in my career where that would be a minor embarrassment, for you it could be a whole lot worse. I'm not kidding. They'd probably move you to a different office, sideline you into some lowly administration role and generally make life very difficult for you. Constructive dismissal. I've seen it before, Rhi. I'm just trying to protect you, that's all.'

'Well, it stinks. And it makes me so unhappy, Jay. I'm not sure how much longer I can carry on like this.' She bit on her lip, emotion welling up inside. 'Perhaps I need to start looking for another job?'

'What? Don't do that.' He sighed. 'Honestly, for me, it's only the thought that I might catch a glimpse of you at work that keeps me going through some days. You're the light in my life, do you know that?' Now it was her turn to sigh; she was really not in the mood for his smooth talking. He reached over, his hand finding the top of her thigh, his thumb rubbing up and down her stockinged legs.

'Stop it,' she scolded him, crossing her legs decisively. 'It wouldn't be so bad if we got to see each other outside of work, if we could do things like a proper couple, but we don't. All we do is meet in the car and have sex. I'm beginning to feel like you're using me.' She wasn't sure where her burst of bravery came from, but she could tell by Jay's expression that it took him by surprise too. He took hold of her hand.

'How can you say that? Do you have any idea how much you mean to me? I adore you, Rhi. I want us to be together, but you know my situation. I was with my ex for over ten years; it takes time to get out of something like that. We're nearly there with sorting out the house and all the finances, but I don't want any last-minute hitches. If she discovers I'm seeing someone new she could make life very difficult for me, and you. I don't want that. I want to get everything sorted as quickly as possible so that you and I can move forward together. I promise you, it won't be like this forever.'

'But how long am I expected to wait, Jay? Another week, another month, three months?'

Jay let out a big breath, his exasperation filling every nook of the car.

'I can't put a date on it, Rhi. I thought you'd understand. I'm doing this for you. For us. My ex doesn't need to know about us, not yet anyway. I've already hurt her enough. I don't want to add to her pain. Can't you see that? I just want to draw a line beneath it and move on. With you.'

Rhianna bit on her lip. Was she being unreasonable? Didn't it show what a caring and considerate person he was to not want to hurt his ex any more than absolutely necessary? Jay continually told her that all he wanted to do was protect her, to shield her from all the aggravation he was going through at home and at work, so that when they could finally be together everything would be just right.

'We've never even been on a real date,' she said, sounding sulky even to her own ears.

'I know that and it makes me feel so bad, but I will make it up to you, I promise. There'll be plenty of dates and holidays and special times in the future. It's all I'm working towards.'

Jay slung an arm around her shoulder and pulled her into his embrace, her head falling onto his chest. She loved his strong masculinity, the sense of safety she felt in his arms. She wrapped her arms around his waist, breathing in his scent. They both knew they had something special together, something worth waiting for. All the hardships would be worth it in the end. Wouldn't they? Rhi sighed, her gaze drifting out of the car window into the darkness of the woods. How could she tell? And how long exactly was she prepared to wait? Her eyes fluttered closed for the briefest moment until they pinged open again and she fumbled against Jay's chest to extract herself from his embrace. She had to remain strong.

'Look, Jay, I think it might be for the best if we take a break from each other.'

'What?' He pulled away, checking her expression, his own masked with confusion. 'You want us to split up?'

'Not split up, just have some time out. Until you've got everything sorted. You need the space to do that.' Instead of whinging and whining at Jay, she needed to be less demanding and more supportive, give him the time and space he needed to sort out his problems. If their relationship was strong enough then it would withstand a short break from each other and everything would come right in the end. 'I'm sorry if I've been putting pressure on you. I haven't meant to; it's just incredibly frustrating being on the sidelines, not having any control over our future. I'm sorry for what you're going through at home, but I have to consider what's best for me too.'

She could hear her mum's cautionary words ringing in her ear. It was the reason she couldn't take Jay home at the moment. Her mum would only voice all those doubts and questions that had been plaguing Rhianna ever since she'd started seeing him.

'No, you're right. You deserve better.' He tapped his fingers on the steering wheel, his mind obviously working overtime. 'Look, I don't want to lose you, Rhi. I've got an idea. Why don't we go away for the weekend? We could book into a small hotel and escape all of the hassle around here. It would be lovely, just the two of us.'

'What?' Rhianna could hardly believe her ears. She'd expected to hear more excuses and apologies. Was this just a false promise, though? 'Do you mean it? When?' Sometime way in the future, she half suspected.

'This weekend. Let's do it this weekend.'

'Really?' So much for insisting that they have a break, but this was everything she'd been waiting for. There was no way she could turn down the opportunity. 'Oh Jay, it would be wonderful.' She hugged him tightly, smiling to herself at this unexpected turn of events. Good job she'd listened to her mum's advice about not taking any rubbish from a man and for sticking up for herself. Not an ultimatum exactly. More like a little nudge in the right direction and clearly it had worked. If she needed any proof Jay was absolutely committed to their relationship, then was there any better evidence than this?

5

Bill Carter took a breather, resting his hands on his thighs, surveying the countryside around him. It was a beautiful sunny spring morning, even if there was a sharp nip to the air. They'd been out since early morning, walking around the park, through the woods, over the heath and finally around the lake, stopping to sit on a wooden bench for a while, watching the antics of the ducks, coots and swans. At times they chatted, but they were equally content to soak up the atmosphere in companionable silence, allowing the peaceful ambience to wash over them.

'Are you ready for some lunch?' Abbey asked her dad, punctuating one of those peaceful moments. She checked her watch and realised they'd walked over five miles that morning.

'You bet. All that exercise has whetted my appetite.' He stood up, smiling, his cheeks displaying a nice rosy glow after their exertions, and held out his arm for Abbey. She joined him, slipping her arm through his, relishing this opportunity to spend some special time with her dad. Whenever they did, they both wondered why they didn't do it much more often.

In the cafe, they found a window seat that offered wonderful views across the park. They were surrounded by tall redwood trees with rolling green fields beyond disappearing off into the distance. Bill could have sat there all day admiring the view, but Abbey prompted him into making a decision. He slipped on his glasses and examined the menu, concentrating for a moment on the job in hand, before opting for a ploughman's lunch while Abbey chose the goat's cheese and red pepper quiche with a mountain of salad from the specials board.

'So, I know we've managed to avoid the subject so far this morning, but dare I ask how the plans for the big day are coming together?'

'We're getting there,' Abbey said, with a wry smile. Last time she'd spoken to her dad, she'd had a good old rant down the phone about the wedding preparations: the invited guests who hadn't responded, the photographer who had only just realised that he was double-booked for that day and the wedding dress that she'd loved at first sight and now irrationally disliked with every inch of her being. 'Had I known how much stress it would cause, I would have suggested doing it at the registry office with just a handful of us there.'

'Well, you do know it isn't too late to change your mind?'

'Dad!' The young couple on the next table turned to look, interrupted by Abbey's noisy exclamation. She lowered her voice, leaning forward across the table. 'Why would you say that? Do you think I shouldn't marry Jason, is that it?'

'I'm saying nothing of the sort, but it's my duty as father of the bride to ask that question if you're expressing even the smallest of doubts.'

Abbey sank back down in her seat, suddenly weary.

'Well, not doubts as such. Not really.' She paused to consider that for a moment before continuing. 'It's just that everything's been getting on top of me. I haven't seen much of Jason either so that's not helping. We were meant to be spending this weekend sorting out the seating plan and doing some shopping for presents, but, of course, that went out of the window with this work thing he's got going on.'

'Yes, what's that all about? Where was it you said that he's gone?'

'It's one of those team-building weekends in the depths of the countryside somewhere. He's been on them before. They take the whole sales department and do all these sorts of games and exercises. It encourages them to push their boundaries and strengthen their relationships with colleagues.' She made quote marks in the air with her fingers. 'Team building! To me, it sounds like hell, but you know Jason, he loves all that stuff. Anyway, he's assured me that things should settle down soon, so hopefully I'll get to spend more time with him when we're finally married. Honestly, I've almost forgotten what he looks like.'

Bill chuckled.

'Are you all done here?' A woman hovered at their table, collecting up their empty plates. Abbey had seen her before in the cafe. Her ash-blonde curls, accented with dashes of silver at her hairline, were swept up in a bun and her face was expressive and open. She seemed to run the place and always had a friendly smile and a cheery word for her customers.

'That was absolutely splendid, thank you,' said Bill.

'Can I tempt you with one of our puddings? They're all listed on the chalkboard over there. I can recommend the sticky toffee pudding with custard.'

'My goodness, I like the sound of that, but I have my figure to think of.' He tapped his stomach with the flat of his hand. 'I've got to fit into my wedding suit in less than six weeks so I'd better give it a miss.'

'Really?' The woman's face lit up. 'You're getting married?

Congratulations!'

'Not me, but I shall be walking my lovely daughter here down the aisle.' Abbey saw her dad visibly puff with pride and she felt a swell of emotion inside. What would the pair of them be like on the big day? In floods of tears before they'd even stepped inside the church, no doubt. She would have to make sure they both had a couple of handkerchiefs at the ready.

'How lovely. Well, if you're half as happy as I was in my marriage, then you'll have a very joyful future ahead of you.'

Bill looked up at the woman, as though recognising a kindred spirit. They were of a similar age, he suspected, and there was something about her friendly and bubbly personality that he immediately warmed to.

'I'd agree with that. Finding that special person and spending your life with them, well, there can be no better achievement.'

Abbey forced a smile, appreciating the sentiment, but struggling to muster up the same sense of enthusiasm. *Life goals.* Something for her and Jason to aspire to. She just hoped everything would fall into place once they exchanged their vows.

'Well, my wedding dress is looking a bit big on me, so I can definitely afford to have some of that sticky toffee pudding. Thank you, it sounds lovely.'

Lizzie – the woman had volunteered her name when she delivered the dessert – was right about something: the pudding was delicious, although Abbey had been unable to finish it off, despite her best efforts. Her dad came to the rescue and helped her out, leaving the bowl empty and both their stomachs achingly full.

'Well, if I don't see you before, best of luck for the wedding,' Lizzie called as Abbey and her dad made their way to the exit of the cafe. Bill gave a cheery wave, thinking he would be back soon to try something else from the impressive menu of homemade food.

Barely able to move after their delicious lunch, they took a leisurely mooch around the visitors' centre, reading about the local habitat and admiring the drawings of the visiting schoolchildren, before heading outside and towards the track that led home.

'Abbey!'

She spun round at the sound of her name to see the wife of one of Jason's colleagues grinning at her, with her two small children in tow.

'Hi, Jessica.'

'Not long to go now to the big day. You must be very excited. Must say, Tim and I are really looking forward to it. We don't get out much these days!'

Abbey laughed. 'Yes, we are too. We're just hoping the weather will be as good as it is today. Aren't we lucky?' She held up her palms to the now warm afternoon sunshine. 'I bet the boys are in their element at the moment, doing all their action man stuff.'

Jessica's expression clouded and her brow furrowed. 'Er... the football, you mean? That's where Tim is now. Well, every Saturday afternoon, come to that. I'm a proper football widow.' She laughed. 'I didn't realise Jason was into the game too.'

'No, no he's not. I was talking about... He's away on a sales team building weekend and I thought...'

There were all sorts of thoughts rushing through Abbey's head. She was certain Jason had told her the whole department was going. She racked her brains trying to recall the conversation, but it was all a bit hazy now. She clearly hadn't been listening properly. There was something about it being a last minute thing, that much she remembered, but she'd zoned out after that, fighting her feelings of irritation over their ruined plans for the weekend. Or maybe – oh God, how embarrassing – Tim hadn't been invited along for some reason. And now she'd dropped Jason right in it.

'Look at your face. Don't worry. Perhaps it was just a couple of them that went, not the whole team. Not sure I'd invite Tim along either if it was down to me!' She chuckled. 'Or maybe, you never know, it might be an elaborate ruse?' Jessica's perfectly manicured eyebrows lifted high into her forehead.

'What?' Abbey checked herself, aware that she'd snapped her reply, even though Jessica's tone had been playful. Abbey softened her tone with a wide smile, but goosebumps were creeping over her shoulders and down her spine. 'A ruse? What do you mean?'

'Well, you are getting married in a few weeks' time. Maybe Jason is out arranging some sort of surprise. I don't know! Anyway, I won't breathe a word to Tim.' She tapped the side of her nose with a finger. 'You know what he's like. Not the most discreet person in the world. I would hate for us to spoil any surprise in the offing. You two... come here!'

Distracted by her little ones, who were running in all directions, looking determined to trip up some unsuspecting stranger, she waved goodbye and set off after them.

'See you at the wedding! Can't wait.'

Abbey smiled and waved. Jessica was perfectly charming, as always, but the impromptu meeting had unsettled Abbey. Tim and Jason did the same job, handling different accounts, so why would one of them go off on a jolly weekend and not the other? Maybe Jessica was right. Perhaps Jason had told a little white lie and was planning something special, scoping out venues for the honeymoon they hadn't organised yet. A swirl of excitement ran around her veins.

'It's a bit odd,' she said, almost forgetting her dad was standing by her side.

'I'm sure there's a perfectly logical explanation,' he said neutrally. 'Speak to that young man of yours, see what he has to say for himself.'

6

Lizzie glanced up at the large pine wall clock in her kitchen and then double checked the time on her watch. Relieved to find that it hadn't stopped working and that, instead, time really was passing that slowly, she busied herself watering her pot plants, putting her dirty mug in the dishwasher and flicking the kettle on again to make another coffee.

It was the time of the week that she looked forward to the most. Sunday morning, when she had the chance to catch up with her daughter, Katy, Katy's husband, Brad, and her little granddaughter, Rosie, who lived on the other side of the world in Sydney, Australia. Thank goodness for modern technology. It might not be the same as seeing your loved ones in the flesh but it was the next best thing. Through reading books, singing songs and chatting away over the ether, Lizzie had developed a close and loving relationship with two-year-old Rosie, the little girl engaging and lighting up at her nana's voice, despite never having met her in real life.

Still, all that was about to change, as Katy and her family were coming to stay for six weeks in the summer and Lizzie could hardly wait. Already she'd prepared the bedrooms ready for their arrival and couldn't help herself from buying extra fun accessories for Rosie's bedroom every time she popped into town. There were multi-coloured fairy lights draped across the pretty white shelf unit, a bedside lamp in the shape of a dolphin, and a fluffy lilac rug on the wooden floor with matching cushions on the bed. In the corner of the room, Lizzie had put together two wooden boxes, one full of books and the other containing puzzles and toys. She really wanted it to be a proper home from home for Rosie and hoped that her little granddaughter would immediately fall in love with her bedroom.

The things they had planned: visits to the local play farm, trips to the seaside, visiting Lizzie's only remaining family member, a sister up in Scotland, and, of course, they would introduce Rosie to Primrose Woods with all its many delights. When Katy was a child she'd loved the park, and had spent many happy days there with her mum and dad, exploring the woods, walking through the bluebells and having long leisurely picnics, followed by games of cricket on steaming hot summer days. These days there were so many additional features at the park, like the sculpture trail with its giant's seat made from wood and fairy doors leading to tiny grottos, that both mum and grandma couldn't wait to explore and rediscover them through the new generation's eyes.

Just before ten o'clock, Lizzie opened up her laptop and there they all were, beaming at her from across the ocean. Her heart lifted as it always did at the sight of them. Rosie with her unruly blonde curls and blue eyes was a proper little character now she was walking and talking.

'Nana, Nana!' She clapped her hands excitedly.

'Hello, sweetheart! How are you, and what's that you have there?'

Rosie held up a patchwork dinosaur that she waved at the screen.

'Ra, ra, ra!' she boomed, making everyone giggle.

'How are you, then, Mum?' Katy asked.

'Very well. We've had a lovely spell of weather here recently so we've been busy in the cafe. I've been out in the garden too, having a tidy up and planting some new bushes. Your dad would be proud of me.' The garden had been David's domain when he was alive and he'd spent every spare moment out there, mowing the lawns and tending the flowerbeds. It was a shock to Lizzie's system when she realised, after several months, that she would need to take responsibility for the garden if she didn't want it to turn into a complete wilderness. Without David's natural instincts and enthusiasm for everything green, she'd struggled at times, killing off the clematis, pulling up plants that she'd wrongly suspected were weeds and cutting the grass when it was too wet, gouging trenches in the lawn. At least now, with the help of her neighbour, she managed to keep it tidy and under control, which was just about as much as she could hope for. 'Anyway, how are you all?'

'Very well, although it's been a funny week, hasn't it, Brad?'

Brad shrugged, looking bemused, a wry smile spreading across his face.

'Really, why's that, then?' Lizzie adjusted herself on the kitchen chair. She was all ears, listening in rapt attention.

'Well...' Katy paused. 'Do you want the good news or the bad news?'

'Oh, come on, tell me,' urged Lizzie, a trickle of alarm running through her blood. 'What is it?' she said, impatient now.

'Well, the thing is... I'm pregnant!'

'What?' Lizzie's hand flew to her face, momentarily dumbstruck by this unexpected turn of events.

'I know, Mum, it was such a shock to us as well. It certainly wasn't planned, but now we've got used to the idea, well, we're very happy. Aren't we, Rosie? What do you think to having a baby brother or sister?'

'Baby, baby, baby,' she chanted, swinging her toy dinosaur around her head gleefully.

'That's wonderful. Another grandchild. It's an absolute blessing.' How she wished she could jump up and wrap them in all a big hug, but even at thousands of miles' distance, it was still fantastic news.

'The bad news, though, Mum, is that we're not going to be able to make the trip home this summer. I'm so sorry. We're all so disappointed. I've spoken to the doctors and they say with my history, what happened last time, that it would be inadvisable to fly. Apparently it could, potentially, happen again and we've decided we can't afford to take the risk.'

'No, obviously,' Lizzie said, concerned. She understood only too well. It had been such a worrying time when Katy was pregnant with Rosie. There were so many false alarms, and she'd been kept under close watch by her local hospital, even having spells of confinement in the ward so they could monitor her more closely. Being so far away, Lizzie's anxiety had been through the roof and she'd felt helpless to support her daughter in what was one of the most important times in a woman's life. It seemed like the longest pregnancy ever and when Rosie finally arrived it had been such a huge relief all around. Now, they were about to embark on the same terrifying process again. 'How are you feeling, Katy?'

'Fine, just shattered most of the time. And this little one is full on from the moment she wakes up until the time she goes to bed, so there's not much chance to rest during the day. Aside from that, everything's good. Brad's looking after me.'

'Well, that's a relief.' Now she knew her daughter was pregnant again, it was as though she could see it in her eyes and in her skin, which had a translucent glow about it. 'It wouldn't surprise me if you fly through this pregnancy without any problems whatsoever.'

'I really hope so, Mum.' There was a plaintive note to Katy's voice and Lizzie's arms ached with emptiness at not being able to reach out and hug her daughter, in the same way as she'd comforted her when she was Rosie's age. It was wonderful, life-enhancing news, but still Lizzie couldn't ignore the sense of loss and unease that she felt at being so far removed from her family.

'When is the baby due?'

'In August. I feel like such a fool for not even realising. You know that I've been tired and out of sorts recently, but I put that down to some kind of bug. Rosie brings all sorts home now that she's at playgroup. We never thought we would be able to have another baby, they said it would be very unlikely after we had Rosie, and we'd come to terms with that situation. So to say we were surprised when we found out the news is an understatement!'

'It is a miracle,' said Lizzie, shaking her head in disbelief.

Lizzie had often wondered if it was all the stress that had played a part in Katy's problems last time around. In the space of a few years, she'd lost her beloved father, moved with her new husband to a far-flung country, leaving her mum behind, started a new job, and then become pregnant. So many life-changing experiences in such a short time. Lizzie had encouraged and reassured Katy when she'd expressed doubts about moving to the other side of the world, telling her the opportunity for Brad to take up a post-doctoral research role at Sydney University was one that couldn't be missed. Although Lizzie was still in the depths of her own grief after losing David, she'd had to push her own feelings to one side. The last thing she wanted was to hold her daughter back from living her own life and following her heart and dreams.

'Are you very disappointed about us not coming home?'

'Oh, love, I'd be lying if I said I wasn't, but I understand completely why it has to be this way. It's absolutely the right thing to do. The health of you and the baby is most important at the moment.'

Katy would never know just how saddened her mum really was. How she was holding it together right now, she had no idea. Such a mix of emotions assaulted her mind and body. Tears were brewing inside, but she couldn't give way to them. Not in front of Katy. She was overjoyed at the prospect of a new baby, but when she might see her family again and meet the youngest generation, she had no idea. It was the one thing that had been keeping her going these last few months, filling her with excitement and hope as she'd crossed off the days on the calendar that hung on the kitchen wall. She chided herself for being so selfish, but the pain she felt inside was real and vivid.

'I really need to see you, though, Mum. I can't bear the thought of another year passing without putting my arms around you. And you and Rosie need to spend some proper quality time together while she's still little. She needs her nana and I need my mum.' Katy was adamant, clearly feeling the same way as Lizzie. They'd always been two peas from the same pod, but she was unable to hide her true feelings in the same way as her mum.

'The thing is, Lizzie.' Brad shuffled forward in his chair, his hands clasped together. 'We wondered if you might re-consider and think about coming out here instead. Once you got here, we're sure you'd love it. We're desperate to show you all the sights. You'll have the best time and get to spend time with these girls too. We could even help to pay towards your fare. We've obviously put some money away for our flights that we won't be using now.'

'That's very kind of you, Brad, but you wouldn't need to do that.' She was genuinely touched by their offer, but when had it ever been about the money? 'It's certainly something to think about,' Lizzie muttered half-heartedly.

'Please, Mum. I know it's a really big ask, but it would mean the world to me. I've been looking online and there are all sorts of different methods that you can try that seem to work for people with a fear of flying.'

Already Lizzie could feel her heartbeat racing and her palms growing clammy. They really didn't need to talk about this now.

'There are courses you can attend too. Some of them use virtual simulators where you learn about the planes and the whole process of flying, and discover how safe it actually is.'

'Ah right,' she said, doing her best to block out Katy's words. It was hard for anyone to understand how deep-rooted her fear of flying went. She wasn't being difficult or awkward, but there was no way on earth she could imagine ever stepping foot on a plane again, certainly not on her own. And someone trying to convince her how safe it is was never going to make a difference. A huge metal contraption rolling about in the air, thousands of miles above the earth – it defied all sensible and rational thought. The last time she'd flown was when she and David returned from a summer holiday to Tenerife. Extremely nervous to begin with, they hit some turbulence and Lizzie had a full-blown panic attack, her whole body trembling, severe pains gripping her chest and nausea sweeping through her. She honestly believed she was going to die. It was the most terrifying experience of her life and she vowed then to never put herself through the ordeal again. There was no need. Well, not until dear Katy moved to the other side of the world.

'I suppose I could take a look. Anyway,' she said, eager to move the conversation on, 'tell me everything about this new baby. Do you have a scan photo to show me? And Rosie, how exciting, you're going to be a big sister?'

Lizzie smiled broadly and made appreciative oohing and aahing sounds as Katy and Rosie gabbled on about all the news.

Brad looked on proudly. She was lucky to have such a delightful and supportive family, she knew that. She just had to remind herself of that fact when they finished the call and all the emotion she'd bottled up, since Katy had told her they wouldn't be coming home this year, rose to the surface. Fat tears rolled down her cheeks, racking her whole body. She'd thought she had no tears left to shed after grieving for David, but here they were again, surprising her with their intensity, stirring up all those old feelings that she thought she'd left behind.

'Oh, David, whatever am I going to do?'

She picked up the silver gilt-framed photo of her husband that took pride of place on the mantelpiece, her fingers caressing his loving image.

'It's bad enough you not being here, but Katy as well, and her babies. I know, I know, I should just get on with it, but it isn't that easy.' She sniffled, drying away her tears with the back of her hand. 'I should get outside, shouldn't I? Get some fresh air.'

She pulled on her cardigan and found her gardening gloves from the wicker basket by the back door, walking outside with a pair of secateurs in her hand. It was at times like these when she missed David the most, being able to pour her heart out to him knowing he would understand exactly how she felt, how he would put an arm around her shoulder and assure her everything would work out fine. It was the simple things. Having that special someone in her life to share the ups and downs, the daily minutiae, was something she missed hugely. She had her friends, but it wasn't the same. They had their own busy lives and families, and she didn't want to be a burden to them. Mind you, if David was still around, she knew exactly what he would be telling her to do right now.

She attacked the buddleia with a vengeance, cutting the branches hard back, finding the snipping sensation strangely therapeutic. In a matter of months the shrub would be back in full bloom, attracting a plethora of bees and butterflies, a timely reminder that things never stayed the same and life moved on, offering an opportunity to embrace the changes. She was naturally disappointed that Katy couldn't come home this year, but it was only a minor setback.

There was always next year, when the new baby had arrived. It might seem like a long while away, but it would pass quickly enough. And it would be all the more special for meeting both of her grandchildren together. She hoped Katy would put any ideas of Lizzie travelling out to Australia right out of her head. Next time she spoke to her she'd tell her to book those air tickets for next summer instead. It was the most sensible solution. Lizzie would have to buy another calendar, though, and start counting those days off, all over again.

7

As soon as she heard the key in the door, Abbey excitedly jumped up off the sofa and rushed into the hallway.

'Woah!' Jason stopped dead in his tracks as he closed the door behind him, his surprise at the sight greeting him evident to see. 'What's going on here?'

He took a step backwards, his gaze wandering up and down her body appreciatively.

'Can I not make a special effort for my husband-to-be?' Abbey wrapped her arms round Jason's neck, standing on tiptoes and kissing him on the lips. 'I've missed you so much. I thought I'd show you just exactly what you've been missing out on.'

She'd discarded her old jeans and sweatshirt for a change, and put on a dress, the red one that clung to her curves and which she knew Jason loved.

'Well, you certainly smell good,' he said, nuzzling her neck and sending shivers down her spine. He smelt good too, different some-how, as though he'd picked up his own new scent while away.

'Well, I don't know if it's my new sweet vanilla perfume or the red wine sauce simmering on the stove. Hope you're hungry. I've got us some lovely fillet steaks with some sauté potatoes.'

'Sounds great,' said Jason, regretting the big greasy cheese-burger he'd picked up on the way home. 'I'm shattered; I might just have half an hour's kip first.' He plonked himself down on the sofa and reached for the remote control, turning on the sports channel and within minutes, with an ease Abbey had never acquired, he was fast asleep.

It wasn't quite the response she'd been hoping for, but then what did she expect? He'd clearly had a very demanding weekend, whatever it was he'd been doing. She'd find out about that later. She hadn't wanted to bombard him with questions the moment he walked through the door. After running into Jessica yesterday, it made her realise just how much they'd drifted apart these last few weeks and months. Jason was putting in so many extra hours at work and she was distracted by everything that needed doing for the wedding. They'd lost sight of each other and had barely had a proper conversation in ages. She had no idea what was going on inside his head, the emotions he was feeling, what he was doing and who he was seeing. They needed to recapture that intimacy or else she'd be walking up the aisle to face a stranger in a few weeks' time.

She gave him an hour, enough time to unwind from the stresses of the weekend, then switched off the telly and popped on some music instead. Some mellow Motown to set a romantic mood. She thought how lovely the room looked with the table laid with a red and white gingham cloth, flickering candles and a large glass of red wine poured. When was the last time they'd had a romantic date night together?

'So tell me, how did your weekend go?' she asked, when she finally managed to rouse him from his slumber and he was seated at the table, eyeing his extravagant dinner with something resembling bemusement. She felt a pang of sympathy, realising he would probably have preferred a bowl of something comforting, eaten from his lap on the sofa, but wasn't that part of the problem? They'd fallen into a pattern of behaviour where they did the same thing day in day out, taking each other for granted like an old married couple. They were just starting out on their married adventure together. They needed to keep their relationship fresh and spontaneous.

'Yeah, it was good, thanks. A bit full-on, but I think it was probably beneficial for the team. Everyone seemed to enjoy it.'

'Sounds good. Did everyone go?'

She tried to make the question sound casual, but immediately noticed a flicker of uncertainty cross his features. He glanced over at her as though it might be a trick question.

'The usual suspects.'

'Ah, right. It was just that I bumped into Jessica Mayne at Primrose Woods yesterday and she said Tim hadn't gone. She didn't seem to know anything about it.'

'Nah, he couldn't make it for some reason.' Jason yawned extravagantly, stretching his arms wide in the air. Then he shrugged, returning his attention to his steak with gusto. Maybe it was no big deal. Perhaps Abbey had read too much into a seemingly insignificant situation or perhaps it was Tim being economical with the truth with Jessica. Although what possible reason he could have for doing that, she didn't know. Her mind was going round in circles. Could Jessica be right? Was there an altogether different reason for Jason being away for the weekend?

'That's a shame,' she said, eyeing him suspiciously through her glass of wine. 'I just wonder if you're being entirely honest with me, Jason.'

'What?' He snapped his head up to look at her. His tone was casual enough, but the tell-tale sign of stress, red patchy blotches, were creeping up his neck. 'What the heck are you going on about? I've had a hell of a weekend, Abbey, I don't need the third degree.'

'I knew it!' She leapt from her chair and dashed around to his side of the table. 'I can always tell when you're lying because you go all blotchy. I know exactly what you've been up to.'

'You do?' Jason looked alarmed. 'Where's all this coming from?' He stood up, palms held in a defensive gesture, edging away from her as though his life might be in mortal danger.

'Jessica.' Abbey grinned and Jason tentatively followed suit, unsure of how he should be reacting. Abbey was smiling, though, which had to be a good sign. 'Do you really think I'm that daft? You don't have a team-building weekend without your team! Jessica suggested you might have something up your sleeve. Like some sort of surprise. For the wedding?' Abbey poked her fingers at his tummy, trying to elicit some sort of response. 'Come on, tell me, what exactly have you been up to?'

'Stop it! Get off!' he yelped, batting away her advances half-heartedly, laughing, giving himself some much-needed thinking time. 'You're mad, do you know that?'

'Yes! But it's good mad, right? Come on, Jason, please tell me. I can't bear the suspense. There was no work weekend away, was there? So what have you been doing all this time?'

'Well...' He so didn't need this right now. It had been a good weekend, but he'd been looking forward to getting home and collapsing in a heap on the sofa. Rhi was a great girl, but he'd discovered that she was very intense and needy, requiring his full-on attention every moment of the day. Now, Abbey was making demands on him too. He was feeling a bit queasy, from the sticky predicament he found himself in and from forcing down the last of that steak, delicious though it was. He had a chocolate fondant to come as well, apparently.

'Well... um... it won't be a surprise if I tell you, will it?'

Good answer, he quietly congratulated himself.

'Oh my goodness, what are you like?' Abbey squealed and dragged Jason by the hand into the middle of the room, where she began to sway in time to the music, Jason a hapless participant. 'Is that what this is all about, our honeymoon?'

'My lips are sealed,' said Jason, a feeling of dread brewing in his chest. He couldn't think about it now. His head was hurting and his stomach aching. Tomorrow, at work, he would google holiday destinations. *What a mess.*

'I'm so excited for our wedding, aren't you? These last few weeks I've been so bogged down with the arrangements that I lost sight of what we are doing all of this for. It will be such a relief when we are finally married.'

'Yeah, it will,' said Jason. 'I do love you, you know? I know I might not always show it in the right way, but we're good together, aren't we, Abbey?' He looked serious now, a plaintive note to his voice. 'After almost twelve years, I'm not sure how I'd manage without you in my life.'

'Oh, you soppy old bugger. So it is a good idea after all, then? Us getting married?'

'Yeah.' He laughed as he pulled her closer, moving in time to the music. 'It was all my idea, wasn't it?'

'What?' She punched him playfully in the side. In truth, it had been a bone of contention for years. Abbey was the one who'd pushed to put their relationship on a more formal footing. Jason's view was that they were happy as they were, so why change it? They'd been together since they were at school, apart from a few spells apart, usually initiated by Abbey after Jason had messed up again, but that was when he was still very immature. Everyone deserved a second chance, didn't they? Okay, so Jason had had more second chances than most, but the one thing Abbey wasn't prepared to compromise on was marriage. If they were truly committed to each other, were planning on buying a house together and starting a family, then there was no reason why they shouldn't be married as well. It had taken a while, but Jason had finally come around to her way of thinking.

She rested her head on his shoulder, enjoying this moment of spontaneity, inhaling the sweet but unfamiliar scent that clung to his shirt. Her hands travelled across his back and down to his waist, pulling out his shirt from his jeans.

'Hey, can we save this until the morning? I'm completely shattered and I'd hate to disappoint.' He tipped her chin upwards, a weary smile on his face.

Abbey groaned. It had been weeks since they were last intimate so would one more day really make any difference?

'Well, I'm already disappointed, but I guess if you're determined to keep your future wife waiting, then what's a girl to do? But you do know when we're on our honeymoon, wherever that might be,' she squealed, unable to hide her excitement, 'then we'll have all the time in the world for each other. Just you and me.'

'Yeah,' he said, his voice cracking.

She pulled him even closer, her hand finding the back pocket of his jeans and exploring inside, feeling a perky buttock cheek beneath the fabric, and giving it a gentle squeeze, but there was something else she found there. Something that caused her whole world to stop turning. Her hand clasped around the small square packet, her fingers running around the edge of the foil, her mind whirling slowly as she tried to make sense of what it could possibly be.

Jason realised a moment too late.

'No, wait. Stop that.' His hand flew round to the back of his trousers to stop her progress, but she already had the mystery item in her hand, whipping it out and into the air space between them, brandishing it like a golden ticket.

'What the hell?'

'Honestly, Abbey, it's not what you think.' He grabbed her by the shoulders, looking into her eyes. 'I can explain. Really I can.'

She pushed him away. There was no need for explanations. Everything made complete and utter sense to her now.

8

Rhianna skipped into work on that Monday morning. She'd had such a brilliant weekend and she hadn't wanted it to end. When Jay had dropped her off round the corner from her house last night, she'd waved him goodbye and then given herself a stern talking-to. She needed to get her giddiness under control. She hated having to lie to her mum, but there was no other choice at the moment. She had told her mum that she'd gone to stay with an old schoolfriend for the weekend and she knew her mum would want to hear all the news as soon as she walked through the door. It had made her toes curl making up stories about what she'd done over the weekend, where they'd visited and what they'd eaten, and she'd been so relieved once she was able to move the conversation on to something else entirely.

She couldn't wait until she and Jay could be together properly and hopefully it wouldn't be long. Once her mum got to know Jay, she knew she would love him just as much as Rhi did.

At work she settled down at her desk, zhuzhed up her hair and applied a sneaky coating of lip gloss in her compact mirror, before firing up her computer and delving into her inbox.

'How was your weekend, Rhi?'

Luke Barnfield, who worked in the same department, popped his head up over his computer screen.

'Good, thanks, I went away with my boyfriend.'

She hadn't been able to stop herself. She wanted to shout it from the rooftops, tell everyone what a wonderful and exciting time she'd had, but she knew it was too soon for that.

'Your boyfriend? I didn't even know you had a boyfriend. You've kept that one quiet.'

'I like to keep my personal and professional life separate,' she said haughtily, hoping Luke might take the hint and stop flirting with her. He was harmless enough, but annoying with his constant chattering and silly jokes. Even though they were of a similar age, he seemed so immature, especially when she compared him to Jay, who was all man, sophisticated, intelligent and just dreamy in bed.

'Fair enough.' Luke shrugged. 'You know you'll be breaking a few hearts around here, though, with that news, especially your office admirer's.'

'Look, I'm sorry, Luke, but I've told you. I really like you as a work colleague, but I could never see you in any other way.'

'Cheers, Rhi,' Luke said, chuckling to himself. 'But I wasn't actually talking about me, heartbroken though I am. I meant the guy from sales, the flashy one.'

Rhianna's brow furrowed, feigning confusion, but she knew exactly who Luke was talking about. Could he possibly know about her relationship with Jay? They'd gone out of their way to keep it a secret, but maybe they hadn't been as discreet as they thought. Was it common knowledge around the office?

'What are you talking about?' It was only five past nine in the morning and already irritation was prickling at her skin.

'You know, um, what's his name... Jason. Slicked-back hair and sharp suits. Walks past here every morning and you go all pink and giggly. That one. You can't have missed him. Actually, come to think of it, he's not been past yet today. Perhaps he's got wind of the new boyfriend.'

'I don't know what you're talking about.' He couldn't even get Jay's name right. She bristled, and put her head down, busying herself on her computer, but Luke's words had unsettled her. If Jay were to find out that people were gossiping about them in the office, he would be absolutely furious. And come to think of it, Luke was right. She hadn't seen Jay this morning. Usually he made a point of walking past her desk first thing and he would give her a cheeky wink, his way of showing her that he was thinking about her until a time when they could be together again. Sometimes she might have to go days without seeing him in private, so those furtive glances and smiles caught along the corridor or in the queue for the canteen at lunchtime, were all that kept her going in the meantime.

She tried to ignore the sense of unease that crept along her body. Something was wrong. Perhaps Jay was ill. They'd had a very full-on and exhausting weekend with so much rich and decadent food, lots of fizz to drink and hours on end spent getting to know each other properly in the luxury of a huge king-sized bed. Maybe she'd worn him out! She giggled to herself. Thinking about it, though, she hadn't received a text from him either this morning.

Surreptitiously, she leant down and looked at her phone in her handbag. No, nothing. She fired off a text.

Everything okay? Haven't seen you this morning. Missing you so much! Keep thinking about the weekend. Was the best time ever. Love you. xx

She stared at the waiting emails in her inbox, but she couldn't focus on them at all. She could see why Luke might be jealous of

Jay, but calling him flashy was a low blow. He was a smart dresser who liked to look after himself. Where was the harm in that?

'Besides, you shouldn't be rude about people you don't know the first thing about. From what I've heard, Jay is one of the best salesmen in the company.' Admittedly, she'd mainly heard that from Jay himself, but it didn't mean it wasn't true.

'Yeah, I give you that. I've heard quite a lot about him too. Not all good. You know he's getting married in a few weeks' time?'

'What?' Now it was Rhi's turn to stick her head up and over her computer. What an idiot! She'd never really liked Luke and now, for some reason, he was deliberately trying to rile her. 'No, we're obviously talking about different people.'

Her mood was becoming more irritable by the moment, what with Luke's ridiculous comments and the fact she still hadn't heard from Jay. Perhaps he was in a meeting first thing. She glanced at her watch. She'd leave it fifteen minutes or so, then she'd wander past his desk on the pretext of visiting the coffee machine.

'No, definitely the same guy. Hey, Indra!' Luke called across the floor to another one of their colleagues. 'You've been invited to Jason's wedding, haven't you?'

'Yeah, not long to go now. About three weeks, I think. Should be a good do!'

Rhi looked from Indra to Luke, trying to make sense of what they were saying. She knew Indra played squash with Jay. A cold trickle of dread ran along her veins at the same time as a flash of heat branded her cheeks. Jay? Jason? Was it possible they could be talking about the same person?

You can call me Jay, he'd told her that first time he'd spoken to her in the car park. She remembered that moment, the seductive smile on his face, the effect it had on her insides. Now she was experiencing a completely different emotion swirling in her stomach. She steadied her breathing, unsure of how she might form a coherent sentence.

'Luke, sorry, who is it we are talking about here exactly? Do you mean Jay, the one who drives the blue sporty BMW?'

'Yeah, that's him. I told you he was a flash so-and-so.'

She stood up and pushed back her chair with such force that it toppled backwards, landing sideways on the floor. The commotion caused Luke and Indra to jump from their seats, rushing to her aid.

'Get off me,' she snapped, pushing their concern aside. 'I'm fine.'

'Rhi!' called Luke plaintively, holding out a hand to her, but she wasn't waiting for anyone.

She stormed off down the corridor, stopping momentarily at the water cooler to grab a cup of ice-cold water. Her throat was scratchy and dry, her head spinning. She took a sip, wetting her lips, her mind a whirlwind of thoughts and emotions. There would be a perfectly logical explanation. Luke and Indra had clearly got the wrong end of the stick. When she got the chance to speak to Jay about it, they would laugh and remark on how everyone had got it completely wrong about them and their relationship. It would be a story they would tell to their friends and family in years to come. As she stalked down the corridor, she glanced in the meeting rooms, but they were both empty. When she reached his department, her heart lifted to see him sitting at his desk, but her joy was short-lived. She could tell immediately something was wrong. His shoulders were hunched, his head was lowered and he was slunk down in his chair.

'Jay?'

Quickly he sat up, spinning round to face her, his expression darkening and crumbling at the same time.

'What are you doing?' he mouthed, looking around him, checking to see who might be witnessing this interaction. There was no smile on his face, no light in his eyes, no vestige of the wonderful man she'd spent the weekend with. 'I'll speak to you later,' he hissed.

'This can't wait, Jay.'

'Jay?' someone said in the vicinity, causing a ripple of laughter around her. Ignoring the heckling, she went on.

'Tell me, honestly, is it true? Are you getting married?' Her voice was strong, unwavering, belying the turmoil she felt inside.

'Have you not received your invitation yet, then, love?' called another voice, accompanied by more laughter.

'Piss off,' she said, to the faceless person, her gaze not wavering from Jay as she gauged his reaction, waiting for him to explain, to tell her it was all a big misunderstanding. Any moment now he would look at her and smile, the way he'd looked at her when they were snuggled up in bed together, with fondness and tenderness. He would step up to the plate and come good for her, like she'd been waiting for him to do for months. Now, though, with each passing second, so painfully slow and humiliating, she realised it wasn't going to happen. He couldn't even look her in the eye.

One... two... three...

'You dickhead! You absolute dickhead, Jay, or... whatever your real name is!' The plastic cup and its ice-cold contents left Rhianna's grasp as though it was an Exocet missile, whizzing through the air and hitting its target in the face with absolute precision.

Rhianna only wished it had been a bucketful.

9

Abbey was used to having difficult conversations. In her line of work she often had to raise sensitive and distressing issues and discuss them in a calm and comforting manner.

Sometimes, very sadly, she had to impart the worst possible news to relatives of her residents at the care home. It didn't become any easier the more times she did it; in some ways it only got harder, but she was able to put her own emotions to one side and concentrate on offering solace to those people in their moment of need.

It was all part of her job, a part she didn't relish, but one that she undertook with a great sense of pride and integrity.

When it came to her personal life, she tried adopting the same approach, keeping calm and relaying news in a dispassionate manner, but it wasn't as easy to put her own feelings to one side. Not in this case, at least. She wanted to rant, throw accusations, tell her entire wedding guest list just what a low-life, despicable piece of scum her ex-fiancé really was, but she could hear her dad's cautionary words ringing in her ears.

Rise above it, love. Don't lower yourself to his level.

Easier said than done when she was having to make phone call after phone call explaining what had happened.

The wedding's cancelled. No, we won't be rescheduling another date. It was a mutual decision. Yes, sad, but it's best for everyone concerned.

Okay, so the bit about it being a mutual decision was a lie, but she hadn't wanted to get into the finer details, which might have stirred a lot of awkward questions. All she wanted was for these excruciating conversations to be over as quickly as possible. She didn't doubt the awful truth would filter through to everyone given time, like a joyless Mexican wave.

The most difficult conversation was the one she had with her dad. She'd rushed straight round to his house as soon as she'd found out about the full extent of Jason's betrayal.

'Are you very disappointed?' she asked her dad, after she'd spilt out the whole story, and was mopping up the tears rolling down her face with a tissue.

'Disappointed? Why would I be disappointed? I'm dreadfully sad for you and angry that a man, someone who purports to love you, can treat you so despicably, but I could never be disappointed in you. No way.' He reached across and placed an arm around her shoulder, pulling her into his side, in the same way he'd comforted her when she was a small girl with a grazed knee.

'It's so humiliating, having to phone all our friends and family to tell them the wedding's off.'

'Well, you have nothing to feel ashamed about. Hold your head up high, young lady. There's only one person in the wrong here and that's...' Bill shook his head, his despair evident, making him unable even to voice Jason's name. '... that idiot boyfriend of yours. I've got no problem with ringing around everyone and letting them know the news.'

'Thanks, Dad, but this is something I have to do for myself.'

There were times over the following few days when Abbey

wished she had offloaded the job onto her dad after all. She had over fifty calls to make, each one increasingly testing her nerves and slowly draining every iota of emotional energy from her. As well as the guest list, there was the florist to ring, the venue, the registrar, the DJ and the photographer to contact too. They would lose hundreds of pounds in deposits, but that was the least of Abbey's concerns. She just wanted to be rid of the problem and she knew that if she personally dealt with every outstanding item that needed seeing to, then the job would get done properly. There was no way she was leaving it to Jason to sort out. Besides, despite the fact he was now living back at his parents' and Abbey had changed the locks on the doors to her cottage, Jason was still in denial about their relationship. He honestly believed they would be able to come back from this and go ahead as planned with their wedding.

'Please, Abbey,' he'd pleaded as she gathered up his personal items, piling them high in the hallway. 'Don't do this. I know how upset you are, and that's all down to me, but we can't throw everything away, the twelve years we've spent together, the future we had planned, all over some stupid fling. It didn't mean anything.'

She didn't want to hear it, but he'd gone on, close to tears.

'I've been under so much stress and I didn't want to offload that on you. I know how much you've had on your plate too. It was a release. That's all. She didn't mean anything to me. I was going to end it before the wedding. I totally intended to devote my whole life to you. I still want to do that, more than anything.'

She sighed, snapping her notebook shut, remembering his protestations and his ridiculous excuses. There was no going back. She never wanted to see the creep again.

She stood up and looked around the living room of her cottage, bought with the small inheritance she'd received after her mother died. It looked brighter and less cluttered now that Jason's possessions had been removed, his car magazines, the tangle of cables for all his devices, and his sports bags and shoes that had been littered everywhere. She'd rearranged the furniture, moving the comfy, squishy armchair onto the side wall, allowing the light to flood in through the front bay window. The flowers her dad had bought her, pink lilies, roses and snapdragons, she'd displayed in a clear glass vase in the fireplace, their colour and beauty making her smile every time she looked at them. There was still a faint whiff of Jason's scent about the place, but she made sure to open the windows a couple of times a day to let the fresh air in and allow any vestiges of his remaining toxicity to escape. She couldn't wait for the day when there would be no trace whatsoever that he had ever lived here.

She picked up her puffa jacket from the hook in the porch, shrugged it over her shoulders and headed out of the front door. As she wandered slowly down the path, zipping up her coat, she thought she caught something out of the corner of her eye, a movement from someone on the other side of the street, someone watching her. She quickly looked up, then breathed a sigh of relief, realising her mind was playing tricks on her. She was seeing things now. Unsurprisingly, she'd been on edge the last couple of days, bracing herself for running into Jason. He'd turned up at the front door a couple of times, desperate to talk, but she'd sent him packing. There was nothing for them to discuss so there was no point in getting into any kind of conversation. It was the same reason she'd been avoiding his phone calls. What was the point of them going over old ground? The sooner Jason got the message their relationship was over for good, the better.

She took a moment by the white picket gate to her house, looking all around her, soaking up the warmth and calm of the late spring day. Down the road to her left was the village green, which was covered in a carpet of bright daffodils, their heads standing to attention, smiling cheerily. She would wander down there later to see them in their full glory. The tree seat around the old oak tree was the perfect place to sit and watch the world go by at any time of the year, but especially so now being amongst the colourful spring flowers. Her local pub, The Three Feathers, overlooked the green, which had a small duck pond at one end, home to a resident family of ducks. Abbey knew how lucky she was to live in such a charming village as Wishwell. It was a picturesque spot and attracted many weekend visitors who came to take photographs of the pretty stone cottages, or to wander around the sanctuary of All Saints' Church, which backed onto green fields dotted with sheep. There was a village store, which looked tiny from the outside but was deceptively large inside and stocked every conceivable essential that you could think of, along with a range of locally sourced fruit and vegetables, eggs, and pickles and chutneys, which in the warmer months were displayed in baskets and wooden shelving units outside the front of the shop.

It was something she hadn't been looking forward to, moving away from Wishwell. She and Jason had talked about selling up and moving to one of the new estates on the outskirts of West-hampton where they would get so much more for their money. There was no way they'd be able to afford something bigger in Wishwell. She breathed a huge sigh of satisfaction knowing she wouldn't need to face that decision now. Her life for the foresee-able future was planted firmly in Wishwell, without that creep, Jason!

She shook herself, banishing all thoughts of her treacherous ex from her mind. Instead of turning left towards the village centre, she turned right, walking along the quiet country road and through the cutting into Breakspear's Pass, picking up the footpath that led along the familiar route to Primrose Woods. Thankfully, Jason had never showed any interest in joining her on her visits to the park so its magic and recuperative powers hadn't been tainted in any way by his presence. It was a Jason-free zone.

She strode out, her head craning upwards to admire the sky-scraping redwoods that lined the beaten path down the hill to her destination. She smiled as she spotted the squirrels' antics. They scurried up trees, leaping from branch to branch with daredevil bravado. She could hear the chatter of birds up above her, calling out to each other, and the sway of the wind as it increased its intensity. There was definitely a lot of activity around her, mainly hidden from view, but she could hear scrabbling and squawking coming from the undergrowth. Then there was another noise, one she didn't recognise, which came from somewhere behind her. She startled, and turned to look, but she couldn't see anybody or anything. Maybe not a noise, then, but definitely a presence, as though someone was following her. She carried on, walking that little bit faster now and with more determination, but still she couldn't shake off the feeling that someone was after her. Her nerves were shot to pieces these days, but she was certain she wasn't imagining things. There was the definite sound of footsteps crunching on the ground. She broke into a jog, looking over her shoulder as she felt panic rise in her chest. There! She wasn't going mad after all. Someone in black jeans and a hoodie ducked behind a tree out of her line of sight, but she'd definitely spotted them. Who was it? What did they want? She picked up her speed, jogging faster now, looking ahead into the distance, hoping she might spot a dog walker or a fellow jogger, someone she could run up to and tell them she was in danger, being followed.

'Hey, wait!' the person called out to her.

Abbey gave another quick glance over her shoulder. The hooded figure, tall, lean and clearly athletic, was running after her, gesturing for her to stop, but Abbey wasn't hanging around for anyone, especially not in the secluded surroundings of the outskirts of Primrose Woods. She sprinted, desperate to reach safety, away from the threat of the thundering footsteps getting closer and closer, but whoever it was they were clearly much fitter and faster than Abbey.

With her breath coming in short, sharp bursts and her heart pounding in her chest, feeling as though it might explode, she almost stumbled over her own feet and had to reach out for the nearest tree to stop herself from toppling over. She paused, hands on her thighs, struggling to get her breath, just enough time for whoever it was to catch up with her.

'Get away, leave me alone.' Abbey turned to face them, fear making her bolshie and brave. She was ready to take off again at any moment as soon as she'd gathered her breath.

'Sorry.' Her pursuer pushed back the hood of their jacket and Abbey gasped. 'I didn't mean to scare you. I just want to talk. Please? It's very important.'

10

Sam Finnegan was settled at the front table of the Treetops Cafe with his laptop, phone and walkie-talkie. Although there was a small office for the rangers in a wooden hut close to the adventure trail in the depths of the woods, he preferred to come and work here, not least because Lizzie kept him well topped up with mugs of coffee and, especially welcome today, bacon butties. This morning it was fairly quiet with only a few tables occupied, but even if it was jam-packed with visitors, with different conversations buzzing in the air, Sam was able to focus on what he needed to do, revelling in the activity around him, but able to shut out the noise and concentrate on the job in hand. Most times Lizzie would come and have a chat, tell him all the news of what was going on at this end of the park, but today she seemed distracted and preoccupied. He hoped she was okay. Perhaps she was expecting a big party of visitors later and was mentally preparing herself.

He watched as she attended a table on the other side of the cafe, and recognised the woman she was serving as the same one he'd spent a pleasant ten minutes chatting to on the bench the other day. What puzzled him was the way the unexpected sighting of Abbey – he even remembered her name and he was notoriously bad at that when he met so many different people in the course of his work – made him feel. A mix of excitement and anticipation stirred in his stomach, a sensation that took him by surprise. He smiled, but she was oblivious to his presence, as she was deep in conversation with her friend. He put his head down, returning his attention to the week's timesheets in front of him.

'Hey, Lizzie,' he called, the next time she wandered past. 'Are you okay?'

She paused by his table, her hands on her hips and eked out a smile.

'Yes, fine.' She smiled. 'How about you, Sam?'

'Me? I'm great. Come and have a sit-down with me.'

Lizzie looked around and spotted Josie behind the counter, who indicated she was happy to man the fort if Lizzie wanted to take a break. She even brought over a couple of cappuccinos for the pair of them.

'So what's happening, then?' Sam asked as he observed Lizzie from across the table. She looked weary; maybe she was fighting off a cold or something.

'Oh, you know, everything's much the same.'

Sam fell silent for a moment, examining Lizzie's features, waiting for her to divulge something more, or to come out with one of her cheery expressions, but instead she aimlessly stirred the froth on her coffee.

'Come on, Lizzie. I know you well enough by now to know when something's wrong. I don't want to intrude, but if it's something I can help with then you know you can talk to me.'

Lizzie could cope with most things and was usually able to put on a brave front so that no one would ever know how she was feeling inside, a technique she'd adopted after losing David, but someone being kind and sympathetic to her today was likely to reduce her to tears. She might have known she couldn't get anything past Sam; he was far too perceptive.

'I have some good news, actually. Katy is pregnant again.'

'Well, that's wonderful.' Before she had chance to say anything further, Sam had jumped up from his seat and dashed around to her side of the table, embracing her in a hug. 'It is wonderful, isn't it?' he said, pulling back and looking closely into her face.

'Yes! Very much so. It's lovely news, but it does mean the family won't be able to come home this summer after all.'

'Really? Oh, that is a shame.' Everything fell into place for Sam. He knew how much Lizzie had been looking forward to seeing her daughter again after several years. Her face lit up when she spoke about the trip and all the different things she had planned for their stay. 'You must be very disappointed.'

Lizzie sighed heavily, unable to hide her true feelings from Sam.

'I am, and it makes me feel like such a terrible person. I know I should be brimming with excitement over the new baby, but it's heartbreaking knowing that I won't get to see them for another year at least. Katy wants me to go out there instead, but I just can't bring myself to do it. I feel so guilty, as though I'm letting my family down. People don't understand how debilitating a fear of flying really is.'

'Katy will understand. She's your daughter. She knows you better than anyone.'

Lizzie hoped that was true, but she suspected that even Katy was growing impatient with her mum's reluctance to fly. It had been almost four years since Lizzie had waved Katy and Brad goodbye. She was banking on seeing her daughter and her family in another year's time, but none of them knew if that would even be possible. If Brad would be able to get the time off work then. And if not then, when might she ever see them again? That terri-

fying thought kept her awake at night along with the fear that the
distance between them, wide enough in miles, would only deepen
the distance between them emotionally.

'Take no notice of me. I'm only feeling sorry for myself. I'm sure
we'll work something out soon enough.' She was relieved at having
offloaded onto Sam; she'd been hugging the news to herself for
days now, her sadness and disappointment coming in waves when
she least expected it. Talking to Sam had been freeing, but she was
conscious of not wanting to bore him to pieces with her woes. Not
that Sam appeared bored in the slightest. Her heart expanded
looking at his handsome face. That's what she loved about him. He
always made time for her and was genuinely interested and
concerned for her wellbeing.

'What about you, Sam? Did you get to see Stephanie again?'

'I did.' He grimaced. 'Although not by choice. After I spoke to
you, I realised I needed to tell her that I couldn't see a future for
the pair of us.'

Lizzie visibly winced and pulled a face at Sam.

'I broke it to her gently, said I didn't think we were compatible
on a romantic level, but she didn't take it well. She said it was too
soon to be making those kinds of decisions and we should give it a
little longer.' He chuckled. 'Might have been an idea if I felt
remotely the same way, but it was never going to work. It took a
while for her to get the message, though. She kept texting me and
then when I didn't reply, she only went and turned up here, which
was a bit much. Anyway, hopefully that's an end to it. I've decided
that I'm putting dating on the back burner for the time being. It's
more trouble than it's worth.'

'You just haven't met the right person yet.'

'That's true, but I don't think you can force these things. Much
better to wait for things to happen naturally.'

Lizzie smiled to herself. She hoped Sam wouldn't be waiting

too long. If she were only thirty years younger she would snap him up for herself. He was such a catch: lovely, kind and good-looking to boot, and as much as she would love to give him advice on his love life, she had to bite her tongue, knowing he probably wouldn't be grateful for her interference.

'Sam?'

He was lost in thought, his attention distracted by something on the other side of the room. She turned to look. Ahhh. More accurately, he was distracted by somebody on the other side of the room.

'That's Abbey; she's one of my regulars. Comes in a couple of times a week for a coffee and a sticky bun. I've only got to know her recently.'

'Yes, I met her here the other day too. She seems...' He hesitated, choosing his word carefully. '... nice.'

'Apparently she's getting married in a couple of weeks' time.'

Sam snapped his attention back to Lizzie as though he hadn't quite understood what she'd said.

'Married?'

'Yes, apparently so.'

'Ah, right.' Sam quickly recovered himself, but Lizzie wondered if it was indifference or disappointment she'd noticed flitting across his features. He lifted his cup to his lips and downed the rest of his cappuccino, his gaze focused on Lizzie now. 'I'm sorry your plans have gone awry. I wish there was something I could do to help, but you know I'm here for you if you want to talk.'

'Thanks, Sam. That means a lot.' The front door opened and a group of people wandered in, their attentions fixed on the chalk-board above the countertop with its vast array of lunch options, the aroma of broccoli and Stilton soup simmering on the stove tempting them forwards. 'Looks like the rush has arrived. I ought to get back to work. See you later.'

On his way out, Sam allowed his gaze to drift across to Abbey, who was still sitting at the table listening intently to her friend. As he passed, she looked up and into his eyes, their gaze locking for the briefest of moments, or perhaps he just imagined that, although there was no mistaking the way her face lit up in recognition as she spotted him. He smiled and nodded, before putting his head down and dashing outside, putting all thoughts of the delightful, charming and seemingly totally unavailable Abbey out of his head.

11

———

Abbey didn't need a formal introduction; she knew exactly who it was standing in front of her without knowing their name or having met them before. The woman, more like a girl really, shrugged off the hood of her sweat top and undid the zip a little, smiling tentatively at Abbey.

'Please, Abbey. I'm sorry for coming after you like this, but I had no other way of contacting you. I'm Rhianna, by the way.'

'I know exactly who you are.' Although putting a name and a face to the woman who had destroyed her future was both fascinating and excruciating at the same time. 'Sorry, but I really don't have anything to say to you.'

Despite herself, Abbey couldn't drag her eyes away from Rhianna. She was young, about twenty or twenty-one, Abbey guessed, with flawless olive skin, unruly black curls that were artfully contained in a ponytail and gorgeous brown eyes. She could see why Jason would be attracted to her, why any hot-blooded male might, but that didn't excuse his behaviour in the slightest. He was supposed to have loved Abbey, but if that were true he wouldn't have gone off with the first gorgeous creature that crossed his path. The feelings she was trying to escape, the ones of anger, hurt and pain, made an unwelcome reappearance, stabbing at her stomach.

'Please, Abbey, I have to explain. I want you to know the truth about what happened between me and Jay.'

'You think I'm interested? I really couldn't care less. Now, if you'll excuse me, I've got somewhere I need to be. Oh, and for your information his name is Jason, not Jay.'

Stupid man. In recent months, he'd started telling people to call him Jay. *Everyone does*, he told newcomers, which was a complete untruth. He thought it made him sound cool, hip, down with the kids. It was about the same time he'd started sporting a baseball cap, worn back to front. In hindsight, she wondered if his mid-life crisis had just arrived early. She turned and marched off, her whole body fizzing with rage. She only stopped when she heard the strangulated wail from behind her.

'Heck, don't cry!'

Rhianna had her head in her hands, looking visibly distressed. This was just what Abbey needed on what was supposed to be her relaxing 'me-time' away from the house. All her instincts told her to walk away and not look back, but the poor girl was in pieces and this was no place for a young girl to be wandering around, hurt and upset. Abbey would never forgive herself if something were to happen to her. She pulled out a tissue from her coat pocket and handed it over to Rhianna. 'Look, shall we head for the cafe? It's about five minutes away from here.'

Rhianna nodded, her whole body shaking, and despite herself, Abbey felt the tiniest pang of sympathy for the girl, even if her overriding feeling was one of irritation. This wasn't how she'd intended her day to go. She marched on, cross now, only turning to check that Rhianna was following her. She would be damned if she was going to make small talk. She'd get her settled in the safety of the cafe with a warm drink and then leave her to her own devices. The girl wasn't her responsibility. Only it seemed Rhianna had other ideas. Or Rhi, as she'd insisted Abbey call her. Once she was sitting at a table with her hands cupped around a mug of cappuccino, she started talking and Abbey wondered if she might never stop.

'I had no idea J... I mean Jason, was in a relationship. He forgot to tell me that important piece of information. It was such a shock when I found out. He told me a completely made-up story. That he'd recently broken up with... you, and he was just tying up all the loose ends.'

Abbey winced. Was that all she had become to Jason, a loose end?

Rhianna went on. 'And once he'd done that, he said we could be together. That's what I was waiting for, living for. I can't believe he would lie to me like that.'

'I can,' said Abbey with no hint of satisfaction.

'He was everything to me.' Rhi clasped her hands together, looking at Abbey imploringly. 'I loved him so much and I honestly thought we had a future together. Now I just feel stupid and used.'

'Well, you do know he's a single man now. You're very welcome to him if you still want him.'

'No way!' Rhi's face was wide-eyed with shock, every wretched emotion etched across her features. 'The thing is, you have to believe me when I say I would never have gone out with him if I'd known the full story. It's a big no-no for me. I've seen the damage lying and cheating can cause – my dad had an affair, which broke up my parents' marriage – and I would never want to be a part of anything like that. I'm so furious with Jason, for putting me through that. I never want to set eyes on that man again.'

That makes two of us.

'Well, that's not going to be easy, considering you both work for

the same company,' Abbey reminded her. She didn't believe
Rhianna's protestations for one moment. Give her a few weeks and
Jason's smooth-talking ways and Rhi would be back under his spell
in next to no time. *Good luck to the pair of them*, she thought.

'Not any more. I walked out on my job. Before they repri-
manded or sacked me for assaulting a colleague.'

'What?' Abbey sat forward in her chair, folding her arms across
her chest, intrigued by Rhi's comment.

'Oh, don't worry, it was only a cup of ice-cold water in Jason's
face. Nothing less than he deserved. There was no way I was going
back to that place all the time he was still working there. I wouldn't
trust myself not to throttle him. I've found myself some shifts at
The Three Feathers in Wishwell until I decide what I want to do
next.'

'Fair play.' Abbey couldn't help but have a sneaky admiration
for Rhi's actions. She only wished she'd done the same. 'It's a
shame about your job.'

'I couldn't care less about the job.'

'Well, if you were hoping to run into Jason at the pub, you'll be
out of luck. He never uses the place. He doesn't like it because they
don't show any of the sports channels or any telly, come to that.
Besides, he's back living with his mum now.'

'Honestly, Abbey, please don't think I took the job in Wishwell
to be near to Jason. No way! If that man's got any sense, he'll stay
well away from me.'

Rhianna was defiant; there was no sign of the vulnerable and
haunted girl that had pursued her in the woods and Abbey felt a
begrudging respect for the young woman with her absolute belief
in her emotions and what she was doing. Abbey couldn't
remember being quite so self-assured at Rhi's age. Perhaps if she
had been, then she wouldn't have wasted the best years of her
twenties on someone who wasn't even worth the time of day.

'I just feel so disappointed in myself that I didn't see through him, that he was able to deceive me the way he did. Most of all, I'm sorry for the hurt and pain that I've inadvertently caused to you. I want you to know how sorry I am, Abbey.'

Abbey wondered how she could ever have doubted Rhi in the first place. She was obviously racked with guilt over what had happened; she'd been wringing her hands together the entire time she was speaking to Abbey, and her red-rimmed eyes were evidence enough of the distress Jason had caused.

'I don't blame you,' said Abbey. How could she when Rhi's life had been turned upside down in the same way as Abbey's had? 'It's Jason who's at fault here, not anyone else. Look, I know it's difficult but don't waste any more emotional energy on that man. He's really not worth it. We've both got to move on with our lives and start afresh.'

'Yes, absolutely. That's what I intend to do. Don't you worry.'

Abbey didn't have any concerns about Rhianna. She was young, smart and capable, and would bounce back from this sordid episode in next to no time. As would Abbey, only it might take her a little longer, she suspected.

'Hello, my lovely. Are you all done here?'

Abbey's mood lifted when she saw Lizzie standing there, with her usual sunny expression. Lizzie collected the empty mugs onto her tray and was just about to leave when she remembered.

'Can't be too long to go now until your big day. I bet you're a mass of nerves and excitement?'

Abbey faltered as she clocked Rhianna's horrified expression, wondering if the mention of the wedding might set her off in tears again. Lizzie gave a nervous chuckle, clearly realising something must be amiss and wondering what it was that she could possibly have said out of turn.

'Um... actually, the wedding's off.'

No point in beating about the bush or dressing it up as something else. All those phone calls she'd made to the people on her guest list had taught her that it was much easier to just come straight out with it.

'No?' Lizzie's shock was evident. 'Well, I'm very sorry to hear that.' Lizzie didn't want to probe, but her heart went out to Abbey. She rested a hand on her shoulder and leant forward to look into her eyes. 'Are you okay, darling?'

Abbey swallowed hard. The genuine concern shown by Lizzie took her by surprise – some of the people on her wedding guest list hadn't even asked about her wellbeing. They were more concerned about missing out on a good old shindig, so the kindness of a relative stranger touched her deeply.

'Yep, I'm fine, thank you.' She blinked back the tears threatening to fall. 'And it's much better to find out now about my delightful intended rather than after the event,' she said, brazening it out.

'Best decision she's ever made,' added Rhi, with feeling.

'Well, more fool him,' Lizzie said, agreeing wholeheartedly. She was so pleased Abbey had the support of her friend when she most needed it. 'You deserve so much better. Tell you what, next time you're in, have a coffee and a bacon butty or a sticky bun with me, my treat.'

'I'd enjoy that,' said Abbey, knowing that Lizzie would listen to the whole story calmly and without any sort of judgement.

'In the meantime, I'll leave you in peace to have a chatter with your friend.'

Abbey bit back the reply on her tongue about exactly the type of friend Rhi actually was, but instead she looked across at the young woman who was smiling at her with those big brown eyes, which were both beguiling and determined in equal measure.

When Lizzie had left to attend to other customers, Rhianna stretched out a hand on the table between them.

'I really hope we can be friends now, Abbey. Something good has to come from this whole fiasco.'

Abbey smiled noncommittally. She might be able to accept that none of this was Rhi's fault, but to ask her to become friends with the beautiful young woman who had so enchanted Jason and shattered all her plans for the future was expecting far too much of her and seriously overestimating Abbey's potential for forgiveness. After today, she'd be happy if she never saw Rhi again. She really didn't need those sort of reminders.

12

Rhianna folded the tea towel over the pumps at The Three Feathers, signalling the end of her lunchtime shift at the quaint village pub. With its low oak beams, inglenook fireplace and stained-glass windows, it really was a lovely environment to work in, much better than the faceless corporate office block she'd been used to. She waved goodbye to Malc and Jan, the landlords, and walked through the pretty beer garden to the car park out the back. She had to admit she'd landed on her feet finding this job so quickly. She had experience of pulling pints from her student days and, along with her can-do attitude, that was enough to quickly win Jan over. The pub had a happy and vibrant atmosphere with lots of friendly customers, and in the quiet spells, not that there were too many of those, she would take a moment on the stool behind the bar, her gaze drifting through the mullioned windows to the village green outside. Rhianna looked forward to coming into work, doing her job, having a chat and a giggle, without the fear of being weighed down by office politics. More pleasingly, there was little chance of her running into Jason. A stint behind a bar may not have featured in her career plan, but sometimes it was good to take some time out to consider what came next. Ultimately, she wanted to find another job where she could use her degree in business management, but for the next few weeks, at least, this would suit her just fine.

The drive home on the quiet country roads through the local villages, passing by the stone cottages, old churches and green playing areas, was much better than doing battle with the busy rush-hour traffic in town. She even drove past Primrose Woods every day, but she didn't give a second thought to all those occasions she'd met Jason there. Just the thought of him and what they'd got up to made her skin crawl. Instead she thought of Abbey and wondered how she was getting on. Abbey had told her how much she loved the park, how it was her happy place, somewhere she escaped to when everything was getting on top of her, so there was no way she was going to confess to Abbey it had been her and Jason's meeting spot, spoiling that illusion for her. She was just pleased that she'd been able to meet Abbey the other week and tell her side of the story. Of course, she hadn't expected forgiveness or anything like that, but she wanted Abbey to know just how sorry she really was.

Arriving home, she put her key in the lock and before she'd even got over the threshold, she heard her mum's voice call out.

'Ah, Rhianna, you have a visitor!'

A *visitor*. For the briefest of moments, a swirl of excitement grew in her stomach as she wondered if it could be Jason, before common sense caught up with her and the excitement was quickly replaced by a flash of anger. He wouldn't dare to come here, would he? Her hackles rose as she primed herself to confront the man who had caused her so much grief.

'Oh, it's you,' she said, relief washing over her as she peered around the living room doorway, spotting Luke perched on the edge of the sofa, a mug of tea in his hands.

He jumped up and produced a bunch of flowers from the side of the sofa, like a magician from a top hat, and presented them to Rhianna.

'Hope you don't mind me popping in, but I was just passing and thought I'd see how you were doing.'

'Isn't that lovely, Rhi?' said her mum, who was beaming at her, eyebrows waggling furiously. 'I'm popping into town now, so I'll leave you two to it. Lovely meeting you, Luke.'

'You too, Mrs West!'

Rhi chuckled as she heard the front door close. 'Sorry about Mum; she gets a bit overexcited at times.'

'Don't worry, she was absolutely lovely. Made me very welcome. I didn't mention anything about work. I wasn't sure how much she knew. Said I was an old friend.'

'Thanks, Luke,' said Rhi, taking the flowers and thinking how pretty they were, grateful for the kind gesture and his thoughtfulness on both counts. In all the time she'd been seeing Jason, he'd never bought her flowers. The only present he'd ever given her was some sexy red lingerie, which, in hindsight, had obviously been more of a present for him.

'You're right, I didn't tell Mum about the details of me leaving. She doesn't know about Jason either,' she admitted sheepishly. 'Just as well, really.' Funny how she'd been keen to keep Jason's presence in her life a secret, knowing her mum would have asked all those awkward questions that she'd been asking herself, and Jason too. Perhaps, deep down, she'd known something was amiss, but was too afraid to face up to it.

Finding a vase in the dresser, she filled it with water and popped the flowers inside, inhaling their lovely fragrant scent. Later, she would trim them and arrange them properly, but she didn't want to keep Luke waiting. She took a seat in the leather armchair opposite him on the sofa.

'I guess we're still hot gossip in the office?' she ventured cautiously.

'Well, I can't pretend it didn't provide a bit of a talking point for a couple of days, but honestly, it's old news now.'

Away from the constraints of the office, Luke seemed different somehow. The suit and tie had been replaced by jeans and a pale blue polo shirt, which set off his naturally bright eyes and blond hair. Usually, he was there with a smart quip or a joke, but his tone was more considered and concerned today.

'At least I won't have to see any of them again. They must have all thought I was completely crazy.'

'To be honest, I think most people were impressed by your spunk. There were a few who would have loved to do the same to Jason, maybe with a bigger mug of water. Me especially.'

Rhianna put her head into her hands and cringed. 'Honestly, I feel like such an idiot. I don't know what I ever saw in him.'

'Well, at least you've found out what he's really like. You deserve so much better than him, Rhi.'

She felt a prickling of shame at her cheeks. Luke had gone out of his way to visit her and check that she was doing okay, when she didn't really deserve his kindness. She'd always been haughty and dismissive of him at work, rejecting his friendly overtures and only deigning to speak to him when she had to.

'So what's next for you?'

'At the moment I'm working at The Three Feathers in Wishwell, just to see me through the next month or so. I'm looking out for other jobs too, but I'm thinking I might go travelling for a while. I never did the whole gap year thing when I was at university so now might be an ideal opportunity. I certainly won't rush into anything, though. I'm taking my time before deciding what comes next.'

'Sounds like a good plan.' He smiled, and drained the last of his tea. 'I ought to be making a move.' He stood up and Rhi felt a pang of disappointment that he was leaving so soon. She realised that she knew so little about him and now she wished she did. Where did he live? What did he do outside work? What were *his* plans and dreams?

'How are you, Luke?' she blurted, in a last-minute attempt to keep him talking.

'Good, thanks.' He nodded, not really giving anything away. 'Anyway, it's great to know you're feeling so positive about the future and things are working out for you.'

He headed for the door.

'Yes, and thanks again for the flowers.'

She wrapped her arms around her chest, unsure of what to do with them otherwise, inclined as she was to hug him, but uncertain if that was the right thing to do in the circumstances. She couldn't suddenly pretend to be best friends with Luke when she'd barely given him the time of day at work. Instead, she took a step backwards to allow him to pass, and gave him a little finger wave.

'My pleasure. See you around,' he said on his way out of the door without looking backwards.

'Yes,' she replied, not knowing if that would actually be the case, but rather hoping that it might be. She needed all the friends she could get at the moment, but especially, now that Luke had reached out to her, she realised she wanted to get to know him so much better, if only he would let her.

13

It had been a couple of weeks since Lizzie had seen Abbey in the cafe, but she hadn't been able to stop thinking about her in the meantime, wondering how she was getting on. Lizzie barely knew the girl, who reminded her a lot of her own daughter, being of a similar age, but the shock of hearing her wedding was off had stayed with Lizzie ever since. Goodness knows how poor Abbey must be feeling. So she was happy and relieved when she spotted her on that Thursday morning, as she walked through the doors of the Treetops Cafe and immediately rushed over to greet her.

'Hello, lovely, how are you? Take a seat in the window over there and I'll bring your order over. What do you fancy?'

'Mmm, a pot of tea and a toasted teacake, please. Are you going to join me?'

'Absolutely. It's good timing; I was just going to take my break.'

A few minutes later, Lizzie was back with the order, placing it on the table and pulling out a chair opposite Abbey. She shuffled up in her seat, her gaze observing Abbey's fine features.

'So how have you been keeping? I've been thinking about you and wondering how you were getting on?'

'Yeah, not too bad.' Abbey gave a wry smile. 'There are bad days, but I suppose that's only to be expected and I try not to dwell on them. I'm keeping busy at work and I've been rearranging the house, making it my own again. If I'm feeling particularly blue then I just come over here and follow one of the trails, or else find a peaceful spot to sit and watch the world go by. Honestly, it works wonders. By the time I get home I always feel heaps better.'

'Good. I always tell people this place has magical properties. It's all the primroses; they're meant to be a doorway into the fairy world. Katy used to love coming here when she was little and spotting the flowers and searching out the fairies – she would even give them names. I was looking forward to showing Rosie when they came over.' She gave a sigh. 'Never mind. There'll be another time.'

'That's so sweet. I never knew that about the primroses. What a lovely tale.'

'Yes.' Lizzie thought it best not to mention that primroses represented eternal love as well. Not at the moment, at least. She was only glad Abbey was feeling the benefits of visiting the woods, as so many others did too. 'Anyway, you're looking well, I must say.'

'It's all the exercise and fresh air I'm getting; I'm sure it's doing me the power of good. After what happened with Jason, I was determined not to crumble. I won't give him the satisfaction. Obviously, there are difficult times, usually in the middle of the night, when all the pain and hurt comes to the surface, but I won't let it get the better of me. It's pretty humiliating to learn that your fiancé has been playing around behind your back for goodness knows how long, but in a way I feel lucky that I found out when I did. Can you imagine if it had come to light after the wedding?'

'So that's what happened, is it? Well, in that case, you had a lucky escape.'

Abbey nodded, her gaze drifting out of the window, thoughtful for a moment. 'Yeah, the saddest thing to me is that we had all those years together, twelve in total, and any good times have now been spoilt by what happened at the end. It just seems such a waste of time.' Abbey was grateful for Lizzie's undivided attention. The older woman didn't interrupt or allow her interest to drift; she listened with genuine warmth and concern and it was easy to open up to her. 'It was my own fault, really.'

'Why would you say that? It doesn't sound as though you did anything wrong.'

Abbey pushed her empty plate to one side and dabbed at her mouth with a napkin, before sighing heavily.

'He did it once before, not long after we first got together. I was so madly in love with him in those days that I forgave him and hoped it was just a blip. I'm not sure I ever fully trusted him after that. I wish I'd had the gumption to walk away then.' She thought of young Rhianna and the way she'd reacted to Jason's behaviour, knowing she would never have hung around even to listen to Jason's excuses. Part of her regretted that she hadn't acted in such an emphatic way herself all those years ago. Where might she be now if she had? Living a different life entirely, she suspected, if only she'd listened to her instincts.

'Well, it shows what a good person you are to be so forgiving. And doesn't everyone deserve a second chance?' Lizzie paused, mulling over her own words for a moment. 'Although, probably not Jason.'

They locked eyes and giggled. Lizzie, she'd quickly discovered, was a kindred spirit.

'Definitely not Jason. Do you know, Lizzie, I think most of my initial hurt and anger was down to pride. I felt stupid and embarrassed that I hadn't worked out what was going on. There were plenty of signs, and I felt so outraged that he could actually do that to me. I still can't believe it. But do you know, putting all of those feelings to one side, I'm actually relieved that it's over. It took me a few days to admit it, but I realised I would be accepting second best by marrying Jason. I'd put so much time and effort into the relationship that I didn't want to give up on it, but I've come to accept that I didn't love him any more. Not really. I loved the idea of him and our relationship, but the reality didn't actually live up to the fantasy inside my head. And it's clear Jason didn't love me.' Abbey nodded decisively, looking around the cafe, relieved to be saying the words aloud, cementing her true thoughts and feelings. 'He's actually done me a massive favour by bringing about the end of our relationship.'

'I think so too. It's no way to start out on married life with all those lies and dishonesty. Remember, not all men are like your ex. There are plenty of good ones out there. It's just a question of finding one.'

'Huh!' Abbey gave an involuntary grunt. 'Honestly, I'm in no hurry whatsoever. I'm just going to concentrate on myself for once, spend more time with Dad and give the garden a bit of an over-haul. If I should meet someone, then they're going to have to be pretty damn perfect and I think that's a bit of a tall order!'

She omitted to tell Lizzie about the times she woke up in a complete panic in the middle of the night, wondering if she might ever achieve her dreams of a happy family life, her biological clock clanking loudly in her ear. In the cold light of day it didn't seem quite so bad, but there was no getting away from the fact that she was fast approaching her thirties. Had she missed her chance of meeting a decent man and having a family together? Sometimes, in those darkest, loneliest hours, it seemed that way. Still, she wasn't going to jump into another relationship just because she felt the sensation of time rushing past her. One thing was for certain, she'd be a lot more wary next time around.

'Look, I wanted to ask you.' Lizzie leant across the table,

clasping her hands together. 'What are you doing a week on Saturday?'

Abbey's features darkened for the briefest of moments and Lizzie was relieved that she'd got the date right after all.

'The sixteenth? That was my—'

'I know,' interrupted Lizzie with a tentative smile. 'Your intended wedding day. I thought it might be nice for you to spend it with someone who doesn't know Jason or the pair of you as a couple. Get away from the house and do something a little different. It's only an idea. If you have other plans then I perfectly understand.'

'No! I think Dad and I were going to head out and grab some lunch somewhere, but there are no definite plans in place.'

'Well, that's perfect, then. Come and have lunch round at mine. Bring your dad too. Only if you want to, of course?'

Abbey smiled, overwhelmingly touched by the unexpected gesture. As it stood, she and her dad were undecided on what they should do on that particular day, just a promise to spend it together. Now Lizzie had made it an easy decision for them.

'To be honest with you, I have been dreading it, wondering how I'll get through it. I shall be so glad when it's over, but it will be good to have something to look forward to. It's very kind of you to offer.'

'It will be my absolute pleasure. And will give me the chance to get to know your dad a bit better too.'

Truth be known, she was thrilled that Abbey had agreed to come. Part of her worried that she was overstepping the mark by even inviting Abbey along in the first place. She wouldn't have wanted to offend her. The women had only met each other a few times, but there'd been a connection from the outset. They'd clicked straight away and chatted along freely as though they'd known each other for years. Perhaps it was because she could relate to Abbey in a similar way to her own daughter, Katy. Already Lizzie was planning what she might prepare for lunch. She didn't have many visitors these days, preferring to get out of the house if she was socialising, so she would enjoy pottering about the kitchen getting everything ready. The most important thing was to ensure Abbey could forget, if only for an hour or two, what it was she should have been doing on that particular day.

It was only later, seeing Sam when he pulled up outside the cafe in his jeep, that Lizzie suddenly realised her mistake. *Damn.* She was out of practice at making social arrangements and now she'd only gone and double-booked for that Saturday. Sam had offered to come along and fix her fence panels in the back garden that had been blown down in the recent storm and she'd promised him lunch for his efforts. Would it really matter that they were all coming on the same day? Well, there was nothing she could do about it now, not when she didn't want to let either of them down. Hopefully it would be a case of the more the merrier.

14

There was no need for Abbey to hurry home. There would be no one waiting for her, no one expecting a meal later tonight, and nothing to do except please herself for the rest of the day. It was an unexpected but hugely welcome consequence of her newly single status. Even if it was still taking some getting used to. In fact, her days were her own for the next three weeks. She'd booked the time off work ages ago, ten days for all the preparation she had to do in anticipation of the wedding itself and two weeks for the non-existent honeymoon that she'd been hoping Jason had been busy organising in the background. Turned out he'd been busy doing other things, with no thought to Abbey or their wedding arrangements.

She briefly considered rearranging her holiday leave until later in the year, but then she decided she probably needed the break to assimilate everything that had happened. Her plan was to do nothing much at all but potter around the house, see those friends who had reached out to her, spend time with her dad and, no doubt, while away the hours here at Primrose Woods.

Stepping outside the cafe, she took a deep breath, embracing the warmth of the late spring day. The park was a patchwork of habitats: woodland, heath, meadows and lakes and ponds. Even though Abbey might walk the same route on several different occasions, there was always something new to discover on each visit.

On her way here this morning, before popping into the cafe for a reviving cuppa and a bite to eat, courtesy of Lizzie, and an unexpected but very welcome lunch invitation, Abbey had walked along the Woodpecker Trail, marvelling at the activity in the trees around her, listening out for the distinctive drumming and drilling of the birds who'd given their name to this part of the park. Occasionally she would spot the distinctive red marking on the head of a bird as it clung on to the bark of a tree, brightening up her day.

Now, she headed in the other direction through the woods, which led to the exit nearest to home. As she got deep amongst the trees, she spotted a group of rangers working together in a fenced-off area where some of the trees were being coppiced. Her gaze sought out Sam, while wondering at the same time why her heart had picked up apace. Clearly her emotions were still all over the place. It wasn't the first time today he'd popped into her mind. When she was sitting in the cafe waiting for Lizzie to join her, her gaze had drifted out of the window, hoping she might spot him, knowing that to catch a glimpse of him would brighten up her day. For some reason he had that effect on her. It was only when Lizzie returned laden down with breakfast goodies that she'd put the thought of Sam out of her head. Now, out in the warm spring air, the mischievous thoughts taunted her again. A cursory glance in the direction of the rangers told her that Sam wasn't a member of this particular working party. As she walked on, though, she heard frenzied scrabbling noises coming from the bushes. She stopped to look, thinking it might be a squirrel or a muntjac deer, but instead she saw a flash of liver and white darting through the undergrowth, before a familiar bundle of fur came bounding towards her, running straight into her legs, the dog's tail wagging furiously.

'Hello, you!' said Abbey, recognising Lady immediately, bending down to make a fuss of the furball who was greeting her like she was her long-lost owner.

'Lady!' Abbey heard Sam's voice first. It reverberated off the trees until he suddenly appeared, his expression fierce and determined as he followed in the wake of his dog. When he spotted Abbey, his face relaxed and lit up in a wide smile. 'Ah, it's you! Nice to see you. Sorry if she's bothering you. Lady, will you get down,' he commanded, as his dog pestered Abbey for even more attention, taking no notice of her master whatsoever.

'It's fine,' said Abbey, laughing, actually grateful to the dog. It gave her an excuse to focus her attentions downwards, rather than looking up and into the direct gaze of Sam that had the odd effect of making her feel exposed and vulnerable. The half-smile on his lips had a similar effect. 'I promise I'm not deliberately leading your dog astray.'

'She obviously likes you and Lady is known to be a great judge of character, so don't worry about it.'

There it was again, that smile, which ignited in his dark, appraising eyes before reaching his wide full mouth. The way he focused his whole attention on her affected her in a funny way, playing havoc with her heartbeat and sending her head into a spin too. Maybe it was because she didn't know how to act around gorgeous-looking men any more, she was so out of practice.

Perhaps that's what it was – maybe he was flirting with her? How would she even know? It had been such a long time. No, he was just being friendly, and she chided herself for reading far too much into their innocent interaction.

'Looks like you're busy?' Abbey gestured to the activity behind him.

'Yes, we're clearing the area of some trees, having a general tidy-up and building up the bank that borders the farmland. We've had a few stray sheep wanting to hang out over here so we're trying to stop their antics.'

'I guess there's always something to do in your line of work.'

'Absolutely. There's never a dull moment but I wouldn't have it any other way.'

There was a genuine enthusiasm and affability that radiated from Sam, which Abbey found extremely appealing. Along with his imposing physical presence, which she was doing her best to ignore. While Sam grabbed Lady and put her on the lead, Abbey shook her head, ridding herself of the fanciful thoughts. She remembered the woman she'd seen with Sam that day and felt a twist of jealousy for someone she didn't even know, for a relationship she didn't know the first thing about and for the fact that Sam was probably much more honest and straightforward in that relationship than Jason had ever been in theirs. How did she know, though? Didn't everyone's relationship look rosy from the outside? And how would she ever be in a position where she felt able to trust a man, especially when her radar for these things had let her down so seriously? She bent down to fondle Lady, who'd been wagging her tail the entire time. At least with dogs you knew exactly where you stood.

'Right, well, I'll let you go back to your trees. I should be getting home.'

'Well, it's good to see you again, Abbey.'

'Yes.' She faltered, his casual use of her name stopping her in her tracks. He'd remembered. 'You too.'

She walked away, her cheeks glowing, trying to quash the ridiculous tsunami of emotions rushing through her body.

'Oh, Abbey?'

'Yes?' She turned, expectant, seeing that friendly smile on his face again.

'Good luck with everything... you know,' he said, circling his hand in explanation.

'Oh, thank you,' she said, at a loss for anything else to say, not understanding at all. 'Good luck to you too,' she added, wondering if now she didn't sound rude. The only conclusion she came to as she went on her way was that she definitely overthought everything when it came to Sam Finnegan.

Back at home, Abbey headed straight upstairs. She'd been putting off this job for far too long. She pulled her wedding dress out of the wardrobe, her stomach churning at the sight of it. The sensation of the luxurious fabric between her fingers made her shudder. Stopping herself from holding her dress up against her body in the mirror for one last time, in case she realised it suddenly was the perfect dress after all, she quickly stuffed the gown into a black bin liner. She'd thought about selling it online, but that didn't sit right with her. The dress now represented her loss and sadness around her wedding day, and she didn't want to pass on any such associations to an unsuspecting prospective bride. Nor did she much fancy explaining why exactly she was selling the unused gown. She would rather give it away not knowing where it might end up, the new owner having no idea of its history. She would take it to one of the charity shops in town and hope that it would find its perfect match. A blind date! It was a gorgeous dress; someone somewhere would look absolutely amazing in it, but that was never going to be Abbey. Not in a million years. What had she been thinking? She chuckled as she wrestled with the billowing fabric as it tried to escape from the bag, conjuring up an image of her mum's face, had she ever got to see the dress. Abbey should have taken it as a sign.

15

Abbey was still on the lookout for signs. When she woke on that Saturday, the morning of what should have been her wedding day, she half expected the sky to be brooding with storm clouds and the rain to be thrashing against the windows of the cottage. Instead, when she pulled back the daisy sprig curtains in her bedroom, the sun was high in the sky and a golden warmth flooded through the paned windows. A perfect day for a wedding.

Abbey paused for a moment to consider how she was feeling. Did she have an urge to break down into tears and sob her heart out, which would be perfectly understandable in the circumstances? But no, her internal musings discovered there were no such feelings. Maybe she was in denial and a huge wave of emotion would overtake her later in the day, but the way she was feeling right now, she didn't suspect so. All she felt was a lightness of body and mind. A freedom. Today brought the much-needed closure on Jason and that particular episode of her life and heralded the start of a whole new beginning.

She picked up her phone from the bedside cabinet to a couple of messages from old friends who hoped she was doing okay and would be in touch soon to arrange a get-together. Some people weren't sure how to react or what to say to someone whose wedding was called off just a few weeks before the big event, but that was okay with her. There would be plenty of time for catching up with all the people she'd been expecting to see today. There was a message from her dad confirming what time he would be round to collect her. And, predictably, there was a message from Jason, pleading with Abbey to speak to him, to give him another chance and telling her that it wasn't too late for them and their relationship. What an idiot! With a flourish she blocked his number and wondered why she hadn't done it sooner.

'Good morning, sweetheart, how are you?' Bill arrived on her doorstep a little while later with a big bouquet of flowers in his hands and a kindly smile on his face.

'Dad, thanks, these are so pretty.' She hugged him tight, resting her head on his chest, blinking away the tears that prickled at her eyes. 'I'm feeling remarkably good, actually, and very pleased about our change of plans for today,' she said, laughing.

'Do you know, I am too,' said Bill with feeling.

'Why did you never say anything, Dad?' She wandered off towards the kitchen in search of a vase, her dad following her down the hallway.

'How could I? You would never have thanked me for it. In some cases, and definitely where your daughter's relationships are concerned, however hard it is, you have to keep your mouth shut and let them, you, come to your own conclusions. I didn't want any bad feelings to come between us. I'm just glad you came to your senses when you did.'

She couldn't blame her dad. He'd been in a difficult position and she realised she'd been in her own little bubble for so long that she probably wouldn't have listened anyway. Her dad was always there at her side, supporting her in all her decisions, and she was guilty, she knew, of taking him for granted. She looked into his sparkly, kind eyes and felt a surge of love for him. She'd neglected him over recent months, too immersed as she'd been in the arrangements for the wedding. She'd make it up to him. They would spend more time together now. Have more days out together.

With the flowers artfully arranged and placed on a sunny windowsill, they decided to walk to Lizzie's house. It was a ten-minute drive so a leisurely amble along the towpath of the canal would take them about forty-five minutes. From Abbey's cottage, they headed into the village and took the footpath through the churchyard signposted to the canal. They wandered through the wildflower meadow to the bottom of the field where they crossed the wooden bridge that straddled the meandering river, pausing there a moment to peer into the water below, before stepping down into the second field and continuing their stroll towards the canal. They were in no hurry and as it was such a gloriously sunny day they were able to pause and watch the narrow boats navigating the locks, smiling at the antics of the ducks and their babies, and stop and chat to various dog walkers and their pets. There was only one moment where Abbey glanced at her watch and wondered what she might have been doing at that particular time had her wedding gone ahead as planned. She realised she would have been at the hairdresser's, having her red hair teased into a French plait, before hurrying home to meet Sarah, the make-up artist. They'd agreed on a palette of soft and golden hues to provide a dewy look, enhancing Abbey's natural features, and she couldn't help imagining herself as a beautiful bride, her skin glowing with happiness as she shared her big day with all her family and friends. She felt a pang of regret for missing out on all those special moments that she'd dreamt of ever since she was a young girl, and wondered if there might ever be another wedding day with another man, but that fleeting thought disappeared as quickly as it arrived. She was right off men at the moment. Funnily enough, she gave scant regard to Jason, which told her she'd made absolutely the right decision.

'Come in, come in!' Lizzie greeted them fondly when they arrived at her charming, white-washed cottage with a yellow rambling rose climbing up the weathered oak porch. She ushered them through the hallway and into the cosy living room with double French doors, which were opened out onto a narrow but long garden that wended its way down to a low fence overlooking a field. The mooching cows made it a picture-perfect scene.

'What would you like to drink? I have a sparkling wine or some elderflower cordial. Or would you prefer a coffee?'

'Sparkling wine sounds good,' Abbey and Bill said, almost in unison, laughing.

'Go and sit on the patio and I'll bring your drinks out.'

As Abbey had suspected, it didn't feel awkward coming to Lizzie's at all. She had greeted them both as if they were old friends and that was exactly how it felt to Abbey – as if she'd known Lizzie for years. They wandered outside to the patio and Abbey turned her face up to the sky, soaking up the midday warmth. It was such a lovely, secluded spot with a weathered table and chairs, surrounded by an abundance of terracotta pots filled with a mixture of pink and red blooms and the scent of lavender wafting in the air. Abbey cast her gaze along the length of the garden to the fields beyond, spotting a figure working there. She took the drink offered by Lizzie, taking a very welcome sip, the bubbles playing on her tongue before something registered in her mind. She snapped her attention back to the figure working in the distance. There was something familiar about his stance, the way he stood with his hands resting on his hips, his height and the broadness of his shoulders. She screwed up her eyes, placing a hand on her brow to check that her eyes weren't deceiving her. More likely it was her mind playing tricks. It was only when the figure turned and looked towards the house that her suspicions were confirmed. It was him! She recognised the brown, unruly curls and the strong, bronzed forearms as they manhandled a fence panel into place. Involuntarily, her heart started thumping in her chest and a heat prickled at her cheeks. Probably a combination of the sun and the effect of the bubbles going straight to her head. And the unexpectedly delightful view too, of course. She was glad when Lizzie reappeared, placing a bowl of olives and a jug of cheese straws on the table, which served as a welcome distraction. Abbey took a seat between her dad and Lizzie, before taking another casual look into the distance. She really couldn't help herself and this time she was relieved, and maybe a tad disappointed too, that the figure had gone, obviously moved on to another part of the field, or maybe she really had been imagining things after all.

She returned her attention to Lizzie, who was explaining to Bill how she managed to keep the garden in such good order. She was happy to do the light work, tending to the patio pots and hanging baskets, and pruning her shrubs, but apparently, her next-door neighbour, Simon, came in to mow the lawn and trim the hedges, and in return Lizzie kept him and his young family supplied with home-baked cookies and cakes. It was an arrangement that worked well for both of them.

'It was my late husband, David, who was the gardener. He had green fingers and would spend hours out here pottering around. It was his pride and joy. I'm afraid I don't have the same gentle touch with the plants. I only have to look at them for them to keel over and die. I've managed these pots here, but that's as far as my expertise takes me.'

'Well, it looks marvellous,' said Bill. 'I think you're doing yourself a great disservice; it's like Kew Gardens out here.'

Abbey smiled to herself, noticing Lizzie blush. She was relieved that the two of them seemed to be getting on so well, avoiding any awkwardness.

'It's true,' added Abbey, who was relishing the sensation of the sun on her skin. 'It's such a beautiful spot. Perfect for sitting out here with your morning cuppa and a book or newspaper.'

Lizzie nodded, encouraged by Abbey's words and interested to see her garden anew through Bill and Abbey's eyes. They were right, of course. It was a lovely spot, but she rarely came out here to sit and enjoy the peace and quiet alone. Where was the pleasure in that? Too much time to sit and ponder about the past and her family on the other side of the world did her no good whatsoever. Much better to keep busy and find jobs to do around the house. Perhaps, though, she should make more use of this lovely space, realising, as she shared the experience with friends, what a treat it was. Especially on a day like today when the weather was so glorious.

'Right, I think we're all done.'

Seemingly from nowhere, a familiar voice rang out and Abbey knew who it was within a heartbeat, her mind and stomach performing somersaults. So he hadn't been working in the field, but in Lizzie's garden, as Abbey had half-hoped and suspected.

'Sorry, I didn't realise you had visitors.' It *was* Sam Finnegan. He came to an abrupt halt as he emerged from around the side path, looking almost as surprised as Abbey felt. He ran a hand through his mussed-up hair, doing a double take as realisation dawned, managing to look entirely gorgeous in the process. 'Hi…' he said, a bemused smile on his lips.

'You know Abbey, don't you, Sam? She's a regular visitor to Primrose Woods and this is her dad, Bill. You'll be ready for a drink now after all that hard work. What do you fancy?'

'A beer would be great, but look, I don't want to intrude…'

'Nonsense,' jumped in Bill. 'You wouldn't be intruding at all, not as far as we're concerned. You're very welcome to join us,' he said, glancing at Abbey, who nodded her approval too, even if she was still taken aback by Sam's appearance here.

'Perfect,' said Lizzie. 'Let me go and fetch that beer.' She quickly departed, leaving her guests chatting away happily, really rather pleased with herself at how she'd handled the situation.

16

Within minutes, after the initial awkwardness had evaporated into the warm air, and Sam had cleaned himself up after the toil of his morning labours, the four of them sat around Lizzie's garden table, enjoying the fizz, nibbles and ambience as though the whole event might have been arranged. Which, of course, it had, even if inadvertently. Lizzie told Abbey and Bill about her family in Australia, showing them the framed photos of Katy, Brad and Rosie that were dotted around the entire house.

'It's such a shame that they're not able to come over now this year, but I have to forgive them because they have the best possible excuse. Katy is expecting a little brother or sister for Rosie. It's such exciting news.'

'Aw, that's lovely,' sighed Bill. 'Will you be going out to visit them when the baby arrives?'

The excitement on Lizzie's features flittered away, replaced with a cloud of anxiety.

'I'm not sure about that. I've not managed the trip yet. I'm not a very good traveller, I'm afraid.' She gave a nervous giggle. 'Of course, Katy would love me to go and I'm desperate to see them all, but I can't see it happening somehow.'

'That's such a shame. You'd be bound to have such a wonderful time with your little grandchildren,' said Abbey, full of enthusiasm, before she noticed Lizzie's pained expression. 'Is it travelling on your own that you're not keen on or is it the flying aspect?'

'Both! But it's mainly getting on a plane. I come out in a cold sweat just thinking about it. Sam will tell you what I'm like.' She tried to laugh it off, looking across at him for support, but Lizzie's fear was clear for everyone to see. If David was still here, she might have considered it. Travelling to the other side of the world together would have been an adventure, but her confidence in doing things alone had all but vanished ever since her 'rock' had left her side. Shame prickled at her cheeks. She knew it might seem ridiculous to other people, but there was nothing anyone could say to her to make it seem any less terrifying.

'I do know how you feel, Lizzie.' He nodded intently, his face full of concern. 'Maybe, though, you shouldn't discard the whole idea out of hand.' Sam's voice was soft and gentle, carefully negotiating the fine line between friendly support and nagging. 'Just think how amazing it would be to see your family again. Sometimes we need to push ourselves to face the things that scare us the most. I promise you it won't be half as bad as you're imagining it to be.'

Lizzie sighed. Could that really be true? She didn't think so.

'What would David be telling you to do if he was here?'

Lizzie locked eyes with Bill, noticing the kindness radiating from his gaze. She liked the familiar way he spoke about David as though he was an old friend, bringing his presence right back into the here and now.

'Oh, he'd be telling me to put my big-girl knickers on and to get myself out there pronto.' She chuckled, hearing his voice now, gently chiding her. And what surprised her most of all was that she could laugh about it with her newly discovered friends. Their interest was genuine and she could tell they weren't judging her; they just wanted to help.

'Ah, well, there you go, then,' said Bill, his eyes wide as he nodded his head, as if encouraging her.

'Okay, okay. I'll have another think about it, but I'm not making any promises to anyone.'

Lunch was a very civilised affair with a selection of cold meats, continental cheeses and a Greek salad served with lovely hunks of bread, and a delicious crisp wine, which helped the conversation flow and the laughter to echo in the air. When there was a natural lull in the conversation, Sam stood up to refill the wine glasses with the very quaffable rosé that was perfect for the time of year. Abbey took a sip, her eyes snagging with Sam's as he picked up his glass and raised it slightly in her direction.

'So, I hear you're getting married very soon?' said Sam, entirely without guile, his face set in a wide smile until he noticed the deathly hush descend upon the group and the not so subtle shift in what, until that point, had been a very happy atmosphere. A cold trickle of fear ran through him as he saw the look of dismay on Lizzie's face.

'Oh... have I got that wrong? It wouldn't be the first time. I'm sorry... I...' He stopped himself, not wanting to make matters worse. His brow creased as he cast a glance around him, his eyes searching out an answer from someone, but there was no escaping the discomfort around the table. He could have sworn Lizzie had mentioned something about a wedding – it had stuck in his mind – but clearly he'd got the wrong end of the stick entirely. And now he had the distinct impression he'd put his size ten boots into something he should have steered well clear of.

'That's my fault,' admitted Lizzie, looking sheepish. 'I must have mentioned it in passing,' she told Abbey and her dad, 'but of course that was a little while ago now before... well, you know?'

'Don't worry,' said Abbey, waving a hand in the direction of Sam's stricken expression. 'You're not wrong. I was meant to be getting married... today actually, but well, let's just say I had a lucky escape.'

'Ah... okay.' His face crumpled in dismay. 'Today, though?'

She couldn't help but feel sorry for him. He looked uncomfortable, rubbing a hand along his forearm. She was surprised he even knew or could remember that she was supposed to be getting married and that he and Lizzie had even talked about the subject before. When had that happened?

'Sounds as though you've been through a tough time?'

She nodded, annoyed by the heat gathering in her cheeks and the prickly sensation in her eyes. She'd been determined not to get upset, but hated that all the attention and focus was on her now when they'd been having such a good time. She'd almost been able to forget that she should have been doing something else entirely today.

'What I tell Abbey is that it was better that it happened before the wedding and not later on,' Bill offered.

'That's true,' said Lizzie. 'And I'm a great believer in the saying, *what's for you won't pass you by*. That's what I've always told Katy.'

Abbey cringed inwardly as they all tried to offer soothing and reassuring words of wisdom. They were only trying to be kind, but she rankled at the idea that they might feel sorry for her. She didn't need anyone's sympathy. For the first time in years, she actually felt in control of her own life. And today of all days, she didn't want to be dragged down by bitter memories. Today was about new beginnings.

'Anyway, Lizzie, it was very kind of you to invite us along for lunch,' she said brightly. 'Such a lovely gesture. I can't think of anything else I'd rather be doing on what would have been my wedding day. Listen, if I ever have another wedding day, a proper one, then you'll all be invited to come along,' she said, trying to lighten the tone.

'And I'm chuffed to be a gate-crasher at this very select gathering,' said Sam, with a lopsided smile. 'I think weddings are overrated affairs at the best of times.'

'Why does that not surprise me, Sam? I have to say you're probably not the best person to comment on these matters.' Lizzie had a smile on her face as she gently scolded Sam and he took it in good humour. 'Sam is one of those... what is it they call them... Oh, I know, a commitment-phobe. And a serial dater, too.'

'Lizzie!' Now it was Sam's turn to chastise his friend. 'That is simply not true.'

'It is! What about that lovely girl, Stephanie. You broke her heart. And she wasn't the first either.'

'Lizzie, please! What will these people think? Honestly! It's just... well, you need to get these things right, don't you?' He looked at Abbey with genuine interest in his eyes, the friendly timbre to his voice reaching her insides. 'There's no point in settling for something that you know ultimately won't be right for you.'

Sam's remark touched a nerve with Abbey. Recently, when she'd thought about her time with Jason, which she tried not to do too often, she'd realised what a sham their relationship had become. She'd spent years trying to make it work, adapting her personality to fit in with Jason's needs, trying to create the loving, close relationship she'd always longed for, but knowing in her heart of hearts that her reality with Jason fell far short of what she'd imagined.

'Absolutely.' She nodded her agreement now to Sam. At least it had taught her a valuable lesson. No relationship, she realised, was better than a bad one. And it sounded as though Sam was of a similar mind.

'Sam, you really are a hopeless case,' Lizzie chided, her laughter tinkling in the air.

Her gentle ribbing of Sam intrigued Abbey. What had happened to the girlfriend she thought she'd seen Sam with and could it really be true that he was afraid of commitment? She suspected that had been Jason's problem too, keeping his options open just in case something better came along. Men! Were they really all the same?

She made a mental note. Next time around, if ever there was a next time, she would need to avoid commitment-phobes, serial daters, liars and cheats. She shuddered. What a minefield it was out there! She pulled herself up short, determined not to believe all men were the same. Lizzie was right, wasn't she – there had to be some good ones out there?

'I think we should have a toast,' she declared, raising her glass in the air, relieved to be back in control of the situation. 'Here's to fresh starts and new friendships.'

'I'll drink to that,' said Sam, with a smile, his eyes locking on to hers momentarily.

'Cheers!' Lizzie, Bill, Abbey and Sam all joined in the refrain.

17

The main snug of The Three Feathers was alive with the sound of animated conversation, laughter and a constant flow of customers to keep Rhianna busy behind the bar. It was why she loved this job so much. There was always something to do and if ever there was a lull in the proceedings, there was always a friendly local perched on a bar stool at the counter, only too willing to have a natter.

Tonight, though, she didn't have time to stop. There was barely a free table in the place. She was just handing over a couple of pints of real ale to Albert, one of her favourite customers, when she took a double glance at someone over on the other side of the bar. There was a group of about eight people, men and women, sitting around the large oak table in the window. She remembered serving one of the guys with a tray of mixed drinks, but it wasn't him who caught her attention now. On the opposite side of the table was someone else, someone familiar. It was the blond, sticky-uppy hair and defined jawline that gave it away and her heart gave a beat of recognition. She hadn't seen Luke since he'd called round at the house a couple of weeks ago, but what she had noticed, and what had surprised her, was how often he'd slipped into her thoughts uninvited. At all sorts of random times. As she climbed into her bed of a night, when she drove along the windy country roads home, when she was sitting having a cup of tea with her mum. And now it was almost as if she had conjured him up and here he was, large as life in her pub. Unexpectedly, a smile spread across her lips. She had no regrets about leaving her job – she just wanted to put that whole sordid episode behind her – but unexpectedly, she did miss Luke. Thinking about walking into the office every morning to be greeted by his cheeky, smiley face and his quick-witted banter made her nostalgic for his friendly advances, even if she had been dismissive and cold towards him most of the time. She cringed when she thought of the way she'd treated Luke. What a bitch she'd been when he'd never been anything but friendly and good-natured towards her.

Now, distracted by those thoughts, she observed Luke, chatting and laughing with the pretty girl sitting beside him, and an unfamiliar emotion stirred within her. Regret tinged with a touch of jealousy. She shook the feelings away. Most of all she was cross with herself. She could hardly recognise the person she'd been only a few weeks ago. She'd been so infatuated with Jay that she'd neglected all her other relationships with her friends, her colleagues and even her lovely mum. She had lots of making up to do in every direction. One thing was for sure: never again would she allow a man to have such an unhealthy hold over her.

She cleared the bar top of the empties, placing them in the dishwasher, cursing Jason to herself, even if she knew he wasn't worth the time or effort. The sooner she erased every vestige of his memory from her mind, the better. Most of the time she found it easy enough, but just occasionally, like tonight, she would be reminded of what she'd been through and the anger would whirl and spin inside.

'Everything okay, my lovely?'

Jan was the best boss ever. She didn't stand over Rhianna the whole time and she gave her confidence and the responsibility of handling the busy bar on her own, only stepping in when she knew for certain an extra pair of hands was needed.

'It's all under control,' she said, smiling. 'I love it when it's as busy as this; the time just flies by.'

'Well, you seem to be a great hit with the customers, which is the main thing. They speak very highly of you. Look, I've just been looking at the sign-up sheet for the new quiz on Thursday night and so far we only have four teams lined up, so see if you can spread the word. We could do with some more players. You know, you could always come along yourself, if you fancy it. You're not working that night, are you?'

'No, I'm not, but I'm not sure...'

Jan gave a wry chuckle of understanding, laying a hand on Rhi's arm.

'Probably a bit lame for you, I'm guessing? Don't worry, it was just an idea. I'm sure we'll find some more takers before Thursday.'

'It's not...' Rhi had been about to explain, but she was waylaid by a customer waiting at the bar to be served. It wasn't that she didn't like the idea of the quiz night. Knowing Jan and Malc and how much effort they put into their events, it was bound to be a great evening. It was just Jan's invitation had taken her by surprise, and she was sad to realise there wasn't a single person she could think of that she might be able to form a team with. Rhi hadn't grown up around here; her mum had downsized to the area when Rhi was at university, finding a place on the outskirts of West-hampton, and Rhi had made the decision to move in with her mum when she finished her studies. She'd quickly found the job where she'd met Jason, but her focus had been very firmly on him and she supposed she hadn't put any effort into making new friends. It was another reason why the job at the pub suited her. It gave her the opportunity to meet a variety of new people and who knew, if the quiz evening turned out to be a success, then there would be other times when she could go along and join in the fun.

'Thanks, love!' As one customer vacated the spot at the front of the bar, another took her place.

'Yes, what can I get you?' she said with a smile before realising who it was standing in front of her. 'Luke, hi! Nice to see you. What would you like?'

Her friendly and welcoming manner was totally at odds with the whirlwind of emotions running around her body. Her heartbeat had gone into overdrive. What was going on? She'd never viewed Luke in a romantic light, even when he'd asked her out a couple of times when they first started working together. She'd simply laughed his approaches away as though the very idea was ridiculous. He stopped asking soon after, she remembered now. A heat stung at her cheeks and she was glad to get started on his long order of drinks, her head down as she concentrated on pulling a pint, aware of Luke's gaze flittering over her features.

'Not seen you in here before?'

'No, it's the squash club's social. First time I've come along.'

'Ah, right.' She placed the full pint glass onto the counter, before reaching for one of the botanical gin bottles and filling a measure. 'I thought perhaps you were with your girlfriend?' said Rhi, emboldened by the air of goodwill radiating from the old beams of the pub.

'My girlfriend?' There was a smile hovering at Luke's mouth and a glint of mischievousness in his eye. 'Were you jealous?'

'What?' She bit back a smile. This was the Luke she remembered. Cheeky and funny, only she hadn't really appreciated him then. Wrapped up in her own life and anticipating when she might next snatch some fleeting time with Jason, she'd found Luke irritating and annoying. Now she realised the heat swirling around her body wasn't down solely to the remnants of the sunny day, but more to do with the young man standing in front of her.

'Jealous?' She feigned insouciance. 'Why would I be jealous? Just curious, that's all.'

'That's nice.' Luke couldn't hide his amusement. 'Nope, no girl-friend,' he said with a resigned shrug, smiling at Rhi, their eyes lingering for more than a moment.

Rhi had learnt more about Luke in the last five minutes – he didn't have a girlfriend and he liked to play squash – than she had in the entire time she'd spent working with him. She placed the last drink of his order in front of him with a smile.

'I don't know if you and your friends would be interested, but we're having a quiz night here on Thursday evening. It's for teams of two to six, if you fancied it? All the details are on the posters. We're hoping to make it a regular event if it's a success.'

'Ah, right. Will you be here?' Luke had always been direct and it might have been one of the reasons why he'd rubbed her up the wrong way in the past, but now she realised it was just his manner.

'No, I don't work Thursdays. Should be a good evening, though.'

'Sure. Well, I'll let the others know. They might want to make up a team. Although I'll probably give it a miss if you're not going to be here,' he said, with a crooked smile.

For the rest of the evening Rhi couldn't get her conversation with Luke out of her head. She replayed it over and over, mulling over the way he'd looked at her, the words he'd said, if he'd been flirting with her or just being friendly. Occasionally she would look up and over in his direction, hoping to catch his eye, but he was always deep in conversation with the girl at his side. Maybe she'd read far too much into her brief interaction with him. Her thoughts drifted back to the day when he'd visited her at home, bringing her flowers. She could have sworn they'd forged a new connection. She'd seen it in his eyes and felt it within her body, and she felt certain he must have felt it too. She'd known instinctively she would see him again – it was just a question of when, only this wasn't how she had imagined it.

Later on that evening, when she came out from behind the bar to collect the empties from the tables, she came to an abrupt halt in the back bar when she spotted another familiar face. She faltered, experiencing the unnerving sensation of seeing someone familiar but in a totally unexpected place. It took only a moment for her to realise it was Abbey. She hadn't seen her since that day in Primrose Woods. For one awful moment, she thought the man with his back to Rhi, sitting opposite Abbey, might be Jason, and dread struck at her chest. Had they rekindled their relationship? Were their wedding plans back in place? She really hoped not. Not because she wanted Jason for herself, but because she thought Abbey deserved so much better than that low-life. She was very relieved to discover it wasn't him after all.

'Hi, Abbey, how are you?' she said nonchalantly, reaching around them to clear the table of their empty glasses.

Abbey's shock at seeing Rhi registered on her face for the briefest moment before she gathered herself.

'Hello, I'd completely forgotten you were working here now. How are you?'

'Good. Much better now. I'm over that lingering, annoying virus I told you about,' she said with feeling.

Abbey spotted the glint in Rhi's eye and the twist of her lip, and she smiled in return. 'That's good to hear. I know what you mean. I had something similar recently. And they can hang around for ages. At one point I thought I might never get rid of it.'

Rhi enjoyed the private joke with Abbey. The man with her was totally oblivious to any undercurrent as he was engrossed in the special beers menu.

Despite herself, she would have loved to ask Abbey about Jason, to find out if she'd heard from him at all. In fact, what she'd have really loved was to have a good old rant about the man who had messed up both their lives because there wasn't anyone else Rhi could really talk to about it. Now was not the time, though. She didn't know if the good-looking guy sitting opposite Abbey was a friend or colleague, or perhaps even a new love interest. If that was the case then she would hate to put her foot in it. Instead, she told them about the upcoming quiz night.

'Sounds fun,' said the man. 'I love a good quiz. Do you fancy it?' he asked Abbey.

'Oh!' She seemed surprised by his offer and from the way her cheeks flushed, Rhi got the distinct impression that there might be a budding romance in the air after all.

'Just the two of us? I hope you're not wanting to win,' Abbey joked.

'Yeah, we probably would need a couple more of us. I could ask Lizzie to come along, and what about your dad?'

'That's a good point.' Abbey was coming round to the idea. 'I'm sure he'd love to join us.' Her dad didn't get out much so this might be an ideal opportunity for him to socialise in a relaxed environment. And when had she ever known him to say no to a trip to the pub?

'Perfect, then,' said the man. 'Looks like we've got ourselves a team.'

'Great,' said Rhi. 'What's your team name? I'll just grab the sheet and put your details down.'

Sam and Abbey looked at each other and shrugged in unison, having no clue what to call their new team, making them both laugh.

'Well, it will have to be something to do with Primrose Woods because that's what we have in common,' said Sam.

'And I don't fancy our chances at all, so what about the Primrose Fancies?' suggested Abbey, laughing.

'Perfect,' agreed Sam.

With Rhi back at their table with the sign-up sheet, jotting down their details, Abbey looked doubtful suddenly, hesitating about what she was letting herself in for.

'You do know, I might well be getting you to one side on Thursday evening and pressing you for the answers,' said Abbey, half-jokingly.

Rhi laughed. 'Sorry, I'm afraid I won't be able to help, even if I was allowed to. I'm not working that night.'

'Damn! My fail-proof plan falls at the first hurdle.'

Sam wasn't put off, his eyes lighting up as he looked between Abbey and Rhi. 'In that case, why don't you come along and join the Primrose Fancies if you're not already on another team?' He glanced across at Abbey, hoping he hadn't overstepped the mark by inviting this girl to join their team when he had no idea of the relationship between the pair of them. Fortunately Abbey nodded, smiling enthusiastically.

'Yes, why don't you. Bring a friend too, if you like. It would be good to have a full team with a cross-section of ages and, honestly, we're going to need all the help we can get. If nothing else, it should be a giggle.'

Rhi was genuinely touched by Abbey's offer of the hand of friendship. After what had happened, she'd be well within her rights to never want to talk to or even see Rhi again, but here she was being nothing but welcoming and inviting her to join their quiz team.

'I'd love to come. And I think I know someone else who might like to join us too.'

18

Lizzie should have realised when she received a video call from Katy on a Wednesday morning that something must be wrong. She was so surprised to see her lovely daughter's face pop up on the screen and hear her familiar voice that her instant reaction was one of delight and happiness. It only took a moment, though, for her to realise there was a problem.

'What's the matter?' she asked, fear pressing at her chest. 'Is it the baby?'

'No, the baby's fine.' Katy stood up and turned sideways to show off her now protruding bump, causing a lump to form in Lizzie's throat.

'And Rosie? Brad? Is everything okay with them, Katy?'

'Yes.' She pushed out her lips, sighing heavily, her frustration all too palpable across the miles that separated them. 'They're all fine. Life hasn't changed for Brad. He goes to work, comes home, normally just after I've finished the bed and bath routine for Rosie – you know, I'm sure he plans it that way – we have dinner and then we go to bed. And then the next day we repeat it all over again.'

Lizzie nodded in understanding but remained silent, knowing instinctively that Katy clearly needed a listening ear.

'Rosie is so clingy and demanding at the moment. It's just me and her all day long and there's no escape. I honestly can't imagine how I will cope with two of them. I don't know if she's feeling insecure because of the baby, but I never get a moment's peace. She wants to be carried everywhere and is so whingy-whiney, it wears me down. Sometimes I just want to have five minutes on my own – is that too much to ask?' Katy exhaled a huge, heartfelt sigh. 'Then when I finally get her down to sleep of a night, I collapse in a heap feeling like the worst mother ever.'

'You're not, Katy, really you're not. You're a brilliant mum, doing the best you can.'

'Huh? How can you say that, Mum? You don't know what it's like here. You don't even really know Rosie.'

The implicit accusation stung Lizzie and a dozen retorts hovered on her lips, but she swallowed them down. It hurt all the more because despite spending hours on the phone with little Rosie, reading stories, playing games and singing songs, she knew deep in her heart that it wasn't enough. She'd never held Rosie, kissed the top of her head, inhaled her delicious baby scent or felt the touch of her skin on her own. The benefit of modern technology in bridging the gap between far-flung relatives was wonderful, but it could never replace the closeness and familiarity that came with holding someone tight in your arms.

'That's true, but that doesn't stop me from loving her with all my heart. Just because I can't be there with you doesn't mean you're not all uppermost in my thoughts.'

'Oh Mum, but it doesn't help. It's not fair that I have to do all of this on my own. I never even wanted to come to Australia in the first place and now I'm wondering if we've made the worst decision ever. Do you know, I'm not even sure if I'm cut out for this motherhood lark. Some days I feel like running away and never coming back. If I could jump on a plane right now and come home I would.'

'Katy, don't say that.'

'It's the truth.'

Lizzie could hear the emotion in Katy's voice, but it was her words that concerned her the most. She sounded defeated and low in a way that Lizzie couldn't recognise in her usually sunny, positive daughter. Of course, there'd been times when she'd been fed up or exhausted before – that was only natural as a young mother – but Lizzie had always been able to find a touch of humour or a glimmer of hope behind Katy's grumbles. Not today, though.

'I can't bear hearing you sounding so sad. Does Brad know how you feel? Maybe talking it through with him might help.'

'Talking doesn't help. Don't get me wrong, he's really supportive, but it doesn't change anything. There's only so much Brad can do when he's working so hard. It's you I need, Mum. We all do. I want you to meet Rosie while she's still little. It would make all the difference. I know how you feel about flying, but...' She sighed heavily, her exasperation filtering across the miles between them. 'It's really not that big a deal. You could take some pills, have a few drinks before you get on the plane, anything... Can't you just do it for me, Mum? Really, I'm that desperate.'

Lizzie swallowed hard, a barrage of emotions assaulting her. She knew Katy didn't fully understand the extent of her phobia, the absolute fear she experienced just at the thought of stepping on a plane. No one really did. If anything, it was a bit of a joke to everyone else. One of Lizzie's little quirks, endearing and funny. Still, that wasn't what was uppermost in her mind right now. She was trying to put on a brave front, but Katy's obvious despair had frightened her. Some things were more important, especially when it came down to your daughter's well-being.

'Please, Mum. I'm begging you,' Katy added, as if Lizzie needed any more convincing.

* * *

Abbey still didn't quite understand how it was that she was seeing Sam Finnegan for the second time in the space of a week. Not that she was complaining. She found him really good company and easy to be around, even disregarding the fact that sometimes he had a disconcerting effect on her equilibrium. When he glanced up at her, his dark brown eyes locking on to hers, it did funny things to her insides. Still, it was good to meet someone new, someone from outside her relationship with Jason, her first new friend made as a single woman. Although she was under no misapprehension that this would be anything other than a friend-ship. She would need to keep her fluctuating emotions under control if she wasn't going to be poleaxed by Sam's charms every time she looked in his direction. Her non-wedding day had turned out to be a much better experience than she could ever have expected. The four of them had sat in the garden all afternoon drinking wine and chatting, so much so that it had been easy for Abbey to forget what it was she should have been doing that day. At one point Sam had produced a bottle of his homemade damson gin, which had been very quaffable, even if it had made her a bit giddy, but then again, if you couldn't get tipsy on your almost-wedding day, then when could you?

When Sam had mentioned how he went into schools and other local community groups to give talks about the work of the Prim-rose Woods Trust, Abbey's interest was piqued, thinking how the residents of the care home might enjoy hearing about the different local habitats and the wildlife found there. She was always on the lookout for new activities and events to entertain the guests at

Rushgrove Lodge, so when Sam suggested that they meet up to discuss the possibilities then she jumped at the opportunity. It was only as she waited for Sam to pick her up from the cottage, peering through the front window in anticipation of spotting his car and her heartbeat increasing with each passing moment, that she realised that this had all the hallmarks of a first date. She was bursting with anticipation and had to give herself a stern talking-to as she hurried up the footpath to greet him, reminding herself that there was only one reason why Sam had invited her out tonight and that was to discuss the work of the Trust. They left the jeep parked outside the cottage and walked the short distance to the pub. She was surprised when they took their seats inside and the conversation took a personal turn, with Sam immediately apologising.

'Look I feel really bad for putting my foot in it the other day, you know... about the wedding. If I'd known I obviously would never have mentioned it. I could have kicked myself afterwards. I really hope I didn't make you feel awkward or uncomfortable.'

'Not at all. You weren't to know. And it's not as if I feel ashamed about what happened.' She shrugged, a rueful smile on her face. 'I'm just keen to put it all behind me and start over. I guess invariably that will mean telling people what happened from time to time. It's not something I'm going to keep secret.'

'I understand, but it must have been difficult on that particular day. I'm sorry. I really hope I didn't upset you.'

'Nah.' She swiped away the very idea with a flick of her hand. 'You didn't,' she said with a smile. Everyone expected her to be tearful and upset, but it surprised her just how little anguish she'd experienced at the end of her relationship with Jason. No deep upset, at least. She felt anger at the way he'd treated her, relief at breaking free from the relationship, and regret for not having done it much sooner, but she didn't miss or pine over Jason. Good riddance, was her current state of mind. She'd wasted too much time as it was so there could be no time for regrets. From now on she was determined to live in the moment and look only to the future. And right now, in this particular moment, she was focused solely on the glass of chilled white wine in her hand and the man sitting opposite her, who was lovely, just lovely. Funny and charming, he spoke passionately and confidently about his work, peppering his tales with little entertaining asides, his brown eyes shining with amusement. She tried hard not to get distracted by those eyes, or by the cut of his jaw, or by the way his hair curled on his collar because she wasn't here for that, although she supposed it was doing her no harm whatsoever to sit back and admire the view.

'Sorry,' said Sam later, as the evening was drawing to a close, and they took the walk back to the cottage. 'It's just occurred to me that I might have railroaded you into taking part in the quiz on Thursday. It's not too late to back out if it's really not your thing?'

'No!' she said, rather too quickly. 'I'm looking forward to it.' Although, if she were being truthful, it was seeing Sam again that she was looking forward to the most.

'That's good,' said Sam, giving her a sideways glance, the corner of his mouth curling upwards. They'd reached the front gate to the cottage. 'I'm looking forward to it too,' he said, before climbing into the jeep, and watching until Abbey was back safely inside the house. She smiled, closing the door behind her, a shiver of excitement running down her spine. She hadn't had such a lovely evening in a long time.

* * *

'Luke!'

As he turned round to look at Rhi, his expression settled into one of puzzlement and Rhi had to wonder if she wasn't about to make a huge mistake. What had she been thinking? After the way she'd treated Luke, why on earth had she thought that this was a good idea, that he would even want to spend the evening with her?

'Yes?' he said, wandering over as the rest of his group left the pub, acknowledging their departure with a wave of his hand. He stood in front of her and smiled, standing in that relaxed but confident stance of his, taking Rhi right back to those days in the office when she would waltz past him, head held high, cup of coffee in hand, barely acknowledging his presence.

'Um, well, you know I mentioned the pub quiz to you earlier...'

'Yeah. Sorry, I ran it past the guys, but they weren't really interested.'

'Ah, okay. What I was going to say was that I've been invited to join a team with a couple of friends of mine. There's a spare place and I wondered if you might like to...'

Her words trailed away and a heat pinged at her cheeks, remembering all those occasions when Luke had asked her if she wanted to join the rest of the team for a drink after work and she'd turned him down flatly. And probably rudely too, she thought, squirming inside.

Now, she wondered if he was remembering the same thing because her offer had elicited a knowing smile from him and a light in his eyes.

'Hey, are you really inviting me along to be your teammate?'

'Well, it was just an idea. I understand if you don't fancy it. It's not a big deal.' She bristled, preparing herself for his rejection.

Luke shrugged, his lip twisting to one side. 'Sounds like a good idea to me. Do you want me to pick you up on the way?'

'Um...' She couldn't help the wide smile from spreading across her face, so wide in fact that she had to turn away, busying herself with the intricacies of folding a tea towel so that Luke wouldn't be able to tell how ridiculously pleased she was at him agreeing to coming along to quiz night. When she'd gathered herself, she turned back with a smile. 'That would be great, if you don't mind.'

'I don't mind at all, Rhi.' He had a sparkle in his eye and Rhi suspected she'd done a pretty bad job at hiding her feelings, if the expression on Luke's features was anything to go by. 'Always happy to help out a friend.'

19

'Let me go and get the drinks. What are we all having?' Bill pushed his chair back and squeezed past the others, taking a mental note of everyone's choice of drink as he did.

'I'll give you a hand,' said Sam, following Bill to the bar.

The pub was heaving that evening, the inaugural meeting of The Three Feathers' monthly quiz being a huge draw for the customers with fourteen teams participating, and Malc, the land-lord, presiding over proceedings with his usual good humour and charm. There was a surprisingly competitive atmosphere amongst the teams and Abbey was scolded by her dad when she got distracted by the answer to a question in the music round, which happened to be Take That.

She, Lizzie and Rhi quickly bonded over their love of the band, chattering away about the gigs they'd attended, who their favourite members were and rating the band's singles in order of preference, before their flight of fancy was interrupted by Bill.

'Abbey, shh, we'll miss the next question.'

Abbey rolled her eyes, and made an action of zipping her lips tight, looking suitably chastised and making the others laugh. It was a relief to be able to chat freely when the interval came around.

'Your young man seems a lovely chap,' Lizzie commented to Rhi.

'Oh no, we're not together like that,' she quickly protested. 'He's just a friend. We used to work together.'

'Ah, I see,' said Lizzie with a knowing smile on her face. 'Well, he seems very fond of you.'

'He is lovely,' agreed Abbey.

Everyone seemed to immediately take to Luke – Rhi's teammates, her mum, the people at work. Despite not knowing anyone this evening, he'd fitted in to the group as if he'd known them all for years and, if it hadn't been for his input in the sports round, then the Primrose Fancies could easily have scored a humiliating duck.

Rhi cast her glance over to the busy bar where Luke was helping the other guys with the drinks. It wasn't only his height that made him easy to pick out in the crowd, but also his shock of white-blond hair, which stuck up endearingly in all directions. He looked like the good-looking member of a boy band. As he turned with a couple of pints in hand, his gaze locked on to Rhi's and he winked, his lovely face opening up in a bright smile. Not for the first time, she wondered why it had taken her such a long time to realise what a great guy Luke was.

'Well, this is fun,' said Lizzie. 'I might not have been much help with the questions, but I am enjoying myself. I'm so glad I came along after all.'

'I hope you weren't thinking of bailing out on us?' Abbey said.

'It crossed my mind.' Lizzie sighed. 'It's just all this business with my daughter. She's really struggling at the moment. I spoke to her yesterday and it just breaks my heart to see her so upset. I've got no choice, I'm going to have to get out there and see her for myself.' The determination she felt masked the wobble in her voice.

'What's this?' asked Sam, who'd returned from the bar with the others, laden down with drinks and snacks. 'Did I hear you right? You're going to visit Katy after all?'

'Yes.' But there was no sense of joy or excitement in Lizzie's reply, only a palpable sense of dread and fear.

'That's wonderful, Lizzie. I'm sure you won't regret it. It will be the best decision you ever make,' said Sam encouragingly.

'Where is it she lives?' asked Luke, sitting down next to Rhi.

'She and her family are in Sydney, Australia. They moved out there about four years ago. I haven't even met my little grand-daughter, Rosie, properly yet – I have this terrible fear of flying, you see – and now Katy's pregnant again. She needs me out there so I've agreed to go.'

'You're going to Australia? That's amazing,' said Rhi. 'I'm going too in a couple of months' time. I've wanted to go for ages.'

'Are you?' asked Luke, looking surprised. Rhi's declaration had caught Abbey's attention too.

'Yes, I've decided to go travelling. It's something I've always wanted to do and I reckon now is the ideal opportunity before I settle down properly to adulthood! Get the wanderlust out of my system. I just need to save up a bit more money and then I'll be on my way.'

'Are you going with some friends?' asked Abbey.

'No, on my own. But that doesn't bother me. In fact, I'm really excited about it and I'm bound to meet plenty of people on the backpacker trail.'

Lizzie looked across at Rhi with awe. The young girl with her mass of black curls and bright, inquisitive eyes had to be at least thirty years younger than Lizzie, but she had a confidence and self-assuredness that Lizzie was certain she'd never possessed. She had to wonder if it was a generational thing, because she couldn't remember a time when she would ever have wanted to take off on her own to the other side of the world. Funny to think she was about to do it now as she approached her sixtieth birthday. She admired Rhi's bravery and independence. She could do with channelling some of Rhi's spirit for herself if she was going to take this huge step of her own.

'Hey, Lizzie, we'll be able to swap stories and photos of our trips.'

'Yes,' said Lizzie, laughing tentatively. It was hard not to be taken in by Rhi's enthusiasm and joie de vivre, and for the first time, with the benefit of a couple of glasses of Prosecco inside her and being amongst the warm camaraderie of her friends, she felt the tiniest kernel of excitement about her upcoming adventure. If only that feeling could last until the morning when she would need to sit down at her computer and start planning her visit.

'Hypnotherapy is very good for phobias and anxiety,' piped up Luke unexpectedly. 'It worked for my dad and his fear of heights. He once drove into a multi-storey car park, up one of those spiral ramps and because it was so busy he had to park on the very top floor. Once he got to the top he was sweating and hyper-ventilating, having a full-blown panic attack. There was no way he would have been able to drive back down again. He had to ring my stepmum to go and collect him. After that he decided to seek some help. The doctor referred him to a private hypnotherapist and after about three sessions, he felt much more in control and calm in those situations. It's really made a difference to him.'

'Really? That's very interesting,' said Lizzie, wondering if it might really help. She'd heard about hypnotherapy before, of course, but never actually believed it would work for her. 'At this point I'd be willing to give anything a try. Thanks, Luke, it's definitely something to think about.'

Moments later, Malc's deep voice reverberated around the bar, giving warning that the quiz was about to restart, and Sam gave his team a pep talk.

'Come on, we need to properly concentrate. We can still win this. And we still have our joker to play.'

Trouble was, the next round was geography, which didn't seem to be anyone's specialist subject and they scored a paltry three points. And holding out on playing their joker, hoping that the next round might be one that appealed to at least one of them, they eventually ran out of time and were forced to play their joker on the very last round, which was a literature round, eliciting a huge groan from everyone, and a barely respectable eight points. Still, at least they were able to laugh about their efforts.

'Actually, considering it was our first time playing as a team, I think we gave a pretty good account of ourselves. Coming fifth out of all those teams isn't too shoddy, I don't think,' Sam said.

'Yeah, it was good fun,' said Abbey. Much more fun than she could have imagined. 'And it's the taking part that counts.'

Sam blew out his lips as though he didn't agree with that notion at all. He'd definitely been the most competitive and was clearly disappointed that they hadn't picked up the trophy – or more accurately, the beer voucher – which amused the others no end.

'So does that mean we're all up for the next quiz night?' suggested Bill, looking around at his teammates. 'I think we've got the makings of a really good team here.'

Lizzie nodded eagerly, Rhi and Luke exchanged sly glances, confirming their agreement, and Abbey was just pleased that her dad had enjoyed himself so much that he wanted to do it again. Plus it gave her the perfect excuse for seeing Sam.

'Definitely,' Sam said. 'And next time there'll be no excuses for us not winning.'

As they gathered outside the pub, Bill took Lizzie to one side, gently laying a hand on the sleeve of her jacket.

'I really admire you, Lizzie, for making the decision to go and see you daughter, despite your fears. It's a very brave thing to do. And you do know, I have absolutely no doubt that it'll be the best thing you ever do.'

Lizzie looked up into Bill's brown, sparkly eyes, touched by his kind words. If only he knew. She wasn't brave and she certainly wasn't worthy of his admiration. Inside she was a quivering, nervous wreck and she hated herself for it, but in some ways his faith in her made her the tiniest bit stronger. The touch of his hand on her sleeve was something of a revelation too.

20

Sam stood in front of an entirely rapt audience of about twenty residents in the spacious lounge of Rushgrove Lodge for the Elderly. It was a bright, airy room with sunflower-yellow painted walls, large windows overlooking the courtyard garden, wing armchairs and vases of fresh flowers dotted around the tables. With an infectious energy radiating around the room, it felt less like a care home and more like an exclusive lounge on a cruise liner.

From her vantage point at the front of the room, Abbey sat between Stella Darling and Reg Catling, two of her favourite residents, where she was able to observe Sam Finnegan up close talking about the duties of the park rangers at Primrose Woods, the conservation work being carried out and the wildlife found in the area. Sam was a natural and confident public speaker, his passion for his subject evident to see, making for an entertaining and enjoyable session. Initially, she listened as intently as the men and women around her, but then she found her attention wandering so that she was focusing much more on the shape of his mouth and the way his lips curled to one side when he made a funny remark, than on the words he was speaking. His bone structure was well defined, his jawline sharply cut with cheekbones that were high and prominent, but all those angles were softened by his thick, brown hair and those dark eyes that flickered with humour and kindness. His tall and broad physical presence filled the room, and in his cargos and green sweatshirt bearing the logo of Primrose Woods, it was definitely a case of him bringing the great outdoors in with his enthusiasm for his work. At the end of his presentation, some of the residents asked questions and he answered them all with good humour and grace. Lady, who was on her best behaviour today, had lain at Sam's feet the entire time, although after the presentation, when the tea and cake arrived, her previous good manners disappeared out of the window as she mooched around the lounge, making friends with all the residents, who were only too happy to indulge her with tidbits of cake.

'Did you find that interesting, Stella?' Abbey asked, handing her a cup of tea.

'It was super,' said Stella. 'What a charming young man, and his dog is absolutely delightful.' Abbey had to smile to herself, wondering if Stella had listened to what Sam had been saying or if she'd been distracted by Sam's good looks too. 'Now, if I was only forty years younger I'd be casting my net in his direction.' Her girlish laugh tinkled around the room as she gave Abbey a gentle dig in the ribs. 'You should snap him up for yourself! Now that you're a free woman again.'

Of all the people she'd had to inform that her long-awaited wedding was cancelled, telling her lovely residents at work had to have been the hardest. They'd all been so excited for her and quizzed her regularly in the build-up to the big day. They'd wanted to know all the details about the arrangements: what flowers she had chosen, the hymns they were having, what her guests would be eating on the day. Their disappointment when she told them the wedding was off was distressing, leaving her feeling as though she'd let them down in some way. Ever since, they'd been determined to pair her off with any poor man that walked across the threshold of the Lodge.

'Stop it now, Stella,' chided Reg. 'I'm sure Abbey doesn't need any advice from you on her love life. It was a very interesting talk. I used to walk up at Primrose Woods in my younger days, before these old legs of mine gave up the ghost. It's such a beautiful place. I used to take the dogs up there and we'd walk for miles in all sorts of weather. Wish I could still do that now.' Reg looked wistful as his gaze flitted out of the windows, remembering past walks and faithful family pets, Abbey didn't doubt. In his room were framed photos of not only his late wife and his family, but also a montage of the animals he'd owned. She recalled him telling her all their names once. Now, he was ruffling Lady's fur as she looked up at him longingly, pleading with him for his last bit of cake. It never ceased to amaze Abbey, the beneficial effect visiting dogs had on the residents. Even the quiet and reserved guests would come alive in the company of the furry four-legged friends who came to visit. Sometimes it was easier to have a deep and meaningful conversation with a dog than it was with another human being.

'We were just saying how much we enjoyed your talk.'

Sam had joined Abbey, Stella and Reg, holding a dainty cup and saucer in his big hands, which made Abbey smile.

'That's good to hear. I always welcome any opportunity to chat about the park. It's good to get the word out and to let people know what we're doing.'

'I was thinking that it might be an idea to organise a trip there soon. We could take the minibus and sit out by the lake.'

'Ooh, I like the sound of that,' said Stella.

'I'd definitely sign up for that one,' agreed Reg.

'Well, you'd be very welcome,' said Sam. 'And we could

organise lunch or an afternoon cream tea in the Treetops Cafe. Lizzie puts on a great display of cakes.'

'How about tomorrow?' said Stella, laughing.

'Let me have a look at the events calendar,' said Abbey. 'I'll see if we can get a date in the diary soon. It'll be something to look forward to.'

Sam was intrigued to see Abbey in her work environment. He knew from their limited interactions in the park, and then at the pub, that she was a caring and compassionate woman, but that was never more apparent than in the way she interacted with her staff and the residents, radiating a sense of calm and reassurance around the Lodge. She clearly loved her job and the people she worked with, treating all the residents as individuals, as though they might be her own family. She chatted away enthusiastically, immersed in the moment, listening intently to what was being said to her. As she spoke, she would lay a hand on their arm or touch their shoulder gently and it was clear from the way the residents reacted to her that they trusted her implicitly and held a real and deep fondness for her too.

As Sam sipped on his tea, his attention kept flittering back to Abbey. He'd always been a sucker for a redhead, but there was much more to Abbey than her natural good looks. Beneath the lightly freckled skin and behind the bright blue eyes, there was a beauty that radiated from within. He'd noticed it on that very first occasion he'd met her in the park, and had been enchanted by her undeniable charm on every occasion since. She had a naturally friendly and chatty manner, but he'd detected a soft and vulnerable side, which brought out his protective streak. Was that because he'd heard about her ex and the broken engagement? From what he'd gleaned, the guy had let her down badly and for some inexplicable reason that troubled him greatly. It was definitely her ex's loss though; to let a woman like Abbey slip through his fingers was more than careless.

Now, his attention was interrupted by a commotion coming from the other side of the room and his heart sank, knowing immediately the cause of the ructions. A great cry went up followed by a good deal of laughter. He turned to see Lady, who had clearly just bagged an oozing cream scone, and was scarpering underneath the buffet table.

'Lady! Bad dog,' he scolded, before remembering where he was and smiling tightly through his annoyance. He dashed across to drag the dog out from her hiding place, but not before Lady had polished off the last of the evidence.

'Aw, let her be,' said one lady, who Sam suspected might have been an accomplice in Lady's misdemeanour. 'Why should she miss out on the cakes?'

'She's been such a good dog all afternoon,' said another. 'She deserves a treat.'

Abbey laughed from the other side of the room as she watched Sam trying to manhandle Lady and carefully negotiate with his previously warm audience, who were now definitely Team Lady.

'You do know he's soft on you, that young man?'

'What?' Abbey turned to look at Stella, whose eyes were wide, a mischievous look upon her face.

'Well, I might be getting on a bit, but I'm not too daft to know what it means when a man looks at a woman in a certain way. And that handsome man over there hasn't been able to take his eyes off you.'

Abbey tutted, shaking her head ruefully.

'Stella Darling, would you behave yourself, please! I know you're desperate to find me a man, but we must be careful what we say,' she said, lowering her voice. 'We don't want to scare off our lovely visitors, do we?'

'You mark my words, young lady!' Stella said solemnly. 'I can tell he's got a good heart, that one, so you'd be wise to not let him get away. You don't want someone else snapping him up from under your nose.'

'What is she like, Reg?' said Abbey, attempting to garner a bit of moral support, but Reg just looked over the top of his glasses at Abbey, shrugging his shoulders, as though he was in full agreement with Stella.

Moments later, Sam re-joined them with Lady back on the lead and firmly under control.

'Abbey, I think I should probably make a move now before this hound inflicts any more damage on the room.'

'Don't worry,' she said, laughing. 'She's been absolutely delightful and a great hit with everyone here. She can definitely come again. You both can. Thanks so much for coming along.'

'It's been my pleasure, and we'd be more than happy to come back again at some point. You know where I am, so you only have to ask.'

She smiled gratefully, thinking of a multitude of questions she might like to ask Sam, with only a few of them to do with his work, but she suspected that wasn't what he had in mind.

Sam navigated the room, saying goodbye in turn to each of the residents, which took much longer than anticipated as everyone was determined to say their own special goodbye to Lady, who revelled in all the attention. Eventually, with all the farewells done, Abbey accompanied them both to Sam's jeep in the car park. Standing alone together, after the hubbub of the guests' lounge, Abbey wrapped her arms around her chest, the cool breeze in the air making her shiver. Stella's words fought for attention in her head and she had to brush them away. Stella was just being mischievous, fanciful, but her comments resonated with Abbey, making her consider if there could actually be some truth to her words. The more she saw of Sam, the more she liked him and there was no denying the impact his presence had upon her whole being. Now with Stella's gentle meddling, Abbey's perspective had shifted so that she looked at Sam in an entirely different light, as someone she would like to get to know much better.

'I hope you'll be coming along on Saturday?'

'Saturday?' asked Abbey, bemused for a moment, wondering if she might have missed an invitation. Her gaze flittered along the contours of his strong jawline, noticing the dark shadow there.

'To our annual open day at the park? We've got lots going on; there'll be a food market, some talks, if you can bear the thought of me rattling on again, and some organised walks. Come along, it should be a good day.'

'Yes, I might just do that,' she said, excited at the opportunity of seeing Sam again so soon, and thinking she could gladly listen to Sam's dulcet tones all day long.

21

Rhi was just finishing off her lunchtime shift at The Three
Feathers when she spotted a familiar car pull up outside. She bent
down to peer through the bay window to check if it really was who
she thought it was, and a shiver of anticipation ran around her
body when her suspicions were confirmed. Disappointingly, she
hadn't seen or heard from Luke since the quiz night. It was such a
fun evening and they'd laughed and teased each other all night
long, so much so that Rhi had been certain that Luke would ask to
see her again, just the two of them, but when he'd dropped her off
that night, there'd been no hug goodnight or invitation to meet up
again soon. She'd been left feeling disappointed and let down.
She'd never been afraid to make the first move if she really liked
someone, but something held her back when it came to Luke. It
was as if it was too important to try and the possibility that he
might actually knock her back, kindly of course, because that was
Luke's way, was too awful to consider. In the ensuing days she'd
found herself thinking about him far too often, replaying their
conversations in her head, trying to figure out what he really

thought about her. Maybe Luke had been tying himself up in knots over their relationship too and that's why he was here. To ask her out on a date. She quickly patted down her hair and ran her tongue across her lips.

'Hello, you!' she said, smiling, when he arrived at the bar, as though his appearance was a complete surprise to her. 'What can I get you?'

'I'm not stopping. I just wanted to drop this off.' He handed over a business card. 'It's the hypnotherapist who helped my dad. Would you be able to pass it on to Lizzie? I thought it might give her a gentle nudge in the right direction.'

'Yes, of course,' she said, taking the card and looking at it more intently than it probably warranted. He hadn't made a special trip to come and visit her at all, but it didn't really matter. He was here now and she was surprised by how happy that made her. 'That's really kind of you to remember,' she said, gathering herself.

'I hope it will help.'

Rhi wondered why it was that Luke had such an effect on her. He had such a sunny and upbeat demeanour that she couldn't help smiling when he was around. Just being close to him made her skin tingle and her heart race. What was that all about? After what had happened with Jason, she'd vowed that she was going to steer clear of men and relationships for the foreseeable future. There was no way she was going to hang around to be at the beck and call of some man. It was far too much trouble and besides, she had so many other more important things she wanted to do with her life. Her plans for her trip to Australia were coming along nicely. She'd already drafted her itinerary and in a couple of weeks' time, when she had the finances in place, she'd be able to book her flight. She couldn't wait! She even had some ideas forming in her head as to what she might do when she returned home. Jan and Malc had told her she would have a job waiting for her at the pub, if she wanted one, which was reassuring, but ultimately Rhi wanted to be her own boss. In her personal life and in her career, she wanted to be in charge of her own destiny.

There were so many different ideas and plans circling for attention in her head that sometimes she could barely keep a hold on them all.

And now here was Luke taking up far too much of her headspace too, when she hadn't wanted him to either. All she knew was that now he was here she didn't want him to leave.

'Look, Luke, I was just about to finish my shift.' She undid the ties to her apron and pulled it off, folding it neatly. 'As it's such a lovely day out there I might go up to Primrose Woods now and drop this off with Lizzie in the cafe. Do you fancy coming?'

Her tone might have been confident, masking her hesitation, but underneath the bravado she felt exposed and vulnerable. Would he laugh in her face like she'd done to him on several occasions in the past? The roles had reversed in their relationship and she found herself wishing again that she knew what Luke was really thinking.

'Yes, why not,' he said with that engaging smile. 'Day off today. Took my dad for a hospital appointment this morning and I've nothing planned for the rest of the day.'

Rhi breathed a huge sigh of relief. She needn't have worried. Luke was far too kind to be deliberately rude.

'I hope your dad is okay?' Rhi picked up her handbag from below the counter and joined Luke on the other side of the bar.

'He's fine, thanks for asking. It was only a check-up. He insists he can go on his own, but I like to be there for a bit of moral support, just in case.'

'Do you live at home?' Rhi asked, grateful for the opportunity to learn a little more about Luke.

'I do at the moment. I used to have a flat with my ex, but when we split up I moved in with my dad and stepmum, Carole. It suits me fine as it's easy for the office but I'm looking to move out again as soon as I know what my plans are work-wise.' Luke's casual mention of his ex intrigued Rhi, stirring a myriad of other questions in her head. She had to ignore the urge to know all the details of their relationship, his ex-girlfriend's name and how they'd met, it was really none of her business, and instead focused on what he'd said about his work.

'Are you thinking of leaving Jansens, then?'

'Yes, as soon as I can. It's just not the same in the office without you, Rhi.' He quirked his eyebrow and grinned, and she couldn't help smiling back, knowing he was teasing her. 'I'll see you there, then, at the car park,' he said, still grinning, as he went out of the front door, leaving Rhi with so many unanswered questions and her heartbeat all aflutter.

Lizzie was delighted to see them when they turned up at the Treetops Cafe a little while later and she found them a table at the front of the cafe near to the main counter so she could chat to them while preparing orders.

'Have a seat and I'll bring you over your drinks and a couple of chocolate treats. We've got some delicious rocky roads on today.'

'So how are the plans for your trip coming along?' asked Luke, sitting down opposite Rhi. He was wearing black jeans with a light grey fitted T-shirt that made his eyes appear even more intensely blue than usual, if that was possible.

'Great.' The skin on her arms prickled with anticipation, although that probably had more to do with being in such close proximity to Luke than her thoughts about going off to Australia. 'I've told them at the pub that I'll be going, probably in August, so there's no turning back now.'

'You're not having second thoughts, are you?'

'No, of course not.' She laughed. 'It's something I really want to do. Some friends of mine who've been travelling in Asia will be in Oz at the same time so we're going to meet up and that's given me a focus to the trip. I'm just looking at flights and timings now.'

Lizzie joined them at that moment, placing the drinks and a selection of sweet treats on the table, just catching the last of their conversation.

'Is this for your trip to Australia? I really must get my flights booked, but I keep putting it off.' She pulled a face. 'Don't tell anyone else that, though, will you?'

'Actually, that's why we're here.' Rhi pulled out the card from her pocket. 'Luke wanted to give you this.'

'It's the name and number of that hypnotherapist I told you about. She's really good and I thought it might help.'

'That's really kind of you to think of me,' Lizzie said, taking the card, turning it over in her fingers and wondering if it might hold some answers. She looked across at Luke and smiled. He was such a lovely young man. Some people you take to from the very first moment that you meet them and Luke definitely fell into that camp, as far as Lizzie was concerned. 'I'll ring her,' said Lizzie, holding the card aloft. 'I promise I will.' Well, she didn't have any choice in the matter now. She'd be letting Luke down if she didn't.

'When are you thinking of travelling?' Rhi asked Lizzie.

'Early August. The baby is due around about the sixteenth so ideally I'd like to go out there a couple of weeks beforehand in case the baby arrives early like Rosie did. Then I can hopefully have a couple of weeks with them after the baby's born to help out with the meals and generally make a fuss of them all, but that's assuming the little one turns up when it's supposed to. And there's no guarantee of that!'

'That's the same month I'm planning on flying out there. If you wanted to, we could sit down together and organise our flights. I want to get mine booked as soon as I can after next pay day.'

'Ooh, that's an idea, Rhi. If left to my own devices I might never get round to doing it. Honestly, with you two spurring me on, I can actually imagine myself stepping on that plane after all.'

'You bet you will. We'll make sure of that, won't we, Luke?'

Lizzie didn't doubt it for one moment. Her friends rallying round to help her made a huge difference to her state of mind. Before, she'd been so caught up in her own head, battling her demons, that it almost rendered her incapable of taking even the smallest of positive steps. Now she felt emboldened by the support. She could get on that plane and she would.

'Looks like I have a customer to serve, so I'll catch up with you both later. Thanks again, Luke, for this, and come and see me when you've got your money together, Rhi, and we'll get those flights booked.' Lizzie gestured to the poster on the pillar. 'You'll both be coming to our open day, won't you? This Saturday? There's lots going on.'

Rhi and Luke looked at each other and shrugged, clearly the first time they'd heard about it.

'Well, I might come along, then,' said Rhi, mulling the idea over in her head. Lizzie had been kind enough to support the pub quiz night so it was only fair that she returned the favour.

'Why don't the pair of you come along together? We'll have some tasty specials on the menu. And we're doing cream teas in the afternoon. I can sort you out with something nice.'

Rhi turned her gaze on Luke, her question implicit in her expression.

'Yeah, sure.' He shrugged nonchalantly. 'I've no other plans that day.'

Lizzie noticed the way Rhi's face lit up at Luke's positive response. Despite Rhi's protestations that she and Luke were only friends, Lizzie suspected that Rhi might hope for something more from their relationship. And anyone could see that they would make a perfect couple even if they hadn't entirely realised it themselves yet. All they needed was a little shove in the right direction from an interested friend, in the very same way that they were gently pushing her in a new direction too.

22

Although there was a promise of sunny spells and warmer weather later in the day, it was grey and overcast over Wishwell that morning and the hair on his bare arms prickled against the cold. All this standing around wasn't helping. He was loitering with intent behind the old oak tree on the village green. If he stayed there any longer, he would attract unwelcome attention. He needed to get over there and do what he'd come here to do. He dug his hands deeper into his pockets. Another minute or two.

He'd done an awful lot of thinking these last few weeks. Mainly about Abbey, but also about his own wants and needs. He'd come to the conclusion that he wasn't very good at relationships, that perhaps in the past he hadn't put the time and effort in that he should have done. Now, he realised he needed to change his ways unless he wanted to end up alone, an old and pathetic Lothario. He'd never been short of female attention and he supposed he'd taken advantage of that position, his head too often being swayed by a pretty face. He'd had every intention of curbing his ways, one day, knowing how much he had to lose, but that day had never really dawned until now. He just hoped he hadn't left it too late, now that he'd realised what it was he wanted from life. Or more accurately, who it was he wanted in his life... Abbey.

Now, he had to let her know how he really felt. Easy enough, he would have thought, but something was holding him back, keeping him rooted to his spot. Probably the thought of her yelling that she wanted nothing to do with him. The awful thought that he might never see her again. If only he could make her understand. She might not realise it yet, but he was convinced their future was destined to be together. There was only one way to find out.

He marched over and rapped on the black ring knocker, the wait feeling interminable until Abbey finally opened the door. Dressed in black spotty pyjamas, hair tied up in a messy topknot, and without a scrap of make-up on her face, she couldn't have looked lovelier. A pain pierced his heart for everything he'd lost. If he'd been harbouring a hope that she might actually be pleased to see him, though, he was very much mistaken.

'Jason!' A dark cloud descended over her features. 'What are you doing here?' She folded her arms crossly.

'Abbey, I've missed you. I want to talk to you. To see if we can find a way...'

'No, absolutely not. It's over, Jason. There's no going back.'

She pushed the door in his face, but he wedged his foot in the gap at the bottom, pleading with her to, at least, hear him out.

'Come on, Abbey. Just give me ten minutes. That's all I ask. Look, it's raining out here and it's absolutely freezing. Let me say what I've come here to say and then I promise I'll leave if you ask me to.'

Abbey sighed. She'd woken up in a sunny, hopeful mood, looking forward to the day ahead, and now her ex was on the doorstep looking, admittedly, as though he'd spent the night beneath a hedge. She supposed she'd never forgive herself if he contracted hypothermia.

'Right, you can have ten minutes, that's all.' She opened the door wide, unwilling to look him in the eye.

'Hey, it looks great in here.' Jason stood in the middle of the small living room, brushing down the rain from his body, looking all around him. 'It's different somehow?'

'Yep.' She had to bite her tongue to stop the snarky retort from leaving her mouth. It was bright, light, the energy so much more positive since Jason had left, but she was in no mood to discuss home furnishings with her ex. 'Look, Jason, just say whatever it is you need to say. I have stuff I need to do today.'

'You're not making this easy for me, Abbey, but hell...' He reached out a hand in her direction, which she pointedly ignored. 'This is my home.' He held up his hands, gesturing around him and Abbey thought it unnecessary to point out that this wasn't actually the case any more. 'I need to be with you, Abs, so that we can spend the rest of our lives together. I know I messed up big time, but I promise you I'll spend the rest of my days making it up to you. I love you; I know I didn't tell you nearly as often as I should have, but you're the most important person in the world to me.'

She suppressed a sigh. What wouldn't she have given for a heartfelt declaration of Jason's love a couple of months ago instead of the cool indifference she'd been more normally greeted with. She'd been a fool to put up with it for so long.

'It's too late. I've moved on, Jason. You need to do the same.'

'You can't have done. Not already. I'm not seeing her any more, if that's what you're worried about.'

She knew Jason's features intimately, every expression, every little mark on his face, but she barely recognised him any more. It was like looking at a stranger.

'I'm not worried in the slightest. I'm just pleased Rhi's seen sense and moved on too. She deserves so much better than you were ever able to offer her.'

'What? Wait a minute.' Jason's face crumpled in confusion. 'How do you know Rhianna?'

She had to bite back the smile twitching at her lips. 'Bright girl. She tracked me down. Wanted to apologise. To explain how she would never have got involved with you in the first place if she'd known the truth. I respected her for doing that. It can't have been easy.'

'No.' Jason shook his head, trying to make sense of what Abbey was telling him, all the fight and good intentions leaving his body, realising there would be no getting past Abbey's intransigence. He looked at her imploringly. 'Is there really no hope for us?'

'None whatsoever. Now, would you please leave.'

Her voice was steely, covering the swirl of emotions churning through her body. Tears gathered in her eyes. How she was holding it all together, she had no idea. The temptation to offload all her hurt and anger onto Jason in a violent tirade was huge, but what would be the point? Besides, she wouldn't want to give him the satisfaction. She turned away, opening the front door with a flourish, stopping herself from forcibly pushing him over the threshold. She breathed a huge sigh of relief when he took the hint and left, the emotion she'd been holding tight escaping in a flood of tears. So lost in the moment, she didn't even notice when someone else came rushing through the still open front door.

'Hey, what's been going on here? I passed Jason on the way out. What's he done now?'

'Oh, Dad!' She'd never been so pleased to see anyone in her life, sobbing into his chest long overdue tears that had been stored up ever since the break-up. She should have known that not shedding a single tear over the collapse of her relationship wasn't a healthy reaction, that they would have to come at some point, but these weren't tears of regret. It was weeks and months and possibly even years of frustration bubbling over. 'What an idiot!'

Her dad patted her back, soothing her as he'd done when she was a small girl. 'He is, love, but he's not worth your tears.'

'No, not Jason, Dad!' she said, through her sobs. 'Me!'

* * *

The sun had finally lived up to its earlier promise and broken through the clouds, and Abbey's tears had long since dried, after a pep talk from her dad given in tandem with some hastily arranged thickly buttered toast and a mug of tea. Her dad was right, of course, Jason wasn't worth her tears, but sometimes the enormity of what had happened hit her like a punch to the stomach. All the dreams and plans they'd made together had escaped like a helium balloon floating off into the sky, never to be seen again. Not that she had any regrets. She knew Jason would never change, but it didn't stop the pain from catching her unawares at times.

With her equilibrium restored, they headed for Primrose Woods as planned and Abbey's mood was immediately lifted by being outside and having her dad at her side, offering comfort and words of wisdom. All her worries and bad feelings flittered away as she stepped through the kissing gate onto the windy track that led to the visitors' centre. Today, though, they didn't have the park to themselves as the place was abuzz with people attending the open day. Not that it bothered Abbey; it was heartwarming to see so many people enjoying this little part of paradise. Couples, dog walkers, family groups, young and old, there was definitely something for everyone, especially since the grey clouds had cleared and people were taking the opportunity to just sit and enjoy the balmy weather. Bill and Abbey headed straight for the food market, marvelling at the number of stalls and the array of local produce on sale. Honey, cakes, speciality oils, cheeses and breads. Abbey was in her element mooching around the different tables and bought a jar of ploughman's chutney, a jar of chilli jam and a coffee and walnut cake for later, which she packed away in her rucksack. All the time she'd been on the lookout for Sam, casually looking around, her gaze attempting to pick out his distinctive figure amongst the crowds, but she hadn't spotted him yet. He was no doubt busy sharing his knowledge about the park with groups of visitors.

'Hello, you two!'

Rhi and Luke, each clutching a whippy ice cream with a Flake, greeted Abbey and Bill enthusiastically. Abbey grinned, much happier to see Rhi than she had been to see Jason this morning. Despite her initial wariness towards Rhi, and her determination to have nothing to do with her, she'd quickly taken to the feisty and fun young woman and she really considered it to be one of the good things to come out of her break-up with Jason, an unlikely but ever-growing friendship.

'We've just come from the cafe,' Luke explained. 'There's a queue going around the block. Lizzie is rushed off her feet, bless her. We gave her a wave, but we didn't have the chance to have a natter.'

'We should go and see her later,' said Bill. 'Maybe it will be less busy after the lunchtime rush.'

'Yes, we will.' Abbey smiled. It wasn't the first time she'd noticed the subtle change in her dad's expression, the way his eyes lit up, every time Lizzie's name was mentioned. He spoke about her lots too, dropping her name casually into their conversations, but not so casually that Abbey hadn't noticed his interest. It made Abbey's heart expand to see something awaken inside him, a spark that had been missing for far too long.

She wondered too what was going on exactly with Luke and

Rhi. They clearly enjoyed each other's company, the conversation and friendly banter flowing naturally between them, but there was an awkward reticence in the way they held each other at a distance, as though either of them might be explosive if they got too close.

'Look who's here!' Abbey's musings were interrupted by Bill's exclamation. She turned to see Sam striding towards them and she could have sworn her heart gave a little leap of happiness at the sight. Mind you, after her set-to with Jason that morning, her emotions were all over the place. Still, there was no mistaking someone else who was leaping with happiness. Lady ran in circles around Abbey's legs, her tail wagging furiously, giving Abbey secret hope that it was because the dog remembered her from before and was giving her the seal of approval. She bent down to make a fuss of her, musing that if Lady's owner ever felt half as excited to see her as Lady did, then that would be a very good thing indeed.

'Just wanted to come and say hello,' Sam said, addressing the four of them, although Abbey wasn't sure if she'd imagined the way his eyes locked on to hers for the briefest moment. 'What a glorious day and such a great turnout too.' He glanced at his watch. 'I'd love to stay and chat, but I'm doing a stint in the visitors' centre. Enjoy the rest of your afternoon. Catch up with you all later.'

Squashing her disappointment, Abbey watched as Sam wandered off into the distance, Lady following at his heel. With a coffee date fixed with Rhi for later in the week, Abbey and her dad said their goodbyes to the young couple and headed away from the throng onto the Heron Trail, taking the leisurely amble around the lake. It was quieter here away from the crowds, the tall trees lending a reverential hush. They spotted a tall grey heron a little further along, standing sentry-like at the edge of the lake, and they stopped for a moment, matching its stillness, just observing its majestic beauty. As they edged further along, the bird, sensing their presence, took flight, soaring through the sky until it swooped down, finding another resting perch further along the lake. Abbey smiled, threading her arm through her dad's, leaning into his side, grateful for his solid presence. She wasn't certain she would have got through the last weeks without him.

'Time for tea and cake?' he suggested, when their meandering led them back to their starting point.

'Good idea.' An even better idea, she decided, when she spotted Sam's tall and rangy figure at the entrance to the Treetops Cafe. Talking with someone. The same attractive and vivacious woman that she'd spotted him with a few weeks previously. Dressed in a white fitted T-shirt, tight-fitting jeans, riding boots and a padded gilet, she looked every inch the country lady today, the perfect partner to Sam's rugged outdoor looks. Treacherously, Lady was now dancing around the other woman's feet in the same way she'd done to Abbey only minutes before. The turncoat. However, the woman was clearly not interested in the dog at all, completely ignoring the high jinks going on around her feet and instead giving her full-on attention to Sam.

'Actually, Dad, I've got a bit of a headache coming on. I might head home if you don't mind.'

'Oh... yes, of course. Come on, then, I'll make you a nice cuppa at the cottage instead.'

'No, you go and see Lizzie. She'll be disappointed otherwise. I'll be fine after a nap. Too much excitement today, obviously.'

'Well, if you're sure, sweetheart?'

'Absolutely.'

To be honest, she was in need of some alone time to nurse her wounds. Her run-in with Jason that morning had upset her more than she'd realised, but even more unsettling was the way her whole being had reacted to seeing Sam deep in conversation with that same glamorous woman. Who was she? She clearly played some part, small or large, in Sam's life. The feeling of jealousy, frightening in its intensity, was instinctive and animalistic. What was wrong with her? Behaving like a love-struck teenager. She'd been entertaining a fantasy that she'd made a special connection with Sam, that he looked at her in a certain way, in a way that might suggest their friendship could be developing into something more personal. Ha! She was clearly delusional. When it came to men, first Jason and now Sam, she really had no idea whatsoever.

23

Putting the key in the lock and closing the door behind her, she breathed a huge sigh of relief. *Home sweet home.* Abbey wriggled off her rucksack, slipped out of her jacket and hung it on the peg beneath the stairs, and emptied her goodies from the food fair onto the kitchen top. The warmth of the late spring day had been replaced by a cool chill and the light outside was fading, so Abbey pulled on her cardigan and lit the wood-burning stove in the living room, which instantly filled the room with a cosy and welcoming glow. She lit the candles on the side tables and pulled down the blinds, revelling in the homely atmosphere. Flicking on the kettle, she popped a tea bag into a mug, and cut into the coffee cake, taking a generous slice. Moments later she settled down on the sofa with her tea, taking a bite from the cake, which was every bit as delicious as its good looks had promised, hitting the required spot perfectly.

Already, Abbey felt so much better. The cottage might be small, but it was her sanctuary, a safe haven away from the stresses and pressures of the outside world. She appreciated it all the more now that Jason no longer lived there, leaving his own personal brand of mess around the place. She was so lucky to have the cottage, a legacy from her mum, along with some other of her favourite bits and pieces that had been handed down to Abbey – an embroidered cushion, a mismatched crockery set and a multi-coloured millefiori paperweight – that had all found their own special nooks and crannies within the cottage. Abbey only had to look at them to conjure up her mum's presence around her when she needed it the most.

After a second cup of tea and another slice of cake, Abbey took a long, leisurely soak in the bath before changing into her pyjamas, ready for an evening in front of the television watching that new cosy crime series that everyone was raving about. She'd snuggled down with her favourite purple fleece blanket wrapped around her, the title credits rolling when there was a rapping at the front door. Abbey's heart sank as she turned to look at the door accusingly. Who could it be on a Saturday night? Not her dad. She'd just been texting him, telling him her plans. If it was Jason again, trying to wheedle his way back into her life, she would not be happy. She'd been remarkably polite to him up until now but her patience was wearing thin. Whoever it was knocked on the door again, and she jumped up to answer it, her hackles rising. She threw open the door.

'Yes,' she snapped, expecting to see Jason, looking sorry for himself, on her doorstep. Instead it was someone else entirely. 'Oh, hello...'

'Yes, ah....' Sam faltered, his gaze flittering over her pink spotty pyjamas. 'This is clearly a bad time. Sorry. I was hoping to catch you earlier at the park, but your dad said you weren't feeling too well. I just wanted to check you were okay?'

'Just a headache,' she managed, trying to make sense of the fact that he was here, looking gorgeous, on her doorstep, feeling touched by his concern for her. 'I'm feeling better, thanks.' Much better with each passing moment, in fact. Although she really wished she hadn't scrubbed her face clean of make-up so that she resembled a shiny peach. And as for the pyjamas, well, at least they were clean and fresh. She collected herself, remembering her manners. 'Would you like to come in?'

'Well,' he wavered, 'I wouldn't want to intrude and it looks as though you might have other plans?'

She laughed, looking down at her bedtime ensemble, brazening it out.

'No plans at all. Come on in, I can fix you a drink.'

Following him through into the living room, Abbey picked up the remote and zapped the telly off. That series might be good, but it could definitely wait until another day. She hurriedly moved the blanket from the sofa, rearranging cushions, suddenly acutely aware of Sam's looming physical presence right next to her. She felt a heat rising in her cheeks.

'Gosh it's warmer in here than I realised,' she said, fanning her face, although that was hardly surprising with the fire burning and the candles glowing and her internal body temperature rising by the second.

'Maybe you're going down with something, if you've not been feeling right?'

'I've just got myself over-tired; I'll be fine after a good night's sleep. What was it you wanted to see me about?'

'Nothing important. I was going to suggest a beer this evening, but no worries. We can always do it some other time... if you want to.'

She nodded keenly.

A silence grew between them before he added. 'To be honest, I just wanted to catch up with you. See how you were doing. We didn't really get a chance to chat today. You don't mind, do you?'

'Not at all.' She turned and headed for the kitchen to break the tension she could feel simmering, opening the fridge. 'A beer or a hot drink?'

'No, I won't, thanks. I'm going to make tracks and leave you in peace. You need to get some rest. I should never have turned up here uninvited anyway.'

'It's fine, really.' Panic gripped her. Now he was here she wanted him to stay, a chance to talk properly. 'I saw you with a woman earlier, at the park?' Abbey threw the question out lightly, she hoped, unable to stop herself from asking. 'Attractive, blonde. I've seen her a couple of times at the park.'

'Ah... Stephanie.' He gave a rueful half smile. 'I hope you didn't think we were... that she was anything more than a friend.'

'I didn't know. You looked very good together. Like a couple. I suppose... well, I did wonder.'

'No. We met online and went on a couple of dates. She was the one Lizzie was talking about at lunch? Don't get me wrong, she's a lovely girl, just not for me. I've told her as much, tried letting her down gently but she's not really getting the message. She keeps on texting and turning up at the park. I'm sure she'll get the idea sooner or later.'

Abbey gave a thought to Stephanie, feeling a pang of sympathy. It sounded as though she was indulging in her own bit of fantasy involving Sam. It was understandable. He was the sort of man who was attractive to women, not only through his natural physical attributes, his height and broad shoulders, his dark good looks, but also by the way he made you feel, as though you were the most important person in the world. He listened intently, as though he really cared about what you were saying. Uncharitably, she wondered if that was a learnt trait or if he was really that lovely, kind and so easy to fall for. Lizzie's words about Sam being a serial dater were ringing an alarm in her head. 'What it is to be so popular,' she said playfully.

His brows lifted, his eyes wide as he appraised her.

'Well, I'm not sure I see it in quite the same way,' he said defensively, 'but anyway, that's not important.' He headed for the front door before turning to look at Abbey again. 'I really hope you're feeling better soon. Look, I don't know if you fancy going out for dinner some time soon?'

His invitation took her by surprise and she spoke before she had a chance to get her thoughts in order. 'Like a date, you mean?'

A small crease appeared on his brow, but there was a definite smile in his eyes.

'If you want to put a name to it, then yes, I suppose we could call it that.'

Did she really want to be the latest in a long line of dates for Sam? Someone he would see on a couple of occasions before becoming bored and moving on to the next woman. Wasn't that what Lizzie had intimated? Leaving her in the same state as poor Stephanie. She wasn't sure if her fragile heart was up to that level of hope and expectation.

'Hey, there's no pressure. Just a chance to catch up over a meal. Only if you want to, of course?'

Sam was waiting for a reply, but she felt conflicted, her heart telling her one thing, her head telling her something else entirely. Still, there was only ever going to be one answer with him standing there looking gorgeous and expectant, the subtle scent of the great outdoors just reaching her nose.

'Yes, why not?' she said, realising she probably sounded distinctly underwhelmed. She softened her response with a smile.

It was only a dinner, she told herself. She was under absolutely no obligation to fall in love with him.

* * *

'What a treat this is!'

Lizzie turned on the kitchen light and filled the kettle, switching it on, while Bill unwrapped the fish and chips, allowing the mouthwatering aromas to fill the room. She quickly put some teabags into mugs and buttered some slices of bread, before fetching the milk from the fridge.

'Come and sit down,' said Bill. 'You've been on your feet all day; you must be exhausted.'

'I'm fine until I stop. That's when it usually catches up with me. But it's been such a good day, I think I'm running on adrenalin.' She shook vinegar over her brimming plate of food. 'I saw so many of my lovely regulars today and met lots of new visitors too. And what a perfect way to round off the day,' she said, looking at her plate overflowing with crispy battered fish and a mountain of golden chips. It was only now she realised how hungry she was. She'd been so pleased to see Bill when he turned up at the cafe just as she was finishing for the day. When he suggested they go for a drink at the pub and then collect a takeaway on the way home, she couldn't have been more pleased. Going back alone to an empty house after a day's work was something she still hadn't got used to.

'I can't remember the last time I had fish and chips.' Lizzie tucked in eagerly. 'Probably not since David died. We used to get a takeaway every few weeks and this was always our favourite choice.'

'I know what you mean.' Bill looked over his fork at Lizzie, savouring his own meal. 'It's those little things that you miss when you lose a partner. A takeaway for one isn't quite the same.'

'Tell me, how is Abbey doing now? She always puts on a brave face when I see her, but I know it must have knocked her for six, the break-up with her fiancé.'

'Yes.' Bill's face darkened. 'To be honest with you, I think that's why she's sporting a headache today.' He told Lizzie about Jason's unexpected visit that morning.

'He's got a cheek!'

'He has, and I think it upset her. Not because she has any feelings left for him, but because she was doing a good job of moving on until he turned up. She wants to forget about the past and look to the future.'

'I don't blame her. She's such a great girl. I took to her the very first moment we met. She deserves to meet someone who will treat her properly.'

'She does. Can't say I was terribly disappointed when she told me the wedding was off. In fact, I was rather relieved. I mean, I always rubbed along pretty well with Jason, but he wasn't right for Abbey. I know I'm her dad, but I never thought he treated her particularly well and she wasn't happy, not really. When you've had a wonderful and fulfilling marriage yourself, it's only natural to want the same for your own daughter, isn't it?'

Lizzie nodded, understanding entirely. Bill was clearly a family man. That much was evident to see in the way he spoke about his late wife, and in his love and concern for his daughter. Often when he spoke about them both, his emotions were bubbling just beneath the surface, and Lizzie liked that about him, that he could be so honest and upfront with her. It gave her the permission she needed to be as equally candid about her own life.

'Children, eh?' Bill reflected. 'You don't stop worrying about them just because they're adults. And in some ways it's much harder than when they're little because you can't interfere too much. You have to let them make their own mistakes. Talking of children, how is your daughter now?'

'She's feeling a lot better, thank you. More positive. I think it's knowing that I'll be seeing her in a couple of months. She's very excited.'

'And you?'

'Ah...' Lizzie's distinctive laugh echoed around the kitchen. 'I have my first session with the hypnotherapist on Monday. I was very nervous even speaking to her on the phone; it took me all morning just to find the courage to make the call, but I needn't have worried. When I finally got through to her, she was lovely and put me at ease. She seems to think she can help me and that I will only need two or three sessions.' Lizzie raised her shoulders to her ears and offered up the palms of her hands to the sky. She couldn't quite believe it herself, but it had to be worth a try. 'I really hope she's right. Everyone's been so supportive. You, Abbey, Rhi, Luke and Sam. I don't want to let anyone down. With you all behind me, I really feel as though I might be able to step on the plane when the time comes. And yes, I am beginning to feel a little excited.'

'Good for you, Lizzie. I know you can do it.'

'This is just the beginning, Bill. Next year, I have a big birthday. I'll be sixty, can you believe?'

'Never!' said Bill, his brown eyes twinkling with amusement behind his trendy tortoiseshell glasses.

Lizzie laughed along with Bill, knowing that she might have mentioned her upcoming big birthday once or twice at the quiz night. 'Anyway, I've decided now is the time to start living life to the full. I've been treading water for far too long. You can't live in the past forever, can you? And I think I might have been guilty of doing that.'

'Well, that's very commendable, Lizzie, and a great way to embrace your future. You're just a youngster, you know that, with plenty of good times ahead of you.'

'We both are, Bill.'

Later, on his way out, Bill kissed her on the cheek and she glanced down at his hands marked with golden sun spots, as they gently brushed her arms. Something else she'd missed recently. The human touch. She smiled and waved him goodbye from her doorstep, feeling an unexpected excitement ripple through her body. She hadn't liked to tell him that she felt sure he would play some part in the good times ahead too.

24

When Abbey and Rhi made arrangements to meet up, there was only one place that immediately occurred to them both.

'Primrose Woods?'

'Perfect,' said Abbey.

In fact, on almost all of her days off, Abbey would invariably end up at the park, if only for an hour, to give herself a break from all the other jobs she needed to do, a welcome fix of fresh air and the great outdoors to lift her mood. She would invariably end up in the cafe for a reviving drink and a catch-up with Lizzie if she happened to be working on that day. The possibility that she might run into Sam was neither here nor there, but certainly added an air of anticipation and excitement to her visits.

As it turned out, it was pretty perfect weather-wise that day. Abbey discarded her zipped sweat top as soon as she headed outside, feeling the heat of the sun on her skin through the fabric. She stuffed it into her backpack in case of rain later. When she met Rhi at the visitors' centre, they hugged like old friends before setting off, walking at a determined pace, taking the path that trailed around the perimeter of Primrose Woods. In the fields beyond the fence, sheep were grazing far into the distance on rolling green hills; they passed horses in another field who came to nod their hellos over the fence, and they stopped for a breather to view the magnificence of Primrose Hall, a seventeenth-century Grade II listed manor house that stood at the heart of the magical estate.

'Isn't it amazing,' swooned Rhi. 'Fancy living in a place like that.'

'It is beautiful. They've done a lot of work on it recently. For years it lay derelict, all the windows were boarded up, but they've done a great job with the refurbishment – it's looking wonderful now. It's recently been used as a location for a Tom Cruise film, apparently, but the rumour is that the new owner will be moving in soon.'

'Wow, how the other half live, eh?'

As Rhi and Abbey walked on, their conversation flowed and they chatted about all sorts of things, the beautiful landscape around them, the weather, their respective jobs, everything and nothing, but they steered well clear of discussing the one person that had brought them together. Although they had only known each other a matter of weeks, it was as if they had always been friends who were comfortable embracing the natural silences that fell between them. It was a couple of hours later when Abbey checked her watched and realised they'd walked over five miles. Her body tingled with the exertion, her skin glowed and she felt a wonderful sense of well-being. Looking across at Rhi, she suspected she was experiencing the same, as she appeared as fresh-faced as when they'd first set off.

'This is my favourite spot in the whole park.' They'd taken a seat on the bench where Abbey had first spoken to Sam, although that wasn't the only reason why she loved it here so much. The views across the park were breathtaking and she liked to sit and watch the world go by. She could get her thoughts in order, feel any worries or stresses slip away.

'I can understand why. It's so beautiful and peaceful here.' They both stared off into the distance, lost in their own thoughts. 'I wanted to ask your advice, actually, Abbey.'

'I'll help if I can.' Abbey turned to look at Rhi. 'What is it?'

'It's about my love life,' said Rhi with a wry chuckle.

Abbey let out an involuntary snort. 'And you think I'm the right person to help on that front, knowing my terrific relationship history?' She laughed, but then an awful thought struck her. 'Please don't tell me Jason's been bothering you as well?'

'Jason? You've heard from him?'

'Yep.' Abbey sighed, not really wishing to visit that old ground. 'He turned up at the cottage the other day, professing his love, asking me to forgive him and for us to give it another go.'

'Really?' said Rhi, hardly able to believe the cheek of the man.

'I told him where to go. Far too politely, of course, but it upset me, realising how many years I'd wasted on someone who simply wasn't worth the time or the energy.'

Rhi reached across and placed a comforting hand on Abbey's arm. 'Nothing's ever wasted. If you hadn't been through all of that with Jason, you wouldn't have arrived at this point. Now, you're much better placed to know what it is you want from your life and what you will and won't accept from a relationship.'

'That's true.' Abbey looked across at Rhi and smiled. She didn't feel remotely qualified to offer Rhi any advice, particularly on the subject of relationships. This young woman was mature beyond her years and seemed to have most things sussed out. Funny, forthright and caring, she was much more self-assured than Abbey had ever been, even if she was trying to change in that respect now. 'What was it you wanted to ask me about? Is it Jason?'

'Good grief, no! That man is history to me. He would know

better than to turn up at my door.' Rhi's face darkened and Abbey laughed at her vehemence. Rhi smiled in return. 'No, it's Luke.'

'Ah, I wondered about you two. You seem to get on very well.'

'We do, and I really like him, but I'm not sure how he feels about me. He asked me out once when we worked together, when I was actually seeing Jason, but I knocked him back. In fact, I was a bit of a cow towards him.' Every time she thought about it, she cringed inwardly, the shame making her cheeks tingle. 'Now I'm single and would really like to see how things might develop between us, but it's almost as if he just sees me as one of the boys, a mate.'

'Maybe he already has a partner, do you know?'

'No, I did a little bit of surreptitious fishing on that front. He had a girlfriend, but they split up. He's definitely single. I don't understand it. He used to be really flirty with me. Now he's not. Perhaps he just doesn't fancy me any more?' Rhi pushed her bottom lip out, pulling her dark curls out from her ponytail and shaking her hair loose, ringlets framing her pretty face.

Looking at her now in all her gorgeousness, and having seen them together, the sparks flying between them, Abbey thought that explanation highly unlikely.

'Well, perhaps he doesn't want to be too pushy, knowing what happened between you and Jason.'

Rhi shrugged. 'I've invited him to a couple of different things, the quiz and for walks, and he's always happy to come along, but he's keeping his distance, emotionally and physically. Who knows, perhaps we missed our moment.'

There was an edge of regret to Rhi's voice.

'There's only one way to find out. Why don't you ask him?'

'Hmmm...' Rhi faltered and Abbey noticed her reticence, the vulnerability beneath her air of innate self-confidence. 'I should, but I don't want to scare him away. Honestly, this isn't like me!' She laughed at her own diffidence. 'I'm usually upfront with guys. I hate playing games. It's much better to put your cards on the table at the outset so you don't end up wasting each other's time, but there's something about Luke that prevents me from being entirely honest about my feelings. I really like having him in my life and I don't want to do anything to jeopardise that. I'd hate for there to be any awkwardness between us.'

'Luke's a lovely, genuine guy. I'm sure there wouldn't be. I think you need to be brave enough to take the next step, find out what it is you both want from each other.'

'Yes, I guess you're right. It's just getting up the nerve to do it, I suppose.'

Funny how easy it was to work out what other people should do in their relationships. If only Abbey had as much insight into her own love life.

As if picking up on her thoughts, Rhi looked at her, observing her features closely, before asking. 'What about you and Sam? How are things going there?' A mischievous smile twisted on Rhi's lips as her beautifully sculpted brows lifted questioningly.

'Good, good...' Abbey nodded, attempting to be serious but wrestling with the ridiculous grin that was trying to spread across her face, something that happened every time Sam popped into her head. 'Although obviously we are just friends.'

'Obviously.' Rhi nodded too, a wry smile on her lips as she appraised Abbey doubtfully. Abbey should have known she couldn't get anything past Rhi. 'It's just... I thought I sensed a little frisson of something going on between the pair of you.'

Abbey threw back her head and laughed. 'A frisson?'

Didn't that sound wonderful? Secretly it thrilled her that Rhi was imagining her and Sam together, as an item, that it wasn't totally out of the realms of possibility that they could be a proper couple. She just had to remind herself to not let her own imagination run away with her.

'Don't tell me you don't fancy him a bit,' egged on Rhi.

'Well, he's a good-looking guy. I'll give you that. But I'm not sure he's the settling-down type. And to be honest with you, it's not my priority right now. Finding a new relationship, that is. If it happens, it happens, but I'm not going out looking for it. Although...' Abbey's brow furrowed, a smile lifting the corners of her mouth.

'What?' asked Rhi, picking up on Abbey's hesitation.

'He has actually invited me out to dinner.'

'What, just the two of you, on a date!?'

Abbey smiled. It wasn't such a daft question she'd asked Sam after all. What was it Rhi had been saying about being upfront about these things?

'Yes, I guess.' Abbey still wasn't sure if that was really the case. She'd put Sam on the spot and he'd been amused by the question, his reply, an attempt to make her feel better, she suspected. She was so out of practice at being a single, available woman that she wasn't sure how to act or what to expect when it came to men. If she thought of it as two newly found friends getting to know each other better, then it seemed so much more manageable. So what, if said newly found friend happened to be a really gorgeous guy.

'There you go! I knew it all along.' Rhi grinned. 'Go for it, Abbey. Don't overthink it. Sam is a great guy. And remember, he isn't Jason. Don't let that one bad experience put you off all men.'

'We'll just have to see how it goes.' Abbey shrugged nonchalantly for Rhi's benefit, but really she was managing her own expectations, not wanting to build up her hopes only to be badly let down again.

They fell silent for a moment, distracted by a group of Dalmatians frolicking in front of them, laughing at their goofy antics. Rhi stretched out her denim-clad, long, slim legs in front of her, clasping her hands together and pushing them forwards in the air.

'You know, I still feel so conflicted about this whole situation. I'm so glad we've built a friendship out of the mess, but I feel really bad about what happened with you and Jason. Every time I think about what he did I feel murderous towards him. I was stupid not to see through his lies and when I think about the hurt I inadvertently caused you, I feel terrible. If it wasn't for me, then your life wouldn't have been upended in the way that it was. You'd actually be married by now.'

'Yes, and what a disaster that would have been! Honestly, Rhi, don't beat yourself up over it. None of it was your fault and you've actually done me a massive favour. Funny thing is, I don't really miss Jason or our relationship, just the idea of them. It goes to show what a sham it was.'

Rhi grinned, putting an arm around Abbey's shoulder. 'Never again, eh? For either of us.' She held up her little finger, locking it around Abbey's pinkie. 'A pact. We vow not to take that sort of rubbish from any man ever again. Agreed?'

'Absolutely,' Abbey said with a wide grin.

'Come on,' said Rhi, dragging Abbey to her feet, before linking arms with her. 'Let's go and see Lizzie. I think we deserve a slice of cake after all that walking and putting the world to rights.'

25

'What are you doing here?'

'Well, that's not very welcoming, Rhi. It's great to see you too. Last time I looked, this place was a pub. I'll have a pint of the special, please.'

At least it was early into a lunchtime shift. There weren't too many customers around to see Rhi's usual sunny demeanour behind the bar transformed into a brewing, fizzing anger. She hadn't been prepared for the strength of her feelings at seeing Jason again. Obviously she'd wondered what she might say and do if she had the misfortune to run into him, but she couldn't have predicted that she would have felt so... well, annoyed, humiliated and, quite frankly, murderous. There was no getting away from the situation, either. Jake and Tracey, the other bar staff, wouldn't be in for another half an hour yet, and she didn't want to disturb Malc and Jan, who were upstairs in the living quarters. She might have walked out on her job at Jansens without a second thought, but there was no way she would do anything to jeopardise her position at the pub.

Instead, she avoided his gaze as she pulled his pint, before plonking his glass on the bar top, the contents slopping over onto the beer mat.

'Can we have a chat, Rhi?'

'No, we can't. I'm working if you hadn't noticed.'

'But it's hardly very busy and I only need a moment to say what I need to say. Look, I realised that you never gave me the opportunity to explain.' He paused, his gaze running over her face. 'Christ, you're looking good.'

She glared at him, examining his features as though she was meeting him for the first time. What she'd ever seen in him she didn't know. His eyes were far too close together, there was an unbecoming curl to his lips and his hair, swept back with gel, made him look creepy. At one time she'd lapped up his compliments; now his smooth-talking ways just made her shudder inside.

'I didn't mean to string you along. I don't want you thinking that you never meant anything to me. You did. You still do. I miss you, Rhi.'

She shrugged away his insincere and annoying words.

'I don't need to listen to this. You messed up, big time, and I made a huge mistake getting involved with you in the first place. It's all in the past now. I've moved on. You need to do the same.' She turned her back on him, wishing he would hurry up and finish his pint before the temptation to pick it up and throw it in his face became too much to ignore. She busied herself with tidying the back bar, but Jason followed her round.

'Come on, don't be like that. We can be together now, like we always talked about. Don't you still want that?'

'Are you mad, Jason?' She turned back to face him, her skin burning. 'Why on earth would I want anything to do with you after the way you treated me? You're nothing but a liar and a cheat. I know my own value and I'm worth so much more than you.'

'You're still angry, I understand that. Maybe a few weeks down the line you'll feel differently. You never know, Rhi?'

Oh, she knew, really she did. How she wished she could wipe that smarmy smile right off his face.

'A few weeks down the line I'll be in Australia and I certainly won't be giving you a second thought.'

'Really?' She'd done it. His self-satisfied smile was replaced with a cloud of confusion. 'How long are you going for?'

'Three months, maybe more. Who knows, I might even stay out there if I find I like it.' So what if she was stretching the truth. Jason should be under no misapprehension that there could be any chance for them whatsoever.

'Shame,' sighed Jason, throwing back his beer. 'How's Abbey doing?'

Through the front bay window, Rhi's attention was distracted. A car pulled up outside, one she recognised immediately, the number plate already etched onto her brain. Luke! Her heart thudded at the realisation. What was he doing here?

'Rhi?'

'What?' she snapped at Jason as she shifted her head to see Luke climb out of his car.

'Abbey? You've seen her, right? You couldn't resist interfering, could you? Ruining my chances with her.'

'You did that all by yourself. You didn't need any help from me.'

'Does she talk about me at all. I just wonder—'

'Honestly, Jason,' she interrupted him, her patience wearing thin. 'You're pathetic, do you know that? Abbey has much better things to do with her time than speak about you.' As she faced him down, she saw a movement in the doorway and turned to greet Luke, but he must have seen her with Jason. Before she had a chance to call out to him, he did an about turn and marched back to his car, jumping in and zooming away. Her breath hitched with disappointment. She couldn't believe it. She glared at Jason, only grateful for the barrier of the bar between them as her hands itched to reach for his throat.

'Ugh! Look what you've done now, you stupid, stupid man!'

* * *

Summer had well and truly arrived at Primrose Woods. Abbey manoeuvred the minibus along the winding track to the car park, a big smile on her face as she listened to the giggles, squeals and chatter coming from behind her. For all the noise her select group of passengers was making, they could well have been mistaken for a bunch of excitable schoolkids rather than a set of septuagenarians and octogenarians.

'Look at those monkey puzzle trees!' Sheila gasped. 'I can barely see the tops of them. They look almost prehistoric. You might half expect to see a pack of dinosaurs come thundering out from the woods.'

'The only dinosaurs around here are us lot of old crocks,' quipped Arthur, which set the group off into more giggles.

'Now, then,' said Abbey, trying to bring some order to the proceedings, 'Sam Finnegan, who came to visit us at the Lodge, has kindly agreed to meet us in the car park and we're going to follow his jeep along the access roads so that we can do a tour of the park. We're very lucky as these roads aren't generally open to the public. We'll get a good view of the lake, the meadows and the woods. Then, as it's such a beautiful afternoon, we'll come back to the viewing point and sit outside for an hour or so before going to the Treetops Cafe for tea and cakes.'

'Your young man is spoiling us, isn't he? He's obviously keen to make an impression.'

Abbey raised her eyes at Stella Darling, shaking her head. 'He's not my young man, as you well know, but you're right, he is being very kind to help us in this way.'

'Maybe not yet,' said Stella cheekily, 'but I reckon it's only a question of time.'

Abbey bit back her smile, not entertaining Stella's teasing at all, but it didn't stop her heart from leaping when she spotted Sam's jeep ahead. His tanned arm appeared from the driver's window and he gestured for her to follow as he took the track into the woods, travelling at a very slow and leisurely pace. The windows of the minibus were open, bringing in the lightest of breezes.

'This brings back memories,' swooned Reg as they trundled along, reaching the lake. 'I always used to bring the dogs down here and they'd be straight into the water, swimming after balls and sticks. Happy times.'

Abbey glanced in the rear-view mirror, warmed by the sight of the ladies and gentlemen on the trip today, their enthusiasm evident as they peered out of the windows, taking in the views. She tried to arrange as many visits out as she possibly could for those residents able to participate because they were a mood-lifter for everyone concerned.

'Goodness me,' said Doris a little while later. 'Is that Primrose Hall? Look what they've done to it!'

'It's beautiful, isn't it?' Abbey agreed. 'It's undergone an extensive restoration over the last eighteen months; it's almost complete. There's a rumour that the new owners will be moving in later this year. Not sure who they are, though.'

'Someone with a lot of money,' said Arthur.

'I remember that it was boarded up for years,' Doris went on. 'It always seemed terribly sad to me, standing there lonely and neglected. It used to be owned by Lord Wexham, but he lost all his fortune through gambling debts and his young glamorous wife ran off with an Italian artist. Lord Wexham never got over it, and died alone and impoverished. That was the story, at least. It's good to see the place restored to its former glory. It's about time some new happier memories were made there.'

'If only they could restore people to their former glory in the same way,' mused Reg. 'Wouldn't that be a thing?'

Later, when they'd parked up outside the visitors' centre, Abbey thanked Sam for the guided tour.

'It's my pleasure. I believe firmly that the park should be available to everyone, old and young, so it's important to do whatever we can to facilitate that. I hope it's been beneficial.'

'Absolutely. Just look at them!'

The group, in their sun hats and glasses, were sitting out on one of the viewing decks, soaking up the warmth of the summer's day, enjoying being a part of the activity around them, passing comment on the unsuspecting passers-by. Abbey watched Sam as he made a point of chatting to them all individually, answering any questions and pointing out features on the landscape around them. Stella monopolised his attention, though, laying a hand on his arm as she told a story, her laughter tinkling in the air, her skin glowing a pretty pink. Abbey smiled, knowing exactly how Stella felt; Sam had the exact same effect on her. She wouldn't tell Stella that she was going out to dinner with him soon or else she would never hear the end of it, with Stella wanting to know all the details and if she ought to buy a new outfit in anticipation of a wedding in the offing.

The afternoon was rounded off with a visit to the Treetops Cafe, where Lizzie put on a delightful spread of sandwiches, biscuits and cakes, before Abbey glanced at her watch and realised she would need to bring the proceedings to a close.

'Oh, it's been such a lovely afternoon,' sighed Doris, with the others murmuring their agreement. Abbey thought so too, a perfect summer's afternoon in fact, helped in no small part, from her point of view, at having spent the time in Sam's company. The more she did it, the more she realised how much she liked that man, the positive impact he had on her state of mind, making her feel so vibrantly alive. A dose of Sam Finnegan should be available on prescription, she decided.

With all the residents safely back in the minibus, their seatbelts on, Sam came alongside her as she waited by the driver's door.

'I hope we're still okay for dinner next Friday?'

'Absolutely, I'm looking forward to it,' she said with a smile, feeling the heat of his gaze on her face.

As she drove away she had a big smile on her face. Her passengers waved goodbye to Sam through the bus windows before Stella piped up from the back. 'So you are going on a date with Sam, then? Well, that's very exciting! Come on, then, spill the beans.'

Abbey laughed. Trust Stella to have been earwigging on their conversation. Abbey shook her head indulgently, putting on the radio to shut out the giggling coming from behind.

26

'Hey, come on in. Sorry for the last-minute change of plan.'

Sam leant forward, kissing Abbey lightly on cheek, the lightest traces of his aftershave reaching her senses as he welcomed her through the door of Badger's Lodge, his home deep among the trees on the outskirts of Primrose Woods.

'Not a problem. Really. Thanks for having me!' Abbey handed over the bottle of chilled white wine she'd been clinging on to for moral support. She wasn't certain why she was so nervous and was doing her best to channel Rhi's positivity and energy. It was one thing to meet Sam in a busy restaurant but quite another to be alone with him in, what Abbey was discovering, was a lovely hide-away in the forest. She glanced around, intrigued to see Sam's place and whether it would offer more clues to his personality. It was definitely a bachelor's pad with a brown leather sofa covered in an assortment of blankets. In front of the wood-burning stove, there were a couple of large wicker baskets, one full with a bunch of pine cones and another stacked with logs. On the mantelpiece there were two photo frames, one showing a picture of a woman laughing and the other with the same woman and a young boy on a pier, the sea visible in the background. She spotted Lady, a plastic cone around her head, snuggled up, as best she could, in her dog bed in front of the unlit fire.

'How is Lady now?'

'Feeling sorry for herself. She ripped the skin off her pad when she was out in the woods today and was hobbling around. I popped her down to the vet and they've wrapped it up and put her on a course of antibiotics. She's very disgruntled about it so I didn't feel I could leave her tonight.'

'Aw, poor girl.' Abbey bent down on her haunches to cuddle Lady, who responded with a gentle wag of her tail. 'We could have done this another time.'

'No way. I was looking forward to it. Besides, I enjoy cooking; it relaxes me. Come through and I'll fix you a drink.'

With a glass of wine in her hand, Abbey relaxed too, watching Sam as he moved effortlessly about the kitchen, sautéing potatoes with garlic and rosemary in a pan. The aromas wafting in her direction were enticing, making her realise just how hungry she was.

'Can I help at all?' she offered.

'No, it's all under control. It's just good to have you here,' he said, turning to her with a wide smile that set fireworks off inside her chest. Maybe it was hot in here but Sam's appearance wasn't helping the situation at all. He was wearing navy chinos with a white shirt, his sleeves rolled up to show off his tanned, strong forearms. He ran a hand through his mop of chestnut hair, a tea towel thrown casually over his shoulder, looking every inch the relaxed chef at home. She'd worn a short-sleeved dress, but still a fire seeped around her body, whether from the heat of the kitchen or being in such close proximity to Sam, she wasn't sure. It was fascinating to watch him in his comfort zone. Jason hadn't known his way around the kitchen at all. He could barely rustle up a sandwich, leaving all the domestic arrangements to Abbey, so having a meal prepared for her was a real treat.

'Let's eat,' he said triumphantly as he placed salmon fillets with a herby crust topping, sauté potatoes and green beans onto plates, before carrying them through to the small table in the living room and pulling out a chair for Abbey. He topped up the wine and raised his glass to her. 'Thanks for coming.'

'My compliments to the chef! This looks absolutely delicious.'

Any worries Abbey may have had about any awkwardness between them was unfounded because the conversation flowed easily as they chatted about the park, their respective jobs and their new-found friends made through the quiz team, all helped along, no doubt, by the free-flowing wine.

'No more!' said Abbey, putting a hand over the top of her glass. 'I have to drive home later.'

'I could get you a taxi.' He held up the bottle to the light. 'It would be a shame to drink the rest on my own. And we haven't even got to the damson gin yet.' Sam smiled, gathering up the empty plates.

'Not the gin! It was delicious, and very addictive, but I'm sure it was to blame for my fuzzy head the next day.' She laughed, the memory taking Abbey back to her nearly-wedding day, a day filled with much laughter and love, a day she would always remember now, but for all the right reasons. She was so grateful to Lizzie for her kindness and thoughtfulness in organising such a special lunch on what could have easily been an awful, upsetting day.

'It's entirely up to you, but don't worry about getting home. I'll make sure you get back safely. You can always collect your car tomorrow,' he said, hovering with the bottle in mid-air, tempting her with that smile.

'Thanks.' She put up no further defence and held her glass up for a top-up. In truth, going home was the last thing on her mind.

She could quite easily sit all night long chatting to Sam. It was Saturday tomorrow so there was no early start and no plans made other than to meet up with her dad at some point for a walk over at Primrose Woods. Right now, she was enjoying the moment, the sensation of letting go, of being here with Sam, savouring the lovely food and wine. Ordinarily, Abbey wasn't a great drinker – she only really drank on high days and holidays – but this was definitely turning out to be one of those high days.

'Eton mess!' Sam presented Abbey with an individual glass bowl, overflowing with meringue, cream and strawberries.

'Wow! Just wow!' Abbey dipped her spoon into the fluffy cream, and popped it into her mouth, allowing it to melt slowly on her tongue. 'I'll have to come again if this is the sort of treatment I can expect.'

'Well, you would be very welcome. Any time...' said Sam graciously.

After pudding, Sam poured a small measure of damson gin for them each and, as they sipped on their coffees, the conversation took a more personal turn.

'So, how are you doing now, after the... um... break-up? It must have been a difficult few weeks.' Sam sat back in his chair, coffee cup in hand, observing Abbey closely, but it didn't feel intrusive. Just one friend looking out for another.

She picked up her cup, lost in thought for a moment. *Jason who?* At times, especially when she was with Sam, it was all too easy to forget about that part of her life, even though she'd spent a large proportion of her adulthood with Jason. He was part of her history now and she wouldn't allow her future to be defined by their break-up.

She blew out her cheeks, giving a wry smile. 'I'm okay, most of the time. Sometimes it hits me, usually in the middle of the night, when I wonder why it all fell apart, why I wasn't enough for him. He was supposed to love me, but clearly he didn't.'

Sam didn't interrupt; he simply allowed Abbey to speak, his brown eyes observing her closely as he nodded in understanding.

'You know it was Rhi he was having the affair with?' She hadn't intended to tell Sam, but the words had tumbled out before she'd had a chance to consider whether it was a good idea or not.

'What?' Sam sat forward in his chair, spluttering on his coffee. 'You are kidding me?'

'No.' She shook her head ruefully. 'They worked for the same company. She had no idea about me or that he was engaged. She believed he was single and was devastated when she discovered the truth. They'd just been away for a romantic weekend while I was at home arranging the final touches to our wedding day.'

'The bastard!' Sam shook his head and then held a hand up in apology for the outburst. 'Sorry...'

'There's no need. It's nothing that I haven't called him myself. Don't think badly of Rhi, though. He told her a ton of lies and made her promises that he had no intention of keeping. She tracked me down. She wanted to let me know how sorry she was and how she would never have got involved with him in the first place if she'd known the true situation.'

'Wow! I assumed you two had known each other for years.'

'No. When she first tracked me down, it was at Primrose Woods, actually. I was outraged, as you can imagine. I wanted nothing to do with her, but she begged me to listen, to hear her side of the story. I soon realised that we had a lot in common; she'd been wronged in the same way as I had.' Abbey gave a rueful laugh. 'We bonded over that and quickly became friends. I really like her, despite not wanting to. Through all of this, she's been most concerned about my feelings. It's really sweet, actually. Anyway, why are we even talking about this?' Abbey flapped her hands in front of her face. She sensed her cheeks were flushed from the wine and the intimacy of the occasion. She'd been so enjoying the evening, she didn't want to put a dampener on the occasion by talking about her pitiful love life.

'Sorry. I didn't mean to upset you.'

'No, it's fine. It's just old news. I don't want to have to think about him any more. He's dead to me.' She made a slicing action against her neck, and Sam recoiled in mock horror. She laughed, hesitating for a moment before asking, 'What about you, Sam? Have you ever come close to being married?'

'Nope. Never.' He shrugged, as though it was an inconsequential question, as if she'd just asked him if he'd ever tried sugar in his tea.

'Really? I think it's a shame to have never been in love before at your age.'

Sam laughed, lifting his brows in surprise. She wondered if she'd insulted him, but from what she knew of Sam, he wasn't the sensitive type.

'You make me sound as if I'm positively ancient and beyond hope!' His eyes shone brightly. 'Anyway, I didn't actually say I'd never been in love before, only that I've never had any plans to marry.'

'Ah, right...' *Interesting!* Now she was desperate to know more, to find out about the real man beneath the confident and outgoing exterior he projected. Opening up to Sam about what had happened with Jason had felt entirely natural, helped in no small part by the delicious food, the conversation and the relaxed ambience. Would Sam choose to be quite so forthcoming, though? she wondered. 'So you have *been* in love, then?' she said lightly, in case he didn't want to talk about it.

'Well... it was a long time ago now. I was a kid, basically. We met in sixth form and... fell in love.' He opened up his palms to the air, as though explaining the eternal mysteries of love. 'I went off to one university, she went to another, but we spent our weekends travelling up and down the country to visit each other, and spent every holiday, every moment we could, together. We were planning on moving in with each other after we finished our studies, but...' There was a hesitation, an audible intake of breath. 'It never materialised.'

'What was her name?'

'Sophie.'

Abbey tried to conjure up a picture in her head of the young Sophie. Slim and pretty with long brown hair, clever and carefree too, she suspected.

'So why...' Abbey started, afraid to overstep the mark. 'What happened? If you don't mind me asking, that is?'

'I don't mind at all. She fell for my best friend, Matt, and they disappeared off into the sunset together. Like they do in the movies. It was a bit of a bummer, actually. I lost my best mate and girlfriend in one fell swoop.'

'That's awful. Being cheated on is the worst thing. It makes you feel so humiliated. I'm so sorry.'

'Don't be. I got over it a long time ago.' He shrugged, but Abbey had to wonder if that whole episode had scarred him much more than he was letting on. Maybe it was the reason why he was a serial dater or commitment-phobe, as Lizzie liked to call him. Although perhaps she'd maligned him unfairly, not knowing the true situation.

Sam stood up and began to clear the table, and Abbey took that as a sign for her to leave. She glanced at her watch and realised she'd overstayed her welcome. Sam had gone out of his way to make her feel at home, the meal had been mouth-watering, the wine far too quaffable, but it was Sam's company that she'd enjoyed the most. She stood up too, and her head immediately spun so that she had to reach out for the back of a chair to steady herself. She'd been sitting too long, her legs were refusing to work properly.

'You okay?'

'Fine. It's been a lovely evening, Sam. Thank you. I'll just my find my bag and call for a cab.' The damson gin had been her downfall again, proving to be just as delicious and potent as she remembered, she concentrated all her efforts on appearing in control and together, when she felt nothing of the sort. A wave of tiredness washed over her. Looking around in search of her bag, her gaze was immediately distracted by Lady, who was still curled up in her basket where she'd been all night long. Occasionally, she'd looked up with those large, brown, sorrowful eyes and a little wag of her tail, but she was clearly out of sorts.

'Poor Lady. I hope she'll be feeling much better in the morning.'

'I'm sure she will. And I hope you'll be feeling okay too,' he said, with a half smile, as he noticed her wobble as she attempted to get up after stroking Lady. 'Look, why don't you stay the night?'

'Sorry?' Sam's invitation took her by surprise, setting off a myriad of emotions exploding in her head like rogue fireworks. What did that mean exactly? She had no idea, her imagination entertaining a whole gamut of possibilities. She looked at him as though he'd asked her to solve a mathematical riddle.

'The spare room is all made up. It'll save you going out there in the cold tonight and you'll be fine to drive back in the morning.' He waited for Abbey to say something, before noticing the confusion flittering over her features. 'Look, I didn't mean to make you feel uncomfortable or anything. I just thought it might be easier, but whatever you think best.'

'Yes!' *Of course.* Now she realised what he meant, she didn't want him changing his mind. Why was she so surprised that Sam was only looking out for her? He was that sort of man, kind and thoughtful. She'd always been the designated driver when she was with Jason, so to be able to enjoy herself with a couple of drinks tonight had been completely freeing. Probably too freeing, she realised now, her head spinning from the wine and the gin. This new independence was wonderful but might take some getting used to. 'Great, if you're absolutely sure, that's really kind of you.'

'I'm absolutely sure,' said Sam, grinning with that wide smile of his that did funny things to Abbey's equilibrium.

Going home right now held no appeal whatsoever, for all sorts of different reasons. Sam smiling at her and Lady thumping her tail were two very good ones to begin with.

27

It took Abbey a few moments, as her eyes fluttered open, to realise she wasn't in the familiar surroundings of her own bedroom at home, but somewhere else entirely. Something had woken her, and she swiped away at an odd sensation tingling at her nose. She grabbed the duvet and turned on her side, pulling it over her head, the events of the previous evening flooding into her mind. She let out an involuntary groan as a pain shot across her forehead. The damson gin! When would she learn? She stretched out her body, reaching for her phone. 9.30 a.m.! Another groan. She never slept in this late. What would Sam think of her? He probably had things to do this morning and instead he would be hanging around downstairs waiting for her to make an appearance. She wriggled up the bed, the movement making her realise, with a start, that she wasn't alone, that there was someone in the room with her, and, more pertinently, in the bed with her. She grabbed the duvet tighter and poked her head over the covers.

'Hello, you,' she said gleefully, and she was rewarded for her appearance with a kiss, several kisses, in fact, on her nose and on her mouth. Abbey giggled, opened her arms wide and went in for a hug, revelling in the full-on attention.

'Lady, get out! You know you shouldn't be in there.' *He's talking to the dog,* Abbey reminded herself as Sam's disembodied voice travelled up the stairs. 'Sorry, Abbey,' he called from the landing now. 'I hope she didn't wake you? Send her out.'

'It's fine, absolutely fine.' she laughed. Lady, without the restrictions of the cone of shame, was clearly feeling so much better than she had yesterday and was eager to get on with today's adventures, harrying Abbey along in the process. 'Give me five minutes and I'll be downstairs.'

Quickly freshening up in the bathroom, closely watched by the dog, Abbey brushed her hair, before piling it on top of her head. She peered more closely at her reflection. She hadn't brought any make-up with her, not expecting to need any, so she would have to channel the au naturel look today. Considering how much she'd had to drink last night, she looked remarkably fresh, but there was something else in her dark green eyes staring back at her from the mirror, something that had been missing for months, or years, even. There was an acceptance, a confidence in the person that she was now. She wasn't trying to be someone else, or altering her personality to fit in with someone else's view of who she should be. She was simply being Abbey and, looking at her reflection, she liked who she saw smiling back at her.

'So what are your plans for today, then?'

Downstairs, Sam had prepared coffee and toast with jams and marmalade, and invited Abbey to join him at the table.

'Well,' said Abbey, sitting down and helping herself to some orange juice. It felt entirely natural to be sharing breakfast with Sam, as though it was a regular weekend occurrence. 'I was going to meet up with Dad for a walk – we usually get together on a Saturday – but I've just heard from him and he says he has other plans. So I've been ditched, which is charming,' she said, laughing. 'I wonder what he's up to? It's not like him to be so secretive.'

'In that case, do you want to do something together? We could head out into the country and go for a walk. Not Primrose Woods, but somewhere further afield.'

'Yes. That sounds... great. I'll have to pop home, change into something more suitable for traipsing through the countryside. What will we do about Lady?'

'Confined to barracks, I'm afraid. I'll drop her off at the office. It's her second home and the rangers on duty will look after her. Shall we say in about an hour's time? I'll come and collect you from the cottage.'

* * *

On her drive home, Abbey could do nothing about the smile spreading across her face even if she'd wanted to. She'd had such a brilliant evening with Sam and it looked as though the fun was going to continue for the rest of the day. Sam's company was exhilarating, making her feel vibrant and alive. For too long, she'd hidden her personality, dampened down who she really was and the saddest fact of all was that she hadn't even realised she'd been doing it. Now she could be herself and Sam, it seemed, liked her just the way she was. There was no point in over-analysing Sam's intentions, what he really thought about Abbey or if their relationship might develop into anything more than friendship. It was too soon for that. *Stop thinking*, she chided herself, *and start living*.

Later, they drove in Sam's jeep to the pretty village of Kissington, where they parked up, before popping into the quaint village shop to load their rucksacks with drinks and energy bars. They headed south on the Ridgeway Trail, taking the marked pathways that led across the fields and through the woods. It was a clear, bright day with a keen wind that whipped across the landscape. Sam took a sideways glance at Abbey, noticing the bloom in her cheeks and the enthusiasm in her eyes. She strode out with determination, clearly loving the great outdoors as much as he did. Occasionally, they would stop to breathe and to simply admire the landscape, the open hillsides and the quiet tranquillity of the small valleys.

'Isn't this wonderful,' she breathed, throwing her arms open wide and relishing the sensation of the cool air on her skin. 'Lady would love it up here, wouldn't she?'

'She would. We'll have to come back some time and bring her along.'

Abbey smiled, thrilled to think that Sam was thinking about a next time.

The more time Sam spent with Abbey, the more he realised what a great girl she was. There was no pretence with her; she was easy company and made him laugh with her honesty and off-the-cuff comments. He liked that she was down-to-earth, and didn't appear to be needy in the slightest. Some of the women he'd dated would never have eschewed their heels and make-up to spend a day outside in the elements, preferring to go walking around a shopping centre all day instead, but in Abbey he'd found a kindred spirit. And, most importantly, she'd been given the seal of approval by Lady. They continued walking along the chalk grasslands, their path in front of them surrounded with wild flowers and fluttering butterflies, an idyllic location, until they reached the top of Avingham Beacon, a local beauty spot that offered far-reaching views over several counties. They stood by the summit stone, the wind whistling around their ears, their hair blowing around their faces.

'Come on, we need to take the obligatory selfie,' said Sam, pulling Abbey into his side, both of them grinning wildly into the camera, snapping the moment for posterity. Before they made their descent on the other side of the beacon, they stood for a few minutes on the brow of the hill, taking in the scenery around them, Sam keeping a protective arm around Abbey's shoulders. The sensation of his touch, even through the thick padding of her jacket, gave Abbey a toasty glow inside.

They continued on their route, a circular walk that took them back, at a much more leisurely pace, to their starting point.

'Ten miles under our belt,' said Sam, looking at his watch when they reached the jeep and deposited their rucksacks inside. 'I think we deserve a cream tea, don't you?'

It wasn't until Abbey came to a standstill that she realised how weary she felt, but in a good, satisfying way. Her legs throbbed from the exertion of their hike and her skin glowed from the effort. Luckily, they were able to find a table tucked away at the back of the village teashop, where Abbey was pleased to take the weight off her feet and was looking forward to the selection of sandwiches, cakes and scones with clotted cream they'd ordered. She took the opportunity to pop to the loo, leaving Sam at the table, her mood happy and relaxed as she negotiated her way through the tables. In the cloakroom mirror she was relieved to discover that she didn't look a complete wreck, as she'd suspected she might. Her red hair had stayed contained within the ponytail and only a few wispy tendrils had escaped, falling around her face, and despite the no-make up look, there was a sparkle in her eyes and a pink blush to her skin. Not that it would have mattered if she'd looked a mess. She was certain Sam wasn't judging her in that way, which was another reason why she found it so comfortable being with him.

As she made her way back to the table, she faltered, noticing that Sam was no longer alone. Someone was sitting in her vacated seat and it took only a moment for her to realise who it was: the woman she'd spotted him with before at Primrose Woods. *Stephanie*? Abbey hesitated for a second, wondering if she should blend into the background, pretend that she needed to go back to the loo, leaving them alone together to chat, but as she momentarily weighed up that proposition, Sam looked up and caught her eye, beckoning her over.

She swallowed hard and wandered over confidently, plastering a big smile on her face.

The other woman looked up, her gaze switching from Sam to Abbey, before something resembling understanding flickered over her features.

'Oh, I'm sorry,' she said, not sounding particularly apologetic. 'I didn't realise you were here with someone.'

Without waiting for Sam to reply, she held out her hand to Abbey as though they were about to go into a business meeting.

'Stephanie.' She had a firm handshake and a determined expression. 'Pleased to meet you.'

'Hi, I'm Abbey. Nice to meet you too.' Up close, Stephanie was even more attractive than Abbey had imagined her to be, so much so that she found her gaze lingering on Stephanie's face, desperately trying to find a flaw in her perfect features. Her hair was a beautiful shade of honey blonde, her eyes a cerulean blue and her skin was smooth and flawless. Not for the first time today, Abbey wished she'd applied a lick of mascara and a touch of lip gloss, not for anyone else's benefit but her own, to bolster her confidence, which was rapidly slipping away by the moment. She gave herself a stern talking-to. Why was she allowing this encounter to make her previous good mood ebb away? Never again, she'd told herself, would she give anyone else the power to make her feel bad about herself, particularly when it wasn't warranted. Besides, she realised now, there was something that was spoiling Stephanie's pretty features. She was cross, very cross, her lips set in an unbecoming pout and Sam was looking more uncomfortable by the moment.

'Is this your new girlfriend, Sam?' Stephanie demanded. 'Is she the reason why you've been blanking me?'

'What? No!' He shook his head as though the very idea was ridiculous. 'Abbey's just a friend.'

Abbey glanced away, relieved to see the waitress making her way over with a tray full of goodies, but feeling the slight of Sam's comment. Perhaps she was being sensitive but his choice of words made her feel inconsequential.

'Looks like our tea is here,' she said brightly, hoping Stephanie would take the hint and leave. If Sam and Stephanie had stuff to discuss then they should do it some other time. Not now. The last thing she wanted was to become embroiled in Sam's love life.

'You should have told me instead of messing me about like this. You said you weren't ready for a relationship. I thought that meant a couple of months down the line we might be able to get back together. I've wasted all this time, waiting for you, Sam, when you never had any intention of seeing me again, did you?'

Sam looked as though he wished he could slide beneath the table, or head out of the back door, away from Stephanie's interrogation and from the prying eyes of those sitting on the neighbouring tables, who were all gawping now. Abbey wasn't sure whether to side with Sam, who was squirming in his seat, or Stephanie, who was trembling and looking as though she might break down in tears at any moment. Abbey had no idea what had gone on between the pair of them, but she knew only too well how much a break-up could hurt.

'I'm sorry, Stephanie. I tried to explain, to let you down gently, but clearly I made a hash of that.'

'Well, thanks a bunch for sparing my feelings. What a bloody hero.' Stephanie pushed back her chair and stood up. 'I hope the pair of you will be very happy together.' She turned to Abbey. 'Just be careful. I'd really hate for him to break your heart like he's broken mine.'

'It's not like that,' Abbey tried to protest, but Stephanie turned, her suppressed emotion palpable in the air, and dashed out of the teashop. Abbey watched her go, unsure of what to do next.

'Do you think you should go after her?'

'No, I don't!' Sam shook his head, exasperated, facing down Abbey's questioning expression. 'Sorry, but I've not actually done anything wrong here. I wouldn't mind, but we only went out a couple of times. I didn't make any promises. What is it with...' He stopped himself, biting on his lip, his gaze dropping to his hands clenched together on the table.

Abbey tilted her head in expectation of him finishing his sentence. What was it he'd been about to say? *What is it with... women?*

'... with her?' He sighed. 'I just don't get it.'

Abbey felt torn, half inclined to go after Stephanie herself. She pushed back her chair, peering out of the window to see if she could spot Stephanie. Whatever had gone on between them, Stephanie was clearly distressed and Abbey hated to see anyone like that. As though reading her mind, Sam leant across the table, laying his hand on hers.

'Don't, Abbey. She's upset, but she'll get over it. Maybe this way she'll finally get the message.'

Abbey looked down at the table overflowing with sandwiches and scrumptious-looking cakes, realising that her previous ravenous hunger had left the teashop at about the same moment as Stephanie had dashed outside.

She turned her focus to Sam, who was pouring the tea, detecting the subtle shift in his mood too. Did she know him half as well as she thought she did? The intimacy she'd imagined between them, having spent an extended length of time together, was hanging on by the slightest of threads. He'd complained that Stephanie hadn't got his message. Perhaps Abbey was guilty of falling into the same trap. Imagining a special connection between herself and Sam, when perhaps it wasn't there at all, with Sam viewing the situation in a totally different light. How could she know?

She sipped on her tea and helped herself to a salmon and cucumber sandwich, nibbling at it morosely. There was no need for any confusion. Sam had made his intentions perfectly clear. She, as Sam had made perfectly clear to Stephanie, was *just* a friend.

28

It didn't really count as stalking when there was no malicious intent. What was wrong with being in the same place at the same time? Coincidences happened all the time. She stood by her car, bag over her shoulder and with her phone in her hand, but with her gaze firmly fixed on the door to the sports centre. He was definitely in there; she'd spotted his silver hatchback on the other side of the car park earlier when she'd arrived, sussing out the place. It was just a question of watching and waiting and, sure enough, her patience was rewarded when she spotted a familiar figure with his distinctive blond hair emerging from the main front doors. She opened the back door of the car and threw her bag in nonchalantly, timing it perfectly so that as she returned to the driver's door, he was just walking past, through the car park, on his way to his own car.

'Hi, Luke!'

'Rhi. How are you?' His face lit up in a smile. 'I didn't know you were a member here.'

'I do the occasional class,' she lied, but with every good intention of taking a class very soon, so it was only the tiniest of fibs.

She'd even taken the precaution of checking there were classes running that morning. 'You?'

'Badminton,' he said with a smile, but, of course, she already knew that. He'd mentioned last time they met that he played on a Sunday morning, so it just took the smallest amount of detective work to find out when he might be leaving the centre.

'Did you win?'

'A couple of matches, yeah.'

Luke looked lovely, all scrubbed and fresh-faced, his hair still slightly damp from the shower. Her instinct was to run to his side and wrap her arms around him, but she didn't want to half scare him to death.

'I was just going for a coffee. Do you fancy one?'

'Yeah, why not?' he said, taking a glance at his watch. Rhi was pleased that he didn't have X-ray vision, so he couldn't see the hiccup motion her heart made. 'Do you want to go to the Treetops Cafe again? We can catch up with Lizzie, see how she's doing?'

'Yes...' She didn't want to give him any reason to change his mind. 'That's great. I'll meet you there.'

If it had been down to her, she would have chosen a different venue. She knew Lizzie wasn't working today, as she'd met up with her earlier in the week, and it was likely the park would be heaving with lots of families, but at least she'd be spending time with Luke and that's all that mattered. She could put out of her mind the reminder of Jason and all the occasions she'd met him at the park, but then they'd never even ventured out of their cars, so it hardly held special memories for Rhi. In fact, whenever she thought about those meetings she'd thought romantic and exciting at the time, it made her skin creep with shame. She could hardly recognise the girl she'd been back then.

When she reached the cafe, Luke had managed to secure a table and gave her a wave from across the room. She wandered across to join him and he greeted her with a wide smile. For a moment, she felt uncharacteristically self-conscious, unsure of how to be with him, just the two of them alone, but it was only a blip because soon their coffees arrived, the conversation flowed and Luke's friendly manner made it easy for Rhi to relax.

'Well, I've finally done it.' Rhi leant across the table, hardly able to contain her news. 'I've booked my flights to Australia so there's no going back now.'

'That's great. When do you go?'

'In August, so not too far away, and I've already started counting down the days. I arranged it with Lizzie so that we're actually flying out together, adjacent seats.'

'Really? That's fantastic.'

'It made sense. We were both planning on going out there at round about the same time anyway.'

'I bet Lizzie will be thrilled to have someone at her side, to give her some moral support.'

'Exactly, and I'll be grateful for the company too. I think Lizzie is actually even looking forward to it now. Of course, she'll have to fly back on her own, as she's only staying out there for about five weeks, while I'll be doing closer to three months, but I'm sure by that point she'll be more than fine with it.'

'It's great, Rhi. I'm really pleased for you. You're following your dreams. Good for you.'

'Yeah, it's exciting.' Rhi felt for the first time in ages that she was taking control of her life, doing something she'd always wanted to do. It really was very exciting, so why was there a kernel of doubt and regret deep inside her chest? She wanted to spill all her hopes and dreams to Luke, for him to be an integral part of her dream, but she could sense his detachment. 'You are coming to quiz night next week, aren't you?' She hoped she didn't sound desperate. 'I really enjoy the quizzes, even if I don't know half the answers.' She didn't add that the main reason she enjoyed those evenings was because it gave her the perfect opportunity to spend time with him.

'Yes, it's in my calendar,' he said with a smile, much to Rhi's relief.

After their coffees, they wandered outside and ventured along one of the woodland trails, walking at a leisurely pace. Within a few minutes they had escaped the crowds and were alone with only the trees and the scurrying wildlife for company. Casually, Rhi slipped her arm through Luke's and he turned to look at her, unable to keep the surprise from his features.

'I'm so glad we've made friends now, Luke. I don't know if I've ever properly apologised for being such a bitch to you at work.'

'Don't worry. You've nothing to apologise for. I was probably a pain in the arse.'

'No, not at all. Well, maybe a bit,' she said, thinking about that before laughing. She did a lot of laughing when she was with Luke, usually about something silly that would set them both off in giggles. 'I just didn't appreciate your sense of humour at the time. I was besotted with Jay, and I couldn't see beyond that. I'm not sure I was a very nice person back then.'

'Hey, we all make mistakes,' he said with a mischievous grin on his face. 'Although I'm not sure I understood what you ever saw in him. Most of the department knew he was a proper idiot and a player too.'

She covered her face with her hand. 'Yeah, I can see that now. It just took me a bit of time to catch up with the rest of you. He came into the pub the other day and just seeing him made my skin crawl.'

'What did he want?'

'To see if I might want to get back with him. Can you imagine? I told him exactly what I thought to that idea. He was lucky he didn't get a pint of beer over his head, but then that would have been a waste of good beer.'

Luke grinned. She didn't mention that she'd spotted him that same day pulling up outside the pub in his car. She still wasn't sure why he'd rushed off like that. Had he received an urgent telephone call? Or was it seeing Rhi and Jason together that had given him second thoughts? She really hoped Luke didn't think she held any feelings for Jason any more.

'Luke?'

He turned to face her.

'Thank you for everything you've done for me. For being a friend. For not judging me for being such an idiot.'

'It's fine. Don't beat yourself up over it. You're moving on with your life and making plans. That's the best revenge. A couple more months and you'll barely remember who Jay is.'

She nodded, knowing that was true, but it wasn't Jay who was taking up all her headspace. It was Luke who featured in her dreams for the future. She was still hanging on to his arm, enjoying the sensation of her body next to his, imagining them as a proper couple. Was that really such a huge leap of the imagination?

'So, come on, then, Luke. You know all about my sorrowful love life. Make me feel better. Tell me about all the mistakes you've made.'

'Me?' He laughed. 'Mistakes? I don't make them. Haven't you realised that about me yet?'

'Ha,' she said, giving him a friendly dig in the ribs. 'I forgot. You're completely perfect, aren't you?'

'Well, you wouldn't be the first person to say that, it's true.'

She shook her head at him, unable to stop the smile from spreading across her face. Nobody was perfect. Everyone had their own funny ways or irritating habits, and she was certain Luke had plenty of his own, but from her particular viewpoint on that particular day, she thought he might come as close to being perfect as she could possibly imagine. Not that she would ever admit to that fact, not to Luke at least. He had the good looks for sure with a tall and athletic build combined with a boyish and confident swagger that was infuriating and endearing in equal measure.

'What happened between you and your girlfriend? The one you shared the flat with?'

He shrugged nonchalantly. 'There was no big falling-out. In hindsight we probably moved in together a bit too quickly. We soon realised that we didn't want the same things from life. She was a party animal and I wasn't and it was clear it was never going to work out between us. We're still friends, though.'

She had to bite on her tongue to stop herself from shouting how she wasn't a party animal either, how they would be a perfect match together, but she managed to stop herself just in time.

The trouble was, the impatience that had been building inside Rhi over the last few weeks was threatening to bubble over. She knew that if she didn't say something now, then she might never do it.

'Luke, there's something I need to ask you.'

'Go on, then,' he said, blindsiding her with that smile again. 'Hit me with it.'

'I just wanted to know... if... well...' This was much harder than she'd anticipated. 'Well... if you... you know... like me...'

'What?' His brow furrowed as he turned to look at her, and she was sure she detected his mouth quirking in disbelief too. 'Of course I like you. I wouldn't give up my Sunday afternoon for just anyone, you know.'

He obviously wasn't going to make this any easier for her.

'No, but I meant, if you liked me in more than a friendly way. Do you understand?'

Judging by Luke's reaction, she wasn't sure that he did understand, but she'd instigated this conversation now and there was no going back.

'You asked me out once. Do you remember? I wondered if you still saw me in the same way.'

'Ah, right.' The penny finally dropped. Luke rearranged his facial features as though he was about to let her down gently. 'That didn't end well, did it?' he said with a wry smile. 'We're friends now. Isn't that what's most important?'

She dropped her arm from his and took hold of his hand instead, pulling him to face her. She was so close to his lovely features that she could lean forward and kiss him, if she really wanted to, and at that moment she really did, but if he wasn't interested in that way, it would be awful and humiliating and mortifying. She didn't want to do anything that might jeopardise the friendship they had.

'It is, but I just wondered if there could be anything more between us?'

'I'm not sure, Rhi. I've always liked you, you know that, but you've only just come out of an intense relationship and now you're off to Australia in a short while. I'm not sure it's the right time for either of us.'

'Yes, but I'll be coming back. I'll only be gone for three months.'

'A lot can change in that amount of time. You never know, you might get out there, meet the love of your life and decide you're never coming back.'

She detected the playful tone to his words, but still she protested.

'I won't!' There was a note of desperation in her voice. She had no intention of having a fling on the other side of the world. This trip was about her own journey of self-discovery, of finding out what it was she really wanted from her life, but she was concerned about what Luke might be doing in the intervening months. It had taken her a long time to realise what a catch he was and now she was worried that she'd missed her opportunity and some other lucky woman might snap him up from under her nose. She sighed inwardly, and followed Luke as he set off again, turning round to beckon her onwards. Now it was his turn to take her by the hand and pull her forwards.

'You've got so much to look forward to, Rhi. Just go and enjoy your travels and don't worry about anything else.'

'Yeah, you're right,' she said, trying to hide her regret, and managing to sound at least enthusiastic at his suggestion. She had no reason to feel hard done by Luke. He'd moved on and she needed to do the same.

'Friends?' he said, putting an arm around her shoulder.

'Definitely,' she said, putting on a brave smile and swallowing down her disappointment. *Friends*. She mulled the word over in her head. That wasn't what she'd had in mind at all. She wanted so much more from Luke and she knew, even if he didn't realise it yet, that they would be absolutely perfect together. She just had to find a way of convincing him of the same too.

29

She closed her eyes, the music washing over her, her body swaying in time to the beat, her mind transported to another place and time. Another person. Until she stopped, bringing herself very firmly back to the present. Her eyes pinged open and she looked up and into Bill's kind face, enjoying the sensation of being held in his arms as he led her around the floor in something resembling a waltz. Lizzie had never learnt to dance properly, but she wasn't going to let that stop her from twirling about the floor as though she were about to win the glitter ball on *Strictly Come Dancing*, even if it meant stepping on Bill's toes a few times. He was far too much of a gentleman to say anything about that.

'Are you having a good time, Lizzie?'

'It's brilliant, Bill, and such a treat. I never realised this would be so much fun.'

It had been his idea to attend the afternoon tea dance and she hadn't needed to think twice about accepting his invitation. She couldn't remember the last time she'd enjoyed herself so much, and just being held by Bill stirred all sorts of feelings within her, emotions she'd never expected to experience again. The Grand

Hotel in town had pulled out all the stops to create a magical atmosphere in the ballroom, with tables dressed with white starched tablecloths, attentive waiting staff in formal attire and a swing band who played a variety of tunes guaranteed to get everyone's toes tapping. They enjoyed a glass of champagne with their tea, which was served in a fancy silver teapot alongside a tiered cake stand covered in an assortment of sandwiches and sweet treats. Lizzie had worn a dress and dug out her sparkly heels from the back of the wardrobe, put on a full face of make-up and worn her hair loose over her shoulders, quite the transformation from her usual daily get-up. When she'd opened the door to Bill, he'd audibly gasped.

'Well, well, look at you! You look absolutely lovely. Give us a twirl.'

She'd giggled and duly obliged, holding out her dress as she spun round on the spot.

'You'll be the belle of the ball. Come on,' he'd said, offering up his arm. 'Your carriage awaits.'

'You're looking pretty dapper yourself, Bill!'

He looked very suave in navy trousers, pink shirt and blue blazer, with a spotted pink handkerchief in his top pocket, his black shoes gleaming with polish. She took his arm, and they walked out to the taxi.

That's what she liked about Bill. He was so easy to be with. There were no awkward silences or uncomfortable moments, and because they had a shared experience of losing their respective spouses, they were able to talk freely and unselfconsciously about their lost loves. They didn't feel embarrassed or afraid by the other's emotions, or worry that they might upset them by mentioning the past. A lot of people didn't know what to say in those circumstances and would hurry the conversation along to a safer subject, but Bill and Lizzie seemed to have an innate understanding of each other, allowing the other to be themselves, giving them permission to speak, or not, as they chose to.

Only today wasn't about the past. It was about the here and now. Lizzie skipped off the dance floor, hand in hand with Bill, her heart thumping loudly in her chest, feeling more alive and vibrant than she had done in years. For far too long, she'd been going through the motions, feeling invisible in her own small world. Bill had arrived in her life and everything had grown larger, more colourful and infinitely more interesting. They took their seats back at the table and Bill topped up their teacups from the posh teapot, cocking his little finger to the side, making Lizzie laugh. She positively beamed, soaking up the atmosphere, looking around at all the tables and at their fellow tea-dancers, who were all dressed in their finery too.

'I'm so relieved my flights are booked now,' Lizzie said, when she'd gathered her breath. 'It feels like a great weight off my mind and this is the perfect way to celebrate.'

'You've done the hardest bit now. Everything else will be a doddle in comparison.'

'I hope so. It makes it easier knowing I'll be travelling with Rhi. If I have a wobble on the day, she'll be there to support me and I know she'll make sure I get on that plane.'

'I'm proud of you, Lizzie. You're going to have the best time ever.'

'I will,' she agreed. Her excitement for the trip was growing by the day. She couldn't wait to see Katy again and to hold her tight in her arms, and, of course, to meet little Rosie for the first time, and the new baby too. She wanted to do all those things a grandmother takes for granted. To fuss over her daughter and the whole family, preparing them meals, taking the little ones for walks to give their parents a rest, and then reading bedtime stories. Just simple everyday tasks that you couldn't really put a value on. She wanted to recapture the closeness she had with Katy and to tell her about everything that had been happening at home, her new set of friends, the quiz nights and now the afternoon tea dance too. Most of all she wanted to spill the beans about Bill. She couldn't put a name to their relationship, but she knew it had brightened up her life entirely. They'd grown close in recent weeks and she knew that Katy would be thrilled to learn that her mum had found someone who made her happy. She'd been on at her for years to join a dating site or a singles club, but Lizzie had always pooh-poohed the idea. She'd had no interest in meeting another man and was resigned to being on her own for the rest of her life, so Bill turning up and filling a gap that she hadn't even realised was there had been a revelation. 'I'll be boring you silly with every small detail when I come home.'

'I won't be bored. I'm looking forward to hearing all about it when you come back and to see all the photos and videos.'

She couldn't wait to share the experience with Bill. In fact, despite only knowing each other for a couple of months, she knew she would miss him terribly when she was away. He was someone who buoyed her up and made everything seem better, bringing out her confidence that had been missing for so long. She didn't know what the future held for her, but she was very hopeful Bill would be a big part of it.

'How is Abbey doing now?'

'Very well. She seems to have regained her sparkle, which is lovely to see. She has the occasional wobble, but that's only to be expected. She's like her mum. Resourceful, adaptable and capable. She'll come through this much stronger, I know she will.'

'That's good to hear. Those girls, Abbey and Rhi, have been so kind to me, and we always have such a giggle together when they come into the cafe. You know, I might have a little get-together at home for us all before my trip. I could invite the girls along with Luke and Sam. What do you think?'

'Sounds like a lovely idea to me,' said Bill. 'If you want me to help with the food or drink, then I'm more than happy to.'

'Then we can host it together,' she said, taking his outstretched hand from across the table.

What a great idea! Lizzie was excited at the prospect of organising a get-together for her friends. The six of them had gelled from the start and each time they met, they grew closer, always revelling in each other's company. They'd had such a great time last night at the quiz evening, even though their performance had been dire, mainly due to playing their joker on the film and TV round, which turned out to be questions on obscure comedy shows that none of them had ever watched before. They scored a pitiful zero points, to much ribbing from the other teams. At least they could laugh about it even if it did mean they finished in a lowly eleventh place at the end of the evening.

It would be lovely to have a farewell do before jetting off on her trip, but especially so for Rhi, who was going away for a longer period of time. She had another ulterior motive for bringing everyone together too. Ever since that lunch date at her house when she'd seen Sam and Abbey together for the first time, she'd thought what a lovely couple they'd make. They'd hit if off immediately and Lizzie had an inkling in her bones that their friendship might develop into something more. Only last night at the quiz, they'd been keeping their distance from each other. Knowing Sam and his reticence when it came to close personal relationships and Abbey having just come out of one, the pair of them might not yet realise what was best for them. A get-together would be a good opportunity for them to get to know each other even better. As for Rhi and Luke, she had no idea what was going on between the pair of them. Despite Rhi's protestations that they were only friends, there was no denying their sizzling chemistry. Perhaps they needed a gentle nudge in the right direction too.

The band started playing their next song, a lively and toe-tapping number, and Lizzie and Bill looked at each other with the same thought in mind.

'Come on, let's go and dance.'

They skipped hand in hand towards the dance floor.

As Bill held her in his arms, sweeping her around the floor, the music romantic and dreamy, Lizzie was dreaming up some plans of her own. The future was revealing itself like a blooming petal, offering exciting, magical opportunities ahead that she was determined to make the most of. She wanted everyone else, her new friends especially, to experience some of the magic too.

30

Abbey strode along the path that led from the kissing gate exit at Primrose Woods and up the leafy hill that took her home. Already, she'd walked five miles over heathland and through meadows, her skin tingling with alertness and vibrancy. She'd decompressed from a particularly emotionally draining shift at work, shaking off all the tension and stress she carried in her shoulders and now she felt ready to tackle the overhaul of her bedroom that she had planned. She reached the top of the hill and was just about to cross the road when she spotted a familiar vehicle which slowed down right in front of her. Treacherously, her heart leapt at the sight of Sam's jeep.

'Hello, stranger.' Sam grinned, resting an arm on the open window. Lady poked her head out from behind him as if in greeting and Abbey couldn't help but smile. Of course, she'd seen him at the quiz night last week, but they hadn't had the chance to talk properly since they'd bumped into Stephanie that day, after which Abbey's emotions had been thrown into turmoil. The strength of her reaction had puzzled her. She'd felt cross towards Sam for the way he'd treated Stephanie, which she knew was

totally ridiculous and unreasonable because it was nothing to do
with her and besides, Sam had protested his innocence. For some
reason, the encounter had managed to stir up her own emotions,
exaggerating and emphasising her vulnerability. She had no real
reason to be angry with Sam. Their relationship was based purely
on friendship, but she'd been nurturing a secret hope that it might
develop into something more. Contemplating the reality of that
meant opening up her heart again to fully trust someone. Was she
capable of doing that with Sam? Or anyone, come to that.

Even with alarm bells ringing in her head, she could do
nothing to stop her body from reacting involuntarily, the way it
always did when she was in Sam's presence. Her entire being
heightened with anticipation of his proximity. She gave herself a
stern talking-to, but her body wasn't listening and did nothing to
extinguish the heat firing her whole being.

'Hi, Sam. Good to see you. And Lady. How's her paw now?'

'She's made a full recovery, thank you. Back to her normal
mischievous self, so all is good in the world. How are you?'

'Good, thanks. Just been for a long walk over the park.'

'Yeah? I've been hoping to catch you. Don't know if you got my
text?' Thankfully, he didn't pause long enough for her to have to
answer. 'I just wanted to clear the air. About the other week. Everything seemed to go pear-shaped after we met Stephanie.'

'It's all forgotten about,' she said, not entirely truthfully. She
had received Sam's text and she'd missed a couple of his calls too,
only because she hadn't known how to react to him any longer.
She'd wanted to ask a dozen questions about Stephanie, if it was
true what Lizzie had said about his fear of commitment, but what
right did she have to interrogate him? He didn't owe her any
answers. Instead, she thought it best to put some distance between
them in the hope that her heightened feelings for Sam might
diminish if she didn't see him for a while. She could put it down as

a fleeting crush that would flutter off into the ether in the same way as it had arrived and the pair of them could return to being friends, without the complication of attraction and desire clouding her view. If only it were that simple. Sam was as gorgeous as ever and she couldn't switch off her feelings as simply as that, however much she might want to.

'Have you got time for that chat now? We could pop to the pub. It's such a lovely afternoon – might be nice to sit in the garden.'

Sorting out her bedroom was a job she'd been putting off for months. Another day wouldn't matter, would it? It was the furthest thing from her mind later when she sat on a wooden bench in the beer garden surrounded by profuse hanging baskets blooming with colour, and yellow and white roses rambling up the walls. Lady sat at her side obediently, the pair of them waiting for Sam as he went in to order the drinks. Why had she even tried to avoid Sam? she wondered, feeling foolish. It wasn't what she wanted at all. Her reaction at seeing him again had shown her exactly what he meant to her, if she needed any reminding. She had to stop overthinking and start living, embracing her more spontaneous and carefree side. Now, with the sun kissing her arms and cheeks, she was determined to enjoy the moment.

'Cheers!' Sam raised his pint of lemonade, touching Abbey's glass of gin and tonic. 'Thanks for coming, Abbey. It's great to see you again. I've missed you.'

Have you? She stopped herself from asking the question aloud. He was smiling a casual smile, but his gaze, genuine and intense, rested on her features. Thinking about it, being honest with herself, she'd missed him too.

'Look, I'm sorry for what happened with Stephanie. You should never have had to witness that. And I know I probably didn't handle it in the best way, but I was annoyed and embarrassed. It had been a great day until that point. Hell...' He ran a hand through his hair, the motion leaving it sticking up all over the place, and she thought how endearing he looked, seeing the vulnerability beneath his self-confidence. 'Let's be honest. It was pretty awkward and not a great way to end our day.'

'It wasn't your fault. You had no way of knowing we would bump into her.'

'True, but I just find it all so frustrating. If you hadn't already worked it out, I'm pretty rubbish at relationships.' He gave a rueful laugh. 'I always seem to mess things up. Without even trying. And I'm still scratching my head over how I could have handled that situation better. Clearly I upset Stephanie and that was never my intention. Anyway, I'm sorry that you were unwillingly dragged into all of that.'

'It's forgotten about.' Abbey waved a hand in front of her face. 'And remember you're talking to someone who knows everything there is to know about messed-up relationships.'

He nodded and smiled, before falling silent. He picked up his glass and looked over the top of it at her.

'The thing is, Abbey, I... like you. I mean I really like you. Ha...' He gave a wry chuckle. 'I told you I was hopeless at this kind of thing, but the truth is... well, I do. The time we've spent together... it's been great and I think we're really good together. I hoped... well, I wanted to see if things might develop between us.' He shrugged, holding his hands up to the air. 'I... I was hoping you might feel the same?'

A heat crept around her entire body and she hoped her face wouldn't give away the extreme happiness she felt inside. She hadn't imagined the spark between them after all, but she couldn't allow her emotions to run away from her. The last thing she needed was a rebound romance that would leave her nursing a broken heart.

'I like you too, Sam.' She hesitated; it didn't seem an adequate way of describing her feelings. Her gaze drifted off around the garden, savouring the beautiful moment of sitting in an English country garden with a gorgeous man who'd just confessed he liked her. She wasn't sure whether to throw her arms around his neck and tell him how he'd been invading her every single thought since the moment they had met or to take a step backwards and play it cool, although the very idea made her smile as she had no concept of how to do that. 'I guess I'm just a bit nervous about getting into a new relationship. I was with Jason for almost twelve years so I'm well out of practice when it comes to dating. And I would never want to go through the same thing again. I'd rather be on my own than be with someone who's going to treat me badly.'

'I've no intention of treating you badly, Abbey.' Sam looked offended, his brow furrowing, trying to make sense of what she was saying. 'Although, I guess, when you're dealing with people's emotions, that can sometimes happen.'

'I know, it's just...'

'Just what?' Sam's response came quickly, putting her on the spot. He dropped his head to one side, his dark brown eyes, always so inviting, observing her closely.

She wriggled in her seat. How could she voice her concerns without sounding accusatory?

'Is this about what Lizzie said?' he pressed, as though reading her mind. 'You know she was only joking, don't you? She's always teasing me about settling down, finding that special person, but to be honest I let it all wash over me. I know she means well, but I don't see the point in being with someone if you know it's not going to lead anywhere. She complains that I have a string of girl-friends, that I'm too fussy, but it's really not the way she makes it out to be.'

'Well, I did wonder,' she said, trying to inject a touch of

humour in her words. 'I really don't fancy being the next name on your long list of women nursing broken hearts.'

'Honestly,' said Sam, reaching across the table and taking Abbey's hand. 'It isn't like that at all. I promise you. And when I see Lizzie again, I'm going to throttle her.' He laughed, recognising the touch of devilment in Abbey's eyes too. 'What do you reckon? Worth taking a chance on? You and me? We could take things slowly and see where it goes.' His hand squeezed hers, his thumb tracing a circle on her palm. 'Obviously, only if you wanted to, of course?'

In that particular moment, basking in the sun, with Sam's caressing gaze flittering over her features and with Lady at her feet, she could think of nothing she wanted more. *Spontaneous and carefree.* She could do this. After all, what did she have to lose, other than her heart?

31

There was only one thing for it: she needed to speak to Lizzie. She couldn't put it off any longer. She'd kept popping into her mind anyway, with Abbey wondering how Lizzie was feeling about her upcoming trip, now that she'd actually booked her flights. On the last couple of occasions she'd popped into the cafe, it had either been Lizzie's day off or else she'd been too busy serving customers to have the chance for a proper natter. They'd exchanged a couple of texts in the meantime, but Abbey felt a distance had grown between them. Probably because Lizzie had so much on her plate getting organised for her holiday.

Today, she wandered into the cafe and pulled out a chair by a window seat, giving Lizzie, who was behind the counter, a wave.

'Hello, you!' Within moments, Lizzie was at her side, ready to take her order of a cappuccino and a slice of millionaire's shortbread, which was Abbey's favourite choice at the cafe. 'How have you been?' She leant over to give her friend a hug.

'Good, busy at work. I don't know where the time goes. I've been up here most days, but keep missing you. How are you feeling about your big holiday?'

'Excited.' Lizzie beamed. 'Nervous too, of course, but with Rhi at my side, holding my hand, it doesn't seem quite so daunting.'

'I bet. Honestly, you two are going to have the best time ever and that's just on the journey out there. I really wish I was coming too.'

Lizzie laughed. 'Actually, I wanted to catch you. I was chatting to your dad the other day about having a get-together at mine before my trip. Just for the Primrose Fancies. To say a big thank you to you all for helping me get to this point. Without you lot I can't imagine ever being confident enough to take this step. Nothing too formal, just some fizz and a small spread. I might tell Sam not to bring the damson gin after last time.' Her laughter tinkled around the cafe. 'Your dad said he would give me a hand.'

'Sounds like a lovely idea. Count me in. So you've spoken to Dad, have you? I can't seem to pin him down these days. He's always busy. Doing what, I just don't know.'

'Look, let me go and collect your order,' said Lizzie, bringing a pause to their conversation. 'I won't be long.'

Already Abbey was looking forward to Lizzie's pre-holiday shindig. The six of them had formed a great bond ever since forming their quiz team, but those evenings were always so noisy and hectic with lots of banter, laughter and friendly arguments, so there was little time to have an in-depth conversation. It would be a good opportunity for them to have a real catch-up before Rhi and Lizzie went off on their travels. She would miss them both while they were away.

Her gaze drifted across to Lizzie, watching as she made the coffee and reached for the chocolate slice from the display of cakes and pastries. Luckily, it was fairly quiet in the Treetops Cafe today. If she was going to ask what she'd come here to ask, then she would have no better opportunity. Only now her resolve was deserting her. A few moments later, Lizzie was back, delivering her order to the table.

'Here you go, lovely. Enjoy!' Lizzie touched Abbey's shoulder before moving away to leave her to enjoy her snack in peace.

'Wait! Do you have a moment? There was something I wanted to ask you.'

Lizzie's brow creased and Abbey felt a pang of guilt, wondering if she might have something to do out the back. It wasn't as if she was rushed off her feet with customers here.

'Well...'

'It's about Sam,' said Abbey, eager now to keep Lizzie's attention.

'Oh!' Lizzie's whole demeanour changed, with a smile lighting her face. What on earth had she been expecting her to ask? 'What's he been up to now, then?' Lizzie pulled out a chair and joined Abbey at the table.

'Nothing. It's just I've been thinking about what you said that first time about Sam. That he'd had a whole string of girlfriends. I just wondered if that was really true? If he is really a ladies' man?'

Lizzie gasped and clapped her hands together in triumph.

'You like him, don't you? I knew it! You two would make such a lovely couple.'

'Stop it!' Abbey couldn't help but laugh at Lizzie's reaction. 'You're getting carried away now. We're just friends at the moment. And I was only wondering.'

'Yes, I could see why you might. Honestly, you and Sam would be perfect together.' Abbey admonished Lizzie with a rueful smile, determined not to get caught up in Lizzie's excitement. 'He's not a ladies' man, no. Take no notice of what I said. I was only teasing. He's such a lovely fella, as you well know, and deserves to find some happiness. It's just that he's pretty hopeless when it comes to his love life. He hasn't met the right woman yet, that's what I tell him.'

Abbey nodded, mildly reassured by Lizzie's words as she went on.

'Sam is like a lot of men. He likes an easy life. He's happy in his job, has a good group of friends, but hasn't really got a clue when it comes to women. He doesn't like confrontation so often gets himself into sticky situations. For him it's easier to live his bachelor life with Lady as the only woman in it, but I think he realises he's missing out. He's admitted as much to me.'

Lizzie had known Sam for years, but they'd only become really close after she'd lost David, her husband. When she'd returned to work after the funeral, Sam made a point of checking in with her on a regular basis and offering her lifts home from work. In the early days, the effort of putting on a cheery front at the cafe was exhausting and often she would step into Sam's jeep at the end of the day and promptly burst into tears. She'd been so grateful for his kindness, the way he'd listened, unembarrassed by her outpouring of grief. Their friendship had grown over the following months with the discovery that they could chat and laugh about anything. Sam did jobs round at Lizzie's place when needed and she enjoyed having someone to cook for, baking him cakes and lasagnes that she sent him home with. They'd even spent last Christmas together when they'd realised they would both be spending it alone otherwise.

'Sam's told me he wants to settle down and have a family one day. He's just waiting for the right woman to turn up...'

Lizzie waggled an eyebrow in Abbey's direction. There would be no one more pleased than Lizzie when Sam finally found that special person.

'I was just curious as a friend. That's all,' Abbey said, knowing she wasn't convincing anyone, not even herself.

'I can tell he likes you, Abbey, if that helps. I saw the way he was looking at you in the pub the other week.'

Lizzie gave a meaningful smile, before her attention was distracted by some activity outside the front of the cafe. One of the rangers' jeeps pulled up and Lizzie screwed up her eyes to see who it might be. The springer spaniel leaping from the back and running up the path, wagging her tail furiously, gave it away.

'Well, talk of the devil!'

Moments later, Sam was standing at their table, and Abbey experienced that same topsy-turvy feeling inside that she always did when she came face to face with him.

'Have your ears been burning?' Lizzie asked. 'We were just talking about you.'

'Really? That doesn't sound good.' Sam grimaced and turned to Abbey. 'What have I told you about not believing everything this woman tells you.'

Lizzie's laughter rang out. 'Don't worry, we were only saying lovely things about you. Anyway, I'm glad you're here. I was telling Abbey that I'm going to have a get-together at mine before my trip. You'll come along, won't you?'

'Try and stop me! I wouldn't miss it for the world. Tell you what, I'll bring along a bottle of my damson gin. That seemed to go down well last time.'

Abbey and Lizzie laughed, exchanging a knowing smile.

'How are the plans going? Are you and Rhi fixed for a lift to the airport? I'm more than happy to drive you there.'

'Thanks, Sam, but we've already booked our taxi. I don't like goodbyes at the best of times so I thought it for the best. I don't want anything that might cause me to have a wobble on the day and seeing your friendly face might set me off.'

'Fair enough, although I try my hardest not to make people cry just by looking at them. Clearly, I need to try harder.'

'Aw, but you know what I mean, don't you?' Lizzie leapt out of her seat, resting a hand on Sam's shoulder. 'What are you having today, some tea and cake?'

'No, I was just about to head home actually and wondered if you needed a lift?'

'Thanks, but I've got another hour or so to do here and then I'm popping into town. I want to pick up some new clothes for my trip. It's all right because I've got a lift organised.'

'Fair enough. What about you, Abbey? I'm going your way.'

'Thanks,' she said, before she had a chance to overthink it. 'That would be great.' She'd already walked her five miles earlier today and spending time with Sam, even if just sharing a car trip with him and Lady, was much more appealing than walking back home alone.

'So what plans do you have for the rest of the day?' Sam asked as they set off in the jeep.

'Nothing terribly exciting. A glass of wine, some supper and then I shall probably settle down with a film, I suspect.'

'Well, that's funny because that sounds exactly like my plans. Fancy coming to mine for supper?'

'But you've cooked for me already. It must be my turn, surely? Come to mine and I'll rustle up something for us both.'

Sam turned to check Abbey's expression, a smile curling on his lips.

'Well, if you're sure. Don't want you feeling obliged to invite me along just because you think you owe me a dinner.'

'Oh, don't worry. Haven't I told you, this is the new me,' she said, matching his smile. 'I don't do anything I don't want to do these days. And really, I'd love to cook for you.' In fact, she couldn't think of anything else she'd rather do this evening. Or anyone else she'd rather be spending her time with.

32

Back at the cottage, Abbey kicked off her trainers and headed straight for the kitchen, opening the fridge.

'Would you like a beer or a glass of wine?'

'A beer would be great, thanks. Do you want me to do the honours?' he asked, taking the beer and the bottle of white wine that Abbey offered.

'The glasses are in the dresser, thanks.'

Lady made herself at home, sniffing at every nook and cranny, following Abbey around keenly. Abbey found a ceramic bowl from the back of her cupboard, filling it with water, and placed it on the kitchen floor. Lady gave an appreciative sniff before lapping it up gratefully and then settling down contentedly in front of the fireplace. Sam made himself useful seeing to the drinks. It was a revelation to Abbey that he was so easy to be around. She knew it was early days and suspected they were both on their best behaviour, but there was no sense of impatience, irritation or judgement that had been a constant worry when she'd been with Jason. It was only now she appreciated how often she'd pandered to his ego and his fluctuating moods.

Later, over creamy tarragon chicken and tagliatelle, the conversation continued naturally.

'I can't believe the change in Lizzie,' said Sam, topping up the wine glasses. 'She seems so much happier and more confident these days. I don't know if that's all down to the hypnotherapist she's been seeing, but if it is, I think we could all do with a few of those sessions.'

'I know, right! It's lovely for her, though. Her excitement is contagious and she and Rhi will make great travelling companions.'

Moments later, Sam's attention was distracted by Lady running around his feet and pawing at his leg impatiently.

'I'm afraid this one has an internal clock with an accuracy to the second. She's after her evening walk. I shall have to take her.'

'Sounds like a great idea. We're pretty much finished here, if you've had enough to eat? We can have some pudding when we get back. And some more wine too, if you like?'

'Are you trying to get me drunk?' he said solemnly.

'Only getting my own back for the damson gin,' she joked.

'You need to tell me if I'm overstaying my welcome. I can always call on one of the rangers to come and collect me and give me a lift home.'

'No, please stay. I'd really like you to,' she said, not wanting to sound desperate, but not wanting their time together to come to an end. Being with Sam ignited every nerve cell in her body, and heightened her feelings of freedom and anticipation at being on the verge of something new and exciting. Ever since she'd first met him, she'd held a part of herself back, afraid of fully letting go, not wanting to be hurt again in the same way as Jason had hurt her. She would never have thought of jumping into a new relationship so soon after Jason, but Sam had somehow carved out a place in her life, so did it really matter if the timing wasn't perfect? She couldn't live in fear, worrying about all the things that might go wrong. Much better to jump in and see where that took her. If nothing else, Sam might turn out to be a stepping stone from the bad and destructive relationship she'd had with Jason to something ultimately more satisfying and worthwhile.

They headed out, walking through the village and across the fields behind the church, Lady galloping ahead. They paused on the small wooden bridge, peering over the edge to watch the water swirling beneath them while Lady ran up and down, over the wooden planks and down to the gate, eager to move them on as quickly as possible. Eventually, Sam gave in to the dog's insistent demands and went ahead, pulling the steel lock of the gate open and holding out his hand to Abbey, as she took the steep step down into the second field.

As they walked on, it felt entirely natural for their hands to stay interlocked and when Sam turned his head to look at her, giving her the benefit of that wide smile, she felt a surge of happiness. The early evening July sun cast a warm orange glow in the sky and the path in front of them wound its way through the wide expanse of field to the second gate, which led onto the towpath. There wasn't a soul in sight, just the two of them, soaking up the scenery, enjoying the moment together.

'Aren't we lucky to live in such a beautiful part of the country? It's only as I've got older that I've really come to appreciate the great outdoors. A few years ago, I could never imagine I would become the sort of person who spends their free time going for long walks in the countryside, for fun as well, but now I just love it and can't imagine my life without it.'

'It really is very beautiful,' he said, his gaze settling on her face and lingering there a moment. 'I always find it very healing, good for the soul to be outside.'

'You didn't grow up around here, though, did you?'

'No, I was a city boy. Grew up in a seventh-floor flat. There weren't many green fields around us so this is as far removed from that as you can imagine.'

'Are your parents still there? Do you get to see them much these days?'

As soon as the words had slipped from her mouth she could see she had spoken out of turn. Why hadn't she stopped to think? Now the palpable pause hung heavily between them.

'Nope. My dad didn't really play a role in my life. I saw him only a few times when he was alive. My mum brought me up on her own. She died a few years back too.'

'I'm so sorry, Sam. I had no idea.'

'No reason why you should.' He smiled, giving her hand a reassuring squeeze, but she felt terrible that she hadn't known about his parents, and had stirred up sad memories.

'It's awful losing your mum. Especially so at what must have been a relatively young age for your mum too.'

'Yeah, she was only in her early fifties.'

'Like my mum, then.'

'Yeah, coming here was a new start for me. I lost Mum shortly after finishing uni, and had to sort everything out at the flat, but there was nothing left there for me to stay for. I'd also recently split from Sophie so it was a pretty bad time. Luckily, I found this job shortly afterwards. Honestly, it was a godsend; it was as though Mum was looking out for me and giving me a push in the right direction. It gave me something to focus on, a proper lifeline. There's no other job I'd rather be doing. I've met some great people and even after all this time I still love getting up and going to work each day. I feel at home here. You can't ask for more than that. I've been at the park over ten years now.'

'Your mum would be so proud of you, of everything you've achieved.'

'I hope so. I think about her a lot. Most days, actually. I wish I could have done more for her, but it wasn't to be. She didn't have the happiest of lives. Never really got over my dad leaving her. He was the love of her life, but he messed her around terribly. He had loads of affairs before they finally split for good.'

'That's so sad.'

'Yeah, it was.' He exhaled a sigh. 'But there's nothing I can do to change what happened. I realise that now. There's no option but to move forward and hopefully not repeat the mistakes of the past.' They'd reached the other side of the field and took the cutaway that led onto the towpath. 'Come on,' Sam said, leading the way.

In a matter of minutes, Abbey's whole perception of Sam had changed. The bits she'd gleaned about him up until now had created an impression of someone confident, carefree and spontaneous, but here she was confronted with another, more vulnerable, side to his nature. The thought that he'd lost his girlfriend, his best friend and his mum all within the space of a few months was devastating. She'd been so wrapped up in her own hurt that she'd never even considered that Sam might have been hurting too.

'Thanks for telling me. I hope I didn't upset you by asking about your family.'

'Not at all. To be honest, I don't talk about that period of my life very often. It's refreshing to be able to share it with you. Thanks. Oh, God!' Sam's attention was suddenly distracted by Lady, who was heading in one direction only. 'Lady, wait! Hang on, I need to grab her or else she'll be straight in the...'

Too late. Lady leapt into the canal, landing with a big splash, ruffling the feathers of a couple of unsuspecting ducks, who quickly departed in the opposite direction. She looked so pleased with herself, her head held high above the water, swimming round in circles proudly.

'That bloody dog!' cursed Sam, and Abbey had to bite on her lip to stop herself from laughing at Lady's antics.

'Come here,' he hissed, hanging over the edge of the canal bank, trying to grab Lady's collar as some passers-by looked on with the same amusement as Abbey.

Later, when Sam was finally able to coax her from the canal and put her firmly back on the lead, Lady enthusiastically shook herself down, showering Abbey and Sam with dirty water.

'I am so sorry about this. I can only apologise for this poor excuse of a hound.'

'Don't worry,' said Abbey, still laughing. 'I love her – she's great entertainment value.'

They continued their walk along the towpath to the next lock before taking the steep path up to the quiet country lane that tracked the boundary to Primrose Woods, completing the loop and taking them back to Abbey's cottage.

'Honestly, Lady, look at the state of you.' The dog wagged her tail furiously at Sam's undivided attention, clearly delighted at having such an eventful walk. 'Abbey will never invite us again, you do know that? You were supposed to be on your best behaviour.'

'She's absolutely fine. And she's one of the better house guests I've had so she'll always be very welcome here, won't you, Lady? Let me go and find a towel.'

'Abbey?' Sam reached out for her arm, pulling her towards him. They were face to face, his gaze roaming her features hungrily, the tension between them sizzling. 'Thanks for everything. This evening, the dinner, for being a great listener. For putting up with my rogue hound.'

She laughed, her entire body tingling in response to his proximity. His hand gently stroked her face, a gesture filled with intimacy.

'It's my pleasure. It's been really lovely and I feel honoured that you felt able to tell me about your parents. I feel I know you a whole lot better now. Thanks for being so honest with me.'

He leant forward, finally placing his lips on hers, so gently and tentatively, his featherlight touch sending goosebumps over her entire body. Her eyes closed, revelling in the moment, his kiss on her lips everything she'd imagined it might be, but it was over far too soon. No sooner had she savoured the taste of him on her lips, igniting her desire for so much more, than he'd pulled away, his gaze caressing her features longingly. His attention distracted, he turned and grabbed hold of Lady, who clearly had ideas of disappearing again, leaving muddy footprints all over the house.

'Oh no you don't!'

The moment lost, Abbey went in search of that towel, still smiling. With Lady cleaned up and finally settled on a blanket in front of the fireplace, a bottle of red wine opened and the glasses poured, they settled on the sofa, having chosen a thriller to watch. The sofa would be Sam's bed for the night. There was a second bedroom upstairs but it was in no way ready for guests. Sorting out the junk in that room was on Abbey's ever-growing job list.

She curled up on the sofa next to Sam, her legs tucked up to one side, her weight falling naturally into Sam's embrace, his enticing body scent playing with her senses. As the opening credits of the film rolled, her mind was distracted by what had happened between them tonight. Something had shifted, they'd grown closer, and that kiss, so brief and enticing, had ignited a longing within her that she knew could only be satisfied by the gorgeous man beside her. Not tonight, though. Within minutes, thinking lovely thoughts, she drifted off to sleep, and stayed there all night long, snuggled up in Sam's arms. It was the best night's sleep she'd had in ages.

33

Two weeks later and the quiz night was drawing to a close at The Three Feathers.

'Well, we're nothing if not consistent!' said Bill.

The Primrose Fancies had given a respectable account of themselves by coming fifth, which, considering they'd spent the entire time chatting about Rhi and Lizzie's forthcoming trip, arguing over the answer to one of the music questions – how many members were in the band The Temperance Seven (nine, apparently, which none of them guessed correctly) – and making plans for Lizzie's farewell party the following weekend, it was something of a triumph.

'You will keep my place open on the quiz team, won't you?' said Rhi as they gathered up their belongings to make the move home. 'I don't want anyone taking my spot while I'm away.'

What she really meant was that she didn't want Luke bringing someone else along, a pretty girl who could step into Rhi's shoes easily, making Rhi just a distant memory, although she could hardly say that aloud.

'Of course we will,' said Abbey, laughing. 'Although I'm not certain we'll have people queuing up to join our team.'

'Well, hopefully that's true. Who knows, perhaps you'll do better without me and Lizzie on the team,' Rhi joked.

'Don't worry,' said Bill, laughing. 'We'll miss you both, but we'll keep your seats warm. It'll certainly be quieter without the pair of you, that's for sure. Isn't that right, Luke?'

'Definitely,' said Luke with a sparkle in his eye.

Rhi wondered if she was being extra sensitive or if it was the nerves and excitement about her trip catching up with her, but her senses were heightened to everyone's moods this evening. In between the normal hubbub of the good-natured quiz, there was a strange, slightly edgy atmosphere radiating around their table, and Rhi was unable to put her finger on what it was all about.

In the interval, in the loos, she caught Abbey and told her about Jason's visit to the pub. He was the last person she wanted to talk about tonight, but she wanted to be totally transparent with Abbey as far as Jason was concerned.

'Why doesn't that surprise me?' Abbey said, meeting Rhi's reflection in the mirror. 'He's pathetic, isn't he?'

'He is, I told him that! He did ask after you. Wanted to know if you still talked about him.'

'Ha, only all the time. You know, it was the best thing we ever did escaping that situation.' Abbey put an arm around Rhi's shoulder as they made their way back to the table. 'We would never have got together for quiz nights if it hadn't have been for Jason so there's something we can be grateful to him for.'

It was true and Rhi was grateful for the opportunity to see Luke again too. He'd picked her up from her house and they'd driven together to the pub, but she sensed he was quieter, more reserved than normal. Lizzie was her usual bubbly self, but you could see that her head was all over the place, flitting here, there and everywhere, probably halfway across the world by now. Fortunately, Bill was doing a good job at settling her down and the pair of them hadn't stopped chatting all night. As for Abbey and Sam, although they hadn't been sitting next to each other, Rhi couldn't help but notice the chemistry sizzling across the table between them, the exchanged glances and the flirtatious smiles. Were they an item now? She really hoped so and she would ask Abbey as soon as she found the opportunity. She sighed inwardly, only wishing she had a similar connection with Luke.

'Are you ready to make a move?' he asked, his keys jangling in his hand.

'Yes.' Rhi stood up, slipping her jacket over her shoulders.

'See you all at mine next Saturday,' Lizzie breezed on the way out. 'I really can't wait.'

* * *

'You'll definitely be coming to the party, won't you?' As they drove through the country lanes back to Rhi's place, her mind was still whirring and she couldn't stop herself from asking. Luke turned to her, his expression bemused.

'You know I am. I'm looking forward to it. Should be fun.'

'Great.' Rhi berated herself for sounding needy. It would be the last time she would get to see Luke before going away and that made her inexorably sad. If he didn't turn up on that Saturday night for whatever reason she would be devastated. If only he knew how he'd got beneath her skin. She wanted to spend as much time with him as she possibly could. 'Why don't you come in for a drink?' she suggested, when they pulled up outside her house.

'Er, I'm not sure. I've got work in the morning and there's some stuff I need to do back at home yet.'

'Please. Ten minutes. A quick coffee. Come on, after next weekend you won't have to see me for another few months. You never know, you might even miss me, then you'll forever regret not coming in for coffee with me.'

He gave a wry smile, shaking his head indulgently. 'You reckon? Go on, then, you've twisted my arm. I won't be able to stay for long, though. I really do need to get back at a decent time.'

Rhi didn't mind; any time spent alone with Luke was a bonus. She was sure, given the opportunity, that they would take their relationship to the next stage. Her feelings were so strong and intense. Luke had to be feeling it too. They'd barely had a chance to talk tonight. The quiz evenings were fun and frenetic, but passed by in a flash and Rhi always thought of everything she'd meant to ask her friends shortly after the event.

Arriving at the house, Rhi put the key in the lock and led the way into the living room, Luke following behind.

'Ah hello, it's lovely to see you again, Luke.' Rhi's mum was sitting in the armchair, her legs tucked beneath her, with a book and a bag of knitting at her side. She zapped the television off with the remote control and sat up straight when she realised she had company.

'And you too, Mrs West.'

'Please, call me Lisa. So did you win?'

'No, we came fifth, which wasn't too shabby compared to last time's performance. We always have such good intentions, but the wheels fell off in the second half.'

'Still, it's always such a good laugh, isn't it? And it's the taking part that matters. Isn't that what you always told me, Mum? I shall miss it while I'm away.'

'And I'll miss you,' said Lisa, gathering up her bits from the sofa. 'But I know you'll have the best time ever, won't she, Luke?

Anyway, you take care; I'm going up to bed now, but hopefully I'll get to see you again when this one returns from her travels.'

Her mum wasn't the only one banking on that possibility. Rhi flicked on the kettle in the kitchen and pulled out a couple of mugs from the cupboard, handing Luke his coffee once it was made.

'So, do you have any plans for the next couple of months?' she asked Luke when they were sitting on opposite ends of the sofa.

'Well, no gallivanting around the world like you, but I have got a second interview next week with a large multinational company. Still in sales, but in a different industry. I need to get out of that place. It's not the best environment, as you know.'

'That's brilliant, you should have told me. A second interview sounds really encouraging. I shall keep everything crossed for you. Where would you be based?'

'It could be anywhere in the country. It might mean relocating, but it would be a good move career-wise. I'll have to see what package they come up with, assuming I get it, of course.'

'Well, that sounds... great! And you're bound to get it,' she said brightly, while inside her heart dropped to her boots. Would she come back from her trip and find that Luke had already gone? Moved to another part of the country. Maybe the universe was trying to tell her something. Perhaps she and Luke were never meant to be together, and this was the final sign, if she needed one.

'You'll keep in touch, though, if you do move away?'

A smile spread across his face. Inscrutable. Unfathomable.

'Of course. There's always social media.'

Didn't people always say that? That they must stay in touch, when inevitably the distance in miles and time would slowly but surely loosen those ties.

'Yeah.' She tried hard not to sound despondent, but the thought that she might not see Luke on a regular basis any more set off a panic inside her. *What about quiz nights and our walks?* she wanted to shout. Clearly she didn't even register on his radar as a consideration when it came to life decisions. Was it really uncharitable of her to hope that he wouldn't get the job after all?

'So are you all packed and ready to go?' Luke asked, seemingly much more comfortable talking about her travel plans than his life plans.

'Pretty much. I've got one huge rucksack and everything is going in there. If it doesn't fit, then it's not coming with me. I really won't need that much, just my clothes.'

'You're a proper adventurer, Rhi. I really admire your spirit.'

'That's one way of describing it, I suppose,' she said, laughing. 'Although my mum might not put it in such flattering terms. Hey, listen, did you think there was something funny going on with the others tonight? It might have been me, but there was a definite atmosphere in the air.'

'Yeah, it was sweet, wasn't it?'

'What? I don't understand. What was it all about?'

'Love,' said Luke, with a grin on his face. 'Lizzie was acting like a teenager with Bill and he was being very attentive and protective towards her. And Abbey and Sam, well, it only needed a match to be lit between the pair of them and the whole place would have gone up in flames.'

'Oh my God!' Rhi mulled over Luke's words for just the briefest of moments. She'd noticed the spark between Abbey and Sam, but Bill and Lizzie too? Love had definitely been in the air tonight for her, but she'd been too wrapped up in Luke to notice what was going on between the others. 'You're right. Why didn't I realise that? And why didn't they say anything?'

'Well, I'm guessing they're both in those early, delicious stages of their relationships where they're still discovering each other, and wanting to keep the magic to themselves for the time being.'

'Right.' Rhi looked at Luke as though she'd just discovered

another part to his personality, trying to hide her amazement. *Magic?* She knew all about that, but how come Luke knew so much about love and relationships? 'You're very perceptive.'

'It's a hobby of mine, people-watching,' he said, with an enigmatic smile. 'Anyway, thanks for the coffee.' He stood up, taking his finished mug out to the kitchen. 'I'll see you next Saturday at the party.'

'Yes.' Rhi jumped up too. She stood to one side to allow Luke through to the hallway and, really, she couldn't help herself. As his body accidentally brushed against hers, her hands reached forward to hug him, standing on tiptoes to kiss him on the lips.

'Rhi, what the heck are you doing?'

He pushed her away, holding her forearms down to stop her advances, scanning her features for some kind of explanation. Seeing Luke's reaction, Rhi jumped backwards, shame tinging her cheeks with heat.

'I'm so sorry, Luke. I didn't think... Well... I just... oh God!' Was he really so repulsed by her that the thought of her kissing him could cause such an intense reaction?

'No, you didn't think.' He shook his head, annoyance bristling off his words. 'You keep doing this, Rhi. Acting on impulse. Jumping into situations before knowing whether it's the right thing for you. You don't want this, not really.'

'Well, sorry, we can't all be as sensible and level-headed as you. And please don't presume to know what I want. Now, I'm really sorry if I offended you. That was the last thing I intended.'

'It's fine, don't worry,' said Luke, his words at odds with the irritation and disappointment radiating from his entire body.

They stood by the front door, the atmosphere between them awkward and intense, Luke fumbling with the unfamiliar lock as he tried to escape.

'I'll see you soon,' he said, when he finally negotiated the door, clearly unable to get out of the house fast enough. Rhi dropped her head in her hands and slid down the back of the front door, landing in a crumpled heap on the floor. What had she done? Her feelings for Luke were clearly not reciprocated and now her worst fears might be realised. She might not even see Luke again before jetting off on her trip abroad and that thought made her incredibly sad.

34

Abbey drove around and around the market square, looking for a place to park, hoping she might be lucky and spot someone just about to leave. Ten minutes later she was considering heading to the multi-storey, when a young man appeared from out of the post office and headed for his white van, giving a thumbs up to Abbey. At last! Once safely in the parking spot, she climbed out of the car and walked along the High Street, the sun kissing her bare arms and legs. It was only then she realised why it was quite so busy this afternoon. The schools had broken up for the summer holidays and the shops were busy with excitable children and their parents, that end-of-term feeling wafting in the air.

Abbey felt a similar feeling in her bones, an appreciation and expectation of things moving on. She'd already seen one major change this summer with the cancellation of her wedding, but now she would be saying goodbye to Lizzie and Rhi, if only for a few months, knowing she would miss them both hugely while they were away. That was the purpose of her trip into town today: to pick up a couple of good luck cards and small gifts for her friends.

More than that, she felt she was on the precipice of something new and exciting in her own life. Sam had admitted to her that he really liked her and while that was hugely flattering and exhilarating, matching her own feelings, it also scared her half to death. Could she really let go and allow herself to fall for Sam? Could her poor heart withstand that level of vulnerability? At the moment it was all fresh, new and exciting, but it must have been that way with Jason once and look what had happened there.

She banished the negative thoughts from her mind. These days her feelings were in a constant state of flux, her heart telling her to seize the opportunity with Sam, her head warning her to keep some distance. *Just in case.* Although that was no way to live her life, she knew. Besides, there wasn't much she could do about her growing feelings for Sam; every time she thought about him she simply melted inside.

Turning in to Bridge Street, she headed for the All That Glitters gift shop with its wide selection of jewellery, candles, specialist china and curios. She had a good old mooch around before her eyes alighted on a little something she thought would be perfect for her friends. Relieved to have found something suitable, she also picked up some cards and gift bags, taking all the items across to the till. With her purchases made, she stepped outside and wandered along the High Street, soaking up the sunny atmosphere. She was going to head straight back to the car but, walking past the little cafe further down the street, she stopped to peer down the side alleyway to see all the tables and umbrellas outside in the walled garden. Realising how thirsty she was, she gave a cursory glance at the menu on the board outside, already having decided a homemade rose lemonade would quench her thirst perfectly. She spotted a table at the back of the courtyard and was just about to head towards it when she felt someone from behind reach out and touch her arm.

'It is you! I thought it was. Are you about to have a drink? That's a coincidence. Me too. Mind if I join you?'

Abbey turned to look, bemused to see Stephanie at her elbow. With her distinctive blonde hair and tall, willowy figure, Stephanie, in a pretty pink sundress, stood out in the crowd. Even if Abbey had wanted to object, she wasn't sure that she could as Stephanie was already telling the passing waitress that they would be taking the remaining free table.

'So are you and Sam together now, then?' Stephanie asked, discarding the menu to one side, and resting her forearms on the table, Abbey feeling the scrutiny of her gaze.

No point in small talk; Stephanie clearly wanted to get straight to the nitty-gritty. Abbey busied herself with her bags, buying herself some thinking time. She didn't have to talk to Stephanie. She could tell a white lie, that she was about to meet a friend, and Stephanie would have to go. She could be even more direct and tell Stephanie to mind her own business, that it was nothing to do with her, which, of course, was true. She could stand up and walk out and have nothing more to do with Stephanie, but there was something that made her stay.

'We're friends. That's all. We've seen each other a few times.' It didn't tell the whole story, how Abbey's feelings for Sam were spiralling out of control, how she really hoped there might be a future for the pair of them.

'I know it's none of my business,' said Stephanie, as if reading Abbey's mind. 'I guess I was just really disappointed that things didn't develop with Sam in the way I hoped they would. Sorry about what happened in the cafe.' She gave an imploring look. 'I was upset, hurt. From the first time I met Sam I thought what a great guy he was. Funny, interesting, obviously really good looking. I thought we could have a future together.'

Abbey nodded, totally able to relate to Stephanie's words. She was relieved when her ice-cold lemonade arrived, taking a refreshing sip.

Stephanie continued. 'I'd been internet dating for about eighteen months and it was just so soul-destroying. Is that how you met Sam too?'

'No, I've never done it. We met through the park, Primrose Woods.'

'Ah, right. You're lucky, then. Don't do it if you can possibly avoid it. You meet so many slimeballs online, or people pretending to be something they're not, so when I met Sam it was as though all my prayers had been answered. He was everything I was looking for in a man, and single and available to boot. I thought we hit it off and I suppose I got carried away, imagining a future that only really existed in my head.'

Abbey swirled the straw round in her glass. Could she be accused of doing the same thing when her head was entertaining all sorts of possibilities involving Sam in the future? She'd imagined the wedding they might have, the house in the country, and even the names they would give the children. It was a good job Sam couldn't read her thoughts or else he might be horrified. She could totally understand how Stephanie might have been swept along on a similar wave of romantic energy.

'I'm sorry it didn't work out for you and Sam.'

'Yeah, it's just one of those things, I guess. I'll get over it. When you see Sam again, tell him I'm sorry. I would tell him myself, but he blocked my number and I wouldn't risk going to see him again. He already thinks I'm a scary stalker lady.'

'Don't worry. I'm sure Sam will understand.'

'Yeah, I guess this kind of thing happens to him all the time,' she said wryly. 'I can imagine he's a bit of a heartbreaker. Look, I hope it works out for you and him, if that's where your relationship is heading.'

Abbey was about to protest when Stephanie held up a hand.

'Really, no hard feelings. I think you make a cute couple. You're probably much better suited to him than I ever was. Besides...' She tapped the table with an excitable flourish. 'I'm moving on! I have a date this weekend and I'm feeling cautiously optimistic. He's a teacher from a neighbouring school so we have that in common at least. This time I'm going to take things slowly, though.' She grimaced exaggeratedly. 'You think I'd know better at my age.'

'That sounds great. I hope it goes well.'

'Thanks. You too,' said Stephanie, finishing off her drink. 'And I'm sorry for what I said last time about being careful of Sam breaking your heart. That was mean of me. I'm sure he's not like that at all, really.'

'Don't worry, it's all forgotten about.' Abbey forced a smile, wishing that were true. Stephanie's comment about Sam being a heartbreaker had struck a chord with Abbey at the time. She'd spent far too long since wondering if it could really be true. Sam may have broken Stephanie's heart, leaving her disappointed and regretful; Abbey only hoped the same fate didn't await her.

35

'Dad!' Abbey's face lit up to see her dad standing on her doorstep that Saturday morning. He very rarely turned up unannounced and seeing him standing there in his navy shorts and yellow polo shirt made her realise just how much she'd missed him lately. He looked so handsome, and yet different somehow. For some reason, they'd forgone their usual weekly walks and get-togethers recently and she'd missed sharing that special one-on-one time with him. 'Come on in. I've just made some coffee. Shall we have a bacon sandwich too?'

'Oh, you've always known the way to my heart. Sounds perfect.'

'We could go to Treetops Cafe and have a full fry-up, if you'd prefer to do that?'

'No!' His response was fast and vehement. 'Let's stay here, then we can have a proper catch-up in private. There's something I need to talk to you about.'

'What's that, then?' she said, immediately concerned.

'It can wait another few minutes. Let's get that sandwich going,' he said, rubbing his hands together gleefully.

It was only when the pan was sizzling and the aroma of bacon was wafting in the air that Abbey wondered what exactly it was her dad wanted to talk about. Something important if he'd made a special trip to her house to discuss it with her. It wasn't how they normally interacted with each other. They didn't mark out special time to talk about certain subjects. They just came right out and said whatever was on their minds. A shiver of concern ran through her veins. She couldn't help but worry.

She sat down beside her dad at the table, pleased to be in his company, enjoying the simple pleasure of sharing a meal, a reminder of times gone by.

'Do you remember the lovely weekend breakfasts we had with Mum?' Abbey wasn't sure why or when it had started, but there was a period in her teenage years when Saturday mornings were something of a ritual, the marking of the start to the weekend with a slap-up breakfast. Sometimes her mum would do a full fry-up with all the trimmings – bacon, eggs, mushrooms, sausages, hash browns, baked beans and plenty of toast and butter – or she might prepare American pancakes with blueberries and cream, and golden syrup, or Dad's particular favourite of smoked salmon and scrambled eggs.

'I do!' Bill beamed at the memory. 'How could I ever forget? Happy days.'

He fell quiet, lost in thought for a moment, his mood altered by the reminder, and she wondered if she shouldn't have mentioned it. Quickly, she moved the conversation on. As they munched on their thick, succulent sandwiches they chatted about the summer heatwave that had arrived as forecasted, Abbey's job, the plans she had for transforming her small and neglected garden into an oasis, and everything else in between, until she could bear the suspense no longer.

'So come on, Dad, tell me. What is it you want to talk about?'

'Ah...' he faltered, clearly rallying himself to come out with whatever it was he was struggling to tell her.

'Oh my goodness,' she gasped. 'You're not ill, are you?'

Her recent conversation with Sam about the sad loss of his parents had resonated with her. It made her realise just how lucky she was to have her dad's constant presence in her life, always there for her, supportive and encouraging. He was her rock and she couldn't ever imagine a time when he wouldn't be around.

'No, why on earth would you think that?'

She let out an audible sigh of relief. 'Because you've been acting peculiarly – secretive, and there's just something different about you. I'm your daughter, Dad. I know when something's up.' Now she stopped to think about it, with her gaze focused on her dad's familiar features, she tried to pinpoint what it was exactly that had changed about him. Maybe he'd lost a little weight, so that his face was a little more angular now and he'd caught the sun, offering his cheeks and forehead a golden glow. He was wearing new clothes too, she realised, the sharp lemon of his polo shirt offsetting his tan nicely and his tailored shorts, crisp and smart. That was it! He didn't look ill at all. Quite the opposite. He looked well and completely refreshed.

'I'm sorry, love. I suppose I have been putting it off. I've not known how to tell you. How you might react.'

'Please, Dad, just spit it out, whatever it is. It can't be anything worse than I've been imagining in my head.'

'Okay, fair enough. Well, the thing is...' He took a deep breath. 'I've met someone.'

'What?' For a moment, Abbey couldn't understand what he meant. Who had he met? Someone at the supermarket, an old friend, a conman about to relieve him of all his worldly goods? Until realisation slowly dawned. 'Oh, you mean, like... someone, a special someone?'

'Yes.' Bill managed to look embarrassed, awkward and happy all at the same time. It certainly explained the new him. The light in his eye, the spring in his step and the almost constant smile on his face.

'Well, that's lovely news. I'm really pleased for you, Dad. What I don't understand is why you felt you couldn't tell me.'

He shrugged his shoulders, rubbing a hand across his forehead. 'I don't know. I wasn't sure how you would react. If you might think I was being disloyal to your mum?'

'Never!' She leant across and hugged her dad tight. 'You deserve to find happiness again. And Mum would think the same once she'd got over the horror of seeing you with another woman!' They laughed in unison.

'Let's hope she doesn't. She always vowed to come and haunt me if I found anyone else!'

'Yeah, but that was just her way and we knew she didn't really mean it.' They pulled a doubtful face together, falling into laughter again. 'Most of all she would want you to be happy. You two were utterly devoted to each other and she knew how much she was loved.' She suppressed a sigh. 'But that was then and, sadly, Mum's not coming back. You can't live in the past forever. Go for it, Dad! That's what I say.'

'Thanks, sweetheart. It's such a relief to be able to tell you.'

'So, when am I going to meet this new lady?' she teased, knowing full well who had brought about this transformation in her dad.

'You already have, love. It's Lizzie.'

Abbey squealed with excitement. 'Of course, it's Lizzie. How could I have not spotted it?' she said dramatically, holding a hand to her chest. 'It's just the best news ever! I adore Lizzie, and you and her together, well, it's simply perfect.'

From the moment her dad had met Lizzie at the cafe, they'd hit it off, chatting easily, laughing together and sharing memories and experiences, finding a common bond. It was funny to think that if Abbey's wedding had gone ahead as planned, then her dad's relationship with Lizzie may never have got off the starting blocks. The same thing could be said for her relationship with Sam. She gave a wry smile to herself. The universe worked in funny ways at times.

'This doesn't change the way I feel about your mum. You do know that? No one could ever replace her. And I never thought I would meet someone new; well, I had no desire to be with anyone else. Then Lizzie came along and it seemed so natural. Everything just fell into place.' Bill's bemusement at this unexpected turn of events was plain to see.

'It's great, Dad. I'm really happy for you both.'

She meant it too. Her dad's sparkle deserted him when her mum died and Abbey, dealing with her own grief, had no way of knowing how to reach him. He put on a brave face for his daughter, and she tried to do the same for him, but they'd both been locked in their own sadness for far too long. Now, it looked as though Lizzie held the key to Bill rediscovering his joy for life.

'That means we'll have double cause for celebration tonight, then.'

'Yes. I wanted to tell you before the party just so that everything was out in the open. Talking of which, what's happening between you and Sam?'

She laughed, her turn now to be hesitant.

'What do you mean?' said Abbey coyly. 'Me and Sam? Is it that obvious?'

'I'm afraid it is. Lizzie and I have been wondering for ages when the two of you might get together.'

'Really?' It pleased her to think that others might have noticed the growing spark between them and it wasn't something that existed only in her imagination.

'Yes,' said Bill with a wide grin. 'I didn't like to say anything, but he's a properly decent chap, that Sam. I could tell he was keen on you right from the start.' He raised a questioning eyebrow.

'I really like him, Dad, and we have grown close. It's just... I suppose I'm a bit wary after what happened with Jason. What if it happens again? If I fall in love and then five years down the line he decides I'm not what he wants after all. I'm not getting any younger and I want to settle down and have a family. I can't afford to make any more mistakes.'

'I know and I can understand how you must feel. But Sam is a totally different character to Jason. Don't judge him on Jason's behaviour. Find out for yourself what he's really like, the man he is. Some things, some people, are worth taking a risk on. Sam might be one of those people.'

'You don't think it's too soon? That I should take my time before jumping into a new relationship?'

Her dad chuckled, shaking his head fondly. 'There are no hard and fast rules, love. If it feels right, if it's what you want, then do it.'

'Yeah,' she said dreamily, an image of Sam's enchanting smile lodging itself in her brain. 'I think you're right. I'm enjoying spending time with him at the moment. I guess we'll just have to see how things go.'

'You've got to grasp any chance of happiness that you can. Life and love, it's so precious. We both know that. Best not to dwell on what might go wrong, but instead focus on what could go right.'

'Thanks, Dad.' She hugged him tight, feeling energised and encouraged by his positive words. 'You and Lizzie, though? It's amazing, such happy news. You'll miss her while she's away.'

'The time will fly by and we'll have plenty more time to enjoy each other's company when she comes home. Lizzie's already making plans for Christmas.' Bill couldn't hide the smile from his face. 'I said I'd pop round later and help her set up for the party.'

He glanced at his watch. 'We've got time for a walk over at Primrose Woods beforehand if you fancy it?'

Abbey stood up and cleared the plates from the table, stacking them away tidily in the dishwasher. 'Definitely. You know how much I love my daily walks there.'

It was funny to think how Primrose Woods had become such an integral part of all their lives, the developing relationships between Abbey, Sam, Lizzie, Bill, Luke and Rhi having grown stronger through the happy times spent at the park.

'It's one of my favourite things to do, in possibly my favourite place in the world and with my favourite person too.' She went across and kissed her dad on the cheek, linking her arm through his. 'What could be any better?'

36

Later that evening, Sam arrived to collect Abbey from the cottage.
A most delightful nervous anticipation coursed around her body
as she heard his car door slam shut. She peeked out of her
bedroom window to see his distinctive broad frame bending down
to open her low, rickety front gate, before sauntering up the front
path. With one final look in the mirror, she ran her fingers through
her hair, teasing it into loose curls, and gave a devil-may-care shrug
to her reflection. It was the kind of mood she was in tonight.
Expectant and excitable.

'Hi!' Did she imagine Sam falter for a moment when she
opened the door? Maybe, although she was certain she hadn't
imagined the appreciation in his eyes.

'Hey! You look lovely,' he said, greeting her with a kiss on the
cheek. She hadn't known what to wear. First of all she tried on her
smart black jeans with a variety of different tops – a tight-fitting
red T-shirt, a floaty, floral blouse and then a long, multi-coloured
tunic – but none of them seemed right for the occasion. In the end
she chose a simple primrose-yellow summer dress that was easy

and comfortable and skimmed her body flatteringly. 'It's great to see you.'

'And you.' Their eyes locked, lingering for a moment, before Abbey checked herself. 'Come on in for a moment while I grab my bags.'

She needed a distraction. Sam standing on her doorstep, in dark blue jeans and a black fitted T-shirt sculpting his tanned biceps, had sent her head into a spin, her body reacting involuntarily to his very masculine presence. He always smelt so good, a heady mix of the great outdoors mingled with just-out-of-the-shower vibes along with citrusy undertones that got beneath her skin and managed to stir all her senses. She shook her head to get rid of those thoughts as she locked the back door and pulled out a bottle of wine from the fridge along with the pasta salad she'd made earlier that afternoon.

'Can you put those down a moment?' Sam relieved her of the items in her hands, placing them on the side table, before taking her hands in his, pulling her towards his body. They stood barely a hair's breadth apart, the electricity between them sizzling. 'I'm not sure I'm going to get through this evening with you looking as beautiful as you do. I'll never be able to drag my eyes away from you.' He touched her face, his fingers gently caressing her cheek, before their lips met and they kissed, tentatively at first, explorative, discovering each other until they both gave in to the desire that had been bubbling beneath the surface for weeks.

When Abbey came up for air, her cheeks flushed and every nerve cell in her body tingling, she met Sam's imploring gaze.

'You have no idea how long I've wanted to do that. I was waiting until I felt you wanted it in the same way too. I hope I'm right about that.'

'You didn't need to wait so long,' said Abbey, realising being with Sam, letting go, was everything she'd imagined it to be and more.

'You know we could call off this evening, say we both have some highly virulent twenty-four-hour bug that we really don't want to pass on to them, and then we could spend the rest of the night here together, just you and me.'

'We can't!' She poked him in the stomach. Even though the idea was wholly tempting, she knew he was only teasing her. 'This...' She kissed him lightly on the forehead. '... will definitely have to wait until later.'

'Spoilsport!'

'Hey, I meant to tell you, guess who I ran into the other day?'

Sam narrowed his eyes, tilting his head to one side. 'Go on...'

'Stephanie.'

'Oh God, no!' Sam's face was a picture of horror. 'Where was this? She didn't come and find you at work?'

'No, we bumped into each other in town. I was just going into the cafe and she invited herself along for a drink.' She chuckled. 'I didn't really have much of a say in that, but it turned out fine. It was actually very civilised.'

Sam grimaced. 'What did she want?'

'To explain why she acted the way she did. She said how disappointed she was; she fell for you big time and honestly believed there could be a future for the pair of you.'

'Right, but she knows now that there's no chance of that?' Sam looked at her imploringly.

'Oh yeah,' said Abbey with a smile. 'She actually asked me to tell you how sorry she was, and she apologised to me as well after saying that I should be careful that you didn't go breaking my heart.'

'So she should!' Sam pulled Abbey closer, his hands resting on her waist, his face a hair's breadth away from hers. 'Stephanie was never right for me. I knew that the moment I met her. When I met you it was a totally different thing. We clicked immediately. I thought you were just so lovely, beautiful inside and out. I couldn't stop thinking about you after that first time we met on the bench. And that's when I knew.'

Abbey could hardly believe what she was hearing as Sam's words washed over her in a warm glow. She'd felt exactly the same.

'Look, take no notice of what Stephanie said.' He cupped her face in his hand. 'I'm really no heartbreaker. And don't listen to Lizzie either, much as I love her. The only people important in all of this is you and me. We can work it out together.'

He leant forward, pressing his lips against hers, and Abbey gasped. It felt so wonderful, so entirely natural that she could have stayed there all night, just luxuriating in his kisses. If only they didn't have a party to attend.

'Come on,' she said, extracting herself from his embrace. She took his hand, laughing as he pretended to resist her attempts to get him out of the house. 'We must go. You know all good things are worth waiting for!'

A few minutes later, as she climbed into Sam's car, she said, 'Anyway, I've got even more news for you. I had an unexpected visit from Dad this morning. He came to tell me that he and Lizzie are seeing each other now. I think they're both really smitten. Isn't that lovely?'

'Wow!' Sam turned to grin at her and she thought how she would never grow tired of seeing his handsome face beaming at her. 'That doesn't surprise me in the slightest. I knew something was up with Lizzie, but I didn't want to press her on it. I thought it was just the excitement of her trip, but suspected there was something more to it than that. She's brighter, more confident, happier. It's good to know that it's down to your dad that she's glowing.'

'I'm so pleased for them both, especially Dad. I worry about him, if he's happy or not. He's been going through life on autopilot ever since Mum died, so to see the change in him is just wonderful.'

'Falling in love can do that to a man,' said Sam, blessing her with that killer smile again, and sending her stomach into free fall at the same time.

By the time they arrived at Lizzie's house, Abbey's heart was still performing topsy-turvy manoeuvres, with Sam's comment playing over and over in her head. Was he talking about his own experience? About falling in love? All she knew was that his words had made her heart soar. Still, she needed to put that aside for now. Lizzie was greeting them at the door and ushered them inside, pointing them in the direction of the kitchen, where Bill was serving drinks. Abbey handed the items she'd brought along to Sam, while Lizzie grabbed her by the arm and took her to one side.

'Abbey, how are you, my lovely?' She clasped Abbey's face in her hands. 'Your dad told me you'd had a little chat this morning.'

'We did, and I'm so made up for the both of you.'

'Really?' Lizzie kissed her on the cheek and hugged her tighter. 'I was worried you might not be happy about the idea.'

'Why ever not?'

'I don't know. Just me being daft. I've not had a man in my life for years. I don't know what the rules are any more.'

Abbey smiled to herself, knowing exactly how Lizzie felt. Young love, old love, in-between love, it had a habit of taking you unawares, when you'd almost given up hope of ever finding it again.

'There are no rules, Lizzie. Dad told me exactly the same thing this morning. You just have to go with the flow.' Abbey sounded as if she knew what she was talking about when in fact she had no idea herself, and was just making it up as she went along. 'And, if my dad was going to meet anyone, then I can think of no lovelier person that I would want him to be with than you, one of my dearest friends.'

'Thanks, sweetheart, that means a lot. And you and Sam look as though you're getting on well?'

Abbey gave an enigmatic smile, her whole body reacting to the mention of Sam's name.

'We are, but it's early days for us,' she said, tempering her own and Lizzie's expectations. Still, though, as she went to find a drink, her gaze searched out Sam, her heart hiccupping as soon as she spotted him. She wished she could put a name to the feelings she was experiencing, racing emotions that took over her whole being. She'd felt nothing like it in years. Not in all the time she was with Jason. It was a complete revelation. Lust, desire, excitement and anticipation all conspired together to put her in a state of giddiness, with a permanent smile spread across her face. So much for her taking things slowly, seeing where events took her. It was too late. She'd fallen, head over heels.

37

Rhi's overwhelming emotion was one of relief to see Luke at the party. She'd half expected him to come up with a lame excuse for not attending so as to avoid seeing her, after the embarrassment of their last meeting, so she was hugely grateful that he was there, looking as handsome as she remembered. Not that she'd spoken to him yet. He was deep in conversation with Bill and Sam, nursing a glass of beer. What could she say to him other than 'sorry'? Would it be awkward between them? She groaned inwardly. It was bound to be, but she didn't want to go away not having seen him one more time.

Lizzie stood by the buffet table and clapped her hands. 'Can I have your attention for a moment, please?'

A cheer went up from her small gathering of guests.

'I won't keep you long, I promise, but I just wanted to say a big thank you for coming along this evening. This little get-together is my way of showing my gratitude to you for all the kindness and support you've shown to me over the last couple of months. I know for certain that without your gentle encouragement – or, more accurately, nagging – I would never have got to the point where I will be actually stepping on that plane on Monday morning, and looking forward to it too, can you believe? Most of all I'm grateful for your friendship. Sam I've known for years and he's always been an absolute rock to me, supporting me through many difficult times.' She blew a kiss in his direction. 'The rest of you I've only come to know in recent months, but I think I've found a bond with each and every one of you, which I hope will continue to grow and develop over the coming months and years. Who knows, maybe the Primrose Fancies will actually get around to winning the pub quiz one of these days. That's what I'm banking on.' She took hold of Bill's hand and squeezed it tight. 'Anyway, that's it – enjoy the rest of the evening, and I'll see you all on the other side.'

Lizzie rushed off into the kitchen and was back moments later, seeking out Rhi.

'This is for you,' she said, handing over a neatly wrapped parcel in pink tissue paper.

'What is it?' she said, bemused. 'You didn't need to buy me a gift.' Rhi carefully unwrapped the present, her eyes lighting up at the sight.

'I hope you'll have room for it in your rucksack.' It was a beautiful leather-bound travel journal engraved with Rhi's name on the front, with a glittered ballpoint pen tucked into the spine.

'I will make room for it. It's beautiful.'

'Well, I thought it would make a lovely record for what you see and do on your trip. And you'll be able to keep all your tickets and mementos in there too.'

'It's brilliant, Lizzie, thank you. I'd meant to buy one for myself but hadn't got round to it, but it would never have been as beautiful as this, so it's the perfect choice.'

Abbey joined them, admiring the journal too.

'That reminds me, I have a little present for you both.' She handed over the two mesh pouches she'd bought from All That

Glitters, giving one to Rhi and one to Lizzie, and they opened them together. Inside was a silver keyring with five lucky charms on each: a horseshoe, a heart, a butterfly, a safety pin and an aeroplane.

'Oh, how lovely,' sighed Lizzie.

'It's gorgeous,' agreed Rhi.

'Well, it's a good luck token for your trips. Not that you'll need it, of course. I thought if you have a wobble at any time, then you would just need to look at the charms to know that we'll be thinking of you and sending you our support across the oceans.'

Later, Sam sidled up to Abbey's side and put an arm around her waist. She looked up into his dark brown eyes, feeling the affection of his gaze.

'Do you feel a bit jealous that it's not you jetting off to sunnier climes?'

Abbey took a moment to think about the question. 'I've never really had a desire to go travelling around the world. My mum always used to call me a home bird and I suppose I am. Never happier than when I'm pottering about the cottage or in the garden, baking cakes, going for a walk in the countryside. All the simple pleasures, that's me. Does that make me sound really uncool and old-fashioned?'

'Not at all. Quite the opposite actually.'

She smiled, basking in Sam's appreciation. 'To be honest, I'd be just as happy with a wet weekend in Wales. There are so many other beautiful places in the UK too that I've not visited yet. I'll get round to it one day. And I like to think I'm doing my own small bit for the planet by not flying abroad.'

'You see, that just goes to show how compatible we are. My idea of heaven would be a wet weekend in Wales with my two favourite girls in the whole world, you and Lady – a cosy cottage by the sea, longs walks on the beaches, pub lunches and exploring some castles. How does that sound?'

Heavenly. Abbey laid her head on Sam's chest as he pulled her into his side. It sounded absolutely heavenly.

* * *

Rhi knew she couldn't avoid Luke all night long. It wasn't as though she could get lost in the crowds as there were only six of them milling about Lizzie's living room, chatting, drinking wine, partaking of the tempting spread of food that Lizzie had prepared. There was a celebratory atmosphere with plenty of laughter tinkling about the room, but Rhi had managed to avoid being alone with Luke, dreading any awkward conversations after the last time. Up until now, that was. She was helping herself to a top-up from the opened bottle of Prosecco in Lizzie's fridge, when she heard his voice.

'Rhi?'

She turned to look at him.

'Have you been avoiding me?' It was delivered with a smile and her body reacted treacherously in the same way as it always did when she saw Luke.

'No.' She felt embarrassment prickle on her cheeks and was grateful that she had something to do with her hands, that she didn't have to face Luke's questioning expression, but there was no avoiding him.

'Rhi?' He said her name slowly, a hint of playfulness to his tone. 'Come on, I know you well enough by now to know when there's a problem. What's up? If it's about the other night, then stop stressing. It's forgotten about.'

'Not by me, it isn't. Every time I think about it I cringe. What's wrong with me? I'm obviously a disaster area when it comes to men and hopeless at picking up on signs. Trying to kiss you like that...' She shuddered. 'I'm sorry for putting you through that.'

'Hey.' He laughed. 'It wasn't that bad. You know, I'm here, I survived it. I've had worse experiences.'

Wasn't that just like Luke? Trying to make light of the situation in an attempt to make her feel better. She didn't deserve him after the way she'd treated him. Trouble was, she could do nothing to change the way she felt. If anything, her feelings for him were growing by the day. Perhaps with the benefit of thousands of miles between them she might be able to put a brake on her unrequited crush.

'Thanks,' she said, unable to hide her sarcasm.

'Come on, don't be like that. In two days' time you'll be flying off on an adventure. Don't let anything spoil that, especially something as inconsequential as this. We're still mates, right?'

Luke embraced her in a hug and she turned her head so that it rested on his chest. *Mates.* Luke knew how to wound her without even trying. He'd forgiven her, though, for her faux pas the other evening, so that was something.

She pulled away, his proximity and his scent far too tempting, worried that she might repeat her earlier mistake and make an even bigger fool of herself. The sooner she stepped onto that plane, away from all the reminders of home, the better. Only she wasn't convinced she'd be able to get Luke out of her system quite so easily. Somehow and at some time, when she wasn't even looking, he'd managed to get beneath her skin, so much so that he was the first thing she thought about when she woke up in the mornings and the last thing she thought about when she went to sleep of a night. How exactly had that happened?

'So what time are you leaving on Monday?'

Rhi reached for the glass of wine she'd placed on the worktop, grateful for the distance between them. She couldn't help wondering, if she'd gone out with Luke in the first place and not that creep, Jason, then the situation might be very different now.

'The taxi's picking us up from here at nine in the morning and then our flight leaves at midday.' She wasn't really in holiday mode yet. Once she got up on Monday and was on her way to the airport, she knew her excitement would build and she knew her time away would whizz by as she already had so much crammed into her schedule. 'I'll give you a wave goodbye as we fly over.'

'Make sure you do,' said Luke with a grin. 'I'll be looking out for you.'

She smiled, outwardly matching his good cheer, but inside she felt a tidal wave of sadness. That was it, then. She was leaving for another continent and it seemed as though it was of little consequence to Luke.

38

'What a lovely evening!' Abbey beamed on the way home as she snuggled up to Sam in the back of the taxi. The woozy, slightly squiffy sensation was only to be expected after all those glasses of Prosecco, and relaxing into the safety of Sam's arms gave her a snuggly and satisfying glow inside. At that moment there was no other place in the world she would rather be.

'It was.' Sam absent-mindedly twirled a finger through Abbey's hair as they drove along the darkened lanes back to her cottage. 'It was great to see Lizzie so excited for her trip. And knowing that Rhi will be there to look after her on the outward flight is reassuring. Rhi's such a great girl. She'll be the best travelling companion.'

'Honestly, she's so confident and capable, that girl. I can't imagine taking myself off at her age and travelling to the other side of the word alone. I really admire her spirit. I can't wait to hear how she gets on and all the fabulous things she'll get up to. It will be something to tell her grandchildren, that's for sure.'

Sam looked down at Abbey, tipping up her chin to look at him. 'You're pretty damn capable in your own right too, though, you know. Kids like Rhi wouldn't have the wherewithal or the stamina for that weekend we have planned in Wales. Takes proper courage to do that.'

Abbey laughed, playfully squeezing his waist, which she discovered to her delight was a ticklish spot and had Sam yelping and wriggling away.

'Stop it. You'll get us thrown out of this cab.'

'I thought Rhi was a bit subdued tonight, actually,' said Abbey, nestling back down on Sam's chest. 'She told me that she and Luke have decided to stay as friends and I think she was a little down-hearted about that, but once she gets out to Australia I'm sure she'll soon forget about her love life here. What she needs to do is to meet a blond, bronzed surfer to take her mind off everything.'

Sam puffed out his cheeks and made a show of exhaling a big noisy breath. 'Thank goodness you haven't got the travel bug, then. I'd hate to think that your head might be swayed by a hunky Aussie surfer just as soon I was out of sight.'

'No... not me.' She giggled. 'Although...' She left the word hanging.

'What?'

'Well, maybe a rugged Welsh sheep farmer might do it for me instead.'

Now it was Sam's turn to tickle Abbey, and she giggled, sputtering into Sam's chest to muffle her squeals of pain and pleasure, not wanting to draw the attention of the taxi driver, until she had to beg Sam to stop.

'Actually,' he said, once calm had been restored. 'I think there's still a chance for Rhi and Luke. I think he's pretty keen on her. He's probably just waiting until she comes home to see if they both still feel the same way about each other then.'

'Yeah, maybe you're right.' Abbey fell silent for a moment, wondering if Sam knew more than he was letting on. 'I'd love to see them get together. They'd be so good for one another. Even though they're complete opposites – he's laid-back and she's a real powerhouse – they seem to really complement each other.'

And didn't Rhi, like Abbey, deserve some happiness with a decent man after her mistreatment at the hands of Jason? They both did. And right now, Abbey was savouring the sensation of snuggling up to Sam, a properly decent man as her dad had described him. From her vantage point, there was no disputing that fact.

Back at the cottage they received a warm welcome from Lady, who had spent the evening curled up on the sofa. She'd made herself right at home at Abbey's place, making it her own, even though she dictated where she would be sleeping: either in front of the wood burning-stove, prime position on the sofa or on Abbey's bed, depending on whether Abbey was sleeping in there too.

Sam didn't make any such presumptions. He'd already remarked how Abbey's sofa was very comfortable as a make-do bed and how that would suit him just fine this evening, although his opinion may have had more to do with the fact that the last time he'd slept there, he'd had Abbey snuggled up beside him, something that had made him very happy. Only tonight, Abbey had other plans in store.

'Come on,' she said, taking him by the hand. There was no way she could wait a moment longer. She had waited far too long as it was. 'Let's go to bed,' she said, leading him up the stairs.

39

Lizzie woke on Monday morning after having had the most restless night of her life. She'd been so worried about missing her alarm that she'd startled awake every hour or so, checking the time before falling into a troubled half-sleep again. At 5 a.m. she admitted defeat and climbed out of bed, the butterflies already building in her tummy. She padded downstairs and filled the kettle, pulling a mug from the cupboard and popping a teabag inside, aware that this would be the last occasion she'd be following her familiar daily routine for a little while. To think that in less than forty-eight hours she would be on the other side of the world, getting to see her daughter, Katy, for the first time in years and finally meeting her dear little granddaughter, Rosie. There'd been occasions when she'd believed she wouldn't see them again until they returned to the UK. Of course, she still felt nervous about the journey ahead of her, but it was a good and exciting kind of apprehension. Thank goodness Rhi would be there to hold her hand.

Drinking her tea in the conservatory, overlooking her little garden, she was glad that her neighbour would be popping round to mow the lawns and water the flower beds in her absence, and Bill had volunteered to keep an eye on the house and pick up any post that arrived. She would miss him, their daily conversations, his sunny smile and his constant encouragement and support, but she knew they would pick up their relationship just where they'd left it, on her return, and she couldn't wait to share with him all the news from Australia. She'd changed her mind about wanting to see him today as well.

'Would you mind coming round on Monday morning before we head off to the airport in the taxi? I think it would help to see a friendly face and I want to give you a final big hug before we leave.'

'I was just waiting for you to ask,' Bill had said, kissing her lightly on the forehead.

She glanced at her watch. It would be another hour or so before Bill arrived, and then Rhi was expected a little later. She gave a wry smile, imagining Rhi still fast asleep in her bed, not getting up until the very last minute, quickly getting showered and dressed, hugging her mum goodbye and heading out of the door with her backpack slung on her back, without a care in the world. Lizzie, by contrast, was sitting, contemplating, and it wasn't helping her nerves in the slightest. She had nothing to do because everything was already done. Her bags were packed, the laundry was cleaned and put away, the dishwater emptied, the houseplants watered, the house as pristine as it had ever been.

She thought about the party the other night and how the house had been abuzz with goodwill and laughter. It had been quite some time since the place had been so full of energy and life. How lucky she was to have found such lovely friends who had quickly become an important part of her life. She would try, while she was away, to find a special souvenir for each of them as a small token of her thanks.

'So you're all packed up and ready to go,' said Bill when he turned up, surveying the multitude of cases and bags in the hallway with amusement.

'I've been packed for days now. Most of it is presents for the family, so I hope I haven't forgotten anything vital. If I have, well, I shall have to do without it.' She chuckled, a carefree laugh that had so enamoured Bill from the first time he met her. He would certainly miss her while she was away, her vitality and enthusiasm, but most of all he was delighted that Lizzie was finally following her dream to see her daughter. 'Thanks for being here. Come on through, and I'll make us a coffee. I could do with the distraction.'

When Rhi arrived a little while later, the excitement levels rose further in the house with lots of nervous giggling and squeals. In her own mind, Lizzie was the same age as Rhi, about to go off on a new adventure, her heart full of love for Bill and for her far-flung family. She couldn't wait to tell Katy about Bill and her new friends, apprehensive and excited at how Katy might react, but knowing instinctively that her daughter would only be pleased for her.

'Is that the taxi?' Lizzie asked, hearing a car pull up outside. She jumped up from her seat and dashed to the front window, peering outside. It was earlier than expected, but it didn't really matter. The sooner they got on their way, the better. She saw the driver climb out of the car, and realised immediately it wasn't their lift. 'It's Luke,' she said, turning to Rhi.

'Really?' Now it was Rhi's turn to jump up from her seat. What was he doing here? she wondered, her heart beating excitedly as curiosity got the better of her. Lizzie went to open the door and Rhi craned an ear to hear what he was saying, but she didn't need to eavesdrop for long because suddenly he was there in the doorway with something clutched in his hand, a smile on his face.

'Let me show you those plants I want you to water for me,' said Lizzie, diplomatically dragging Bill away into another room.

Left alone together in Lizzie's living room, Rhi felt uncharacteristically self-conscious. 'This is a surprise.'

'I thought I'd pop by on my way to work to wish you good luck and, oh, to give you this,' he said, as though it was an afterthought. He handed her a neatly wrapped parcel and Rhi's heart lifted, not knowing what could be within the pretty paper. Her fingers tingled with excitement as she carefully uncovered what was inside. She gasped, pulling out a turquoise woven threaded bracelet with a silver clasp. On it were two silver cubes, one engraved with the word 'Australia', the other with 'Safe travels'. 'I think the idea is that you can add other blocks to the bracelet as you go along, a reminder of all the different places you get to visit on your travels.'

Rhi wasn't sentimental, but Luke's lovely gesture was so unexpected and personal that it touched her deeply inside in a way that she would never have imagined possible. She blinked away the tears prickling at her eyes.

'It's beautiful.' She slipped it onto her wrist, her fingers struggling to fix the clasp until Luke stepped in to gently close it tight, his hand lingering on her arm. 'I'm never going to take it off. Thank you.' She looked up into his piercing blue eyes, feeling lost there again, taking all her willpower to drag her gaze away from him. 'I would kiss you, but after how badly that ended the last time, I won't,' she said, with a wry smile.

'I'll be disappointed if you don't. Come here,' he said, pulling her into his embrace and kissing her gently on the lips. She had no time to think before the sensation of his mouth upon hers was sending ripples of pleasure along her entire body. She'd dreamt of kissing Luke on so many occasions and now, when she'd least expected it, it was happening and it turned out to be everything she'd imagined it to be and so much more.

'See, that wasn't so bad, was it?' she said, coming up for air and smiling.

'Not bad at all,' he agreed with a smile, his blue eyes shining with affection.

Now she had him in her arms, she didn't want to let him go. Hundreds of different thoughts and ideas assailed Rhi's mind as she stood in such close proximity to Luke, his scent toying with her nostrils. How could she possibly make sense of any of them?

'So...?' she ventured. There was so much she wanted to say, but she had no idea where to even begin. 'What do you think... you know, about us... Do you...?'

'Hey, stop. Let's not. Not now. We're friends, right?' He took hold of her hand and squeezed it tight. 'That's all that matters. I didn't want you going away thinking there was any bad feeling between us. There isn't. You're going to have the time of your life and I can't wait to hear about all your adventures when you get home again.'

'Yeah,' she sighed, knowing he was right. And, at least, Luke was looking to the future, to a time when she would be home again. There could be no promises or expectations, but Rhi knew in her heart that spending three months on the other side of the world wasn't going to make a blind bit of difference to the way she felt about Luke. She only hoped it might be the same for him. 'Good luck with the job,' she called after him as she waved goodbye from the doorstep, her heart fluttering as her fingers played with the new bracelet on her arm.

He turned round and gave her a thumbs up, that distinctive broad grin on his face. It would be the image she carried all the way around Australia and home again.

'The taxi should be here any moment now,' said Lizzie a few moments later, when Luke had left. She glanced at her watch, popped to the loo for the umpteenth time that morning and then peered out of the window again, as though the very act might hurry the taxi along. Just then her phone rang and she leapt to answer it. If her nerves had been playing up when she first woke up, they were positively in overdrive now.

Rhi noticed Lizzie's face crease with concern as she listened on the phone.

'Oh dear, are you sure? Is there no one else that could take us? I see, yes, I do understand. No, never mind. We'll get something sorted.'

When Lizzie came off the phone, her face was ashen white and neither Rhi nor Bill were under any misapprehension as to what the telephone conversation had been about.

'It was the taxi firm. They can't come now. The car has broken down on the side of the road and all the other drivers are out on the school run. He said they might be able to get someone to us in an hour and a half, but that's far too late. Oh, I knew something was bound to go wrong. Perhaps it's a sign from the heavens that I shouldn't get on that plane after all.' With every word that she spoke, her voice cracked further with emotion.

'Now don't talk like that, love. If only I had my car I'd willingly drive you there, but it's in the garage until tomorrow.'

'Let me phone Sam, see if he's available.' Lizzie paced up and down her living room, clearly flustered. 'He did offer to drive us but I'd already booked the taxi by then. I just hope he can come now or else I don't know what we'll do.'

'Try him first, then, and if he can't do it, we'll find someone else who can. I promise you, we'll get you both to the airport, one way or another.'

'Don't worry, Lizzie,' said Rhi, rushing to her side and putting a comforting arm around her shoulder. 'This is just a blip.'

'I can't be doing with blips. What happens if we miss our flight? How will I ever explain that to Katy? She'll think I've done it on purpose to avoid getting on that plane. I'm not sure I could go through all this again.'

'Come on, love.' Bill took hold of Lizzie's hand. 'Don't fret. Give Sam a call.'

Fortunately, Sam picked up immediately and before Lizzie had finished explaining what had happened, he told her he was on his way. After what seemed like an interminable wait, but was actually only ten minutes, Sam's jeep pulled up outside the house, a sight that lifted Lizzie's mind.

'Thank goodness you're here.' Lizzie could have wept as she walked up her front path to greet Sam and quickly noticed he had a passenger with him.

'Abbey, I'm sorry to drag you both out like this. I've just remembered, it's your day off, isn't it? I hope we haven't spoilt your plans.'

'Not at all. We were just going to have a lazy day so there's nothing to worry about. Come here,' she said, able to detect how wobbly Lizzie was just by looking at her. She wrapped her in a big hug. 'There's nothing to worry about. You'll be at the airport in plenty of time.'

'Thank goodness,' said Lizzie with a heartfelt sigh. 'Sam saves the day again!'

'Are we ready to go?' He reappeared after having loaded all the bags in the back of the car.

'Sam, you are an absolute sweetheart. I can't thank you enough.' Lizzie and Rhi climbed into the car and Lizzie wound down the window, a big smile on her face, her relief evident to see.

'What are you two doing there?' she said to Bill and Abbey, standing on the kerbside. 'Please come with us. There's plenty of room in the car. That's all right with you, isn't it, Sam?'

'Of course, the more the merrier! Jump aboard!'

With Lizzie clutching on to Bill's arm in the back of the car and Abbey on her other side, and Rhi in the front passenger seat, they finally got on their way to the airport. Sam's presence brought a sense of calm and authority to the proceedings and Lizzie's previous panic dissipated into the air, surrounded as she was by her friends. Rhi gazed out of the window, drinking in the changing landscape, her fingers twiddling with the bracelet on her arm, her mind replaying her kiss with Luke. She could go away without any sense of regret now, knowing that there was no bad feeling between the pair of them. If anything, there'd been the beginnings of a new connection and the memory of that sweet, delicious and all-too-fleeting kiss would keep her going while she was away.

'We made it!' exclaimed Lizzie when they finally arrived at the airport, and Rhi went off to find a trolley for all the bags. 'Thank you all for getting us here. There was a moment when I thought all our plans might crumble.'

Bill and Lizzie hugged so tightly that Abbey had to wonder if Lizzie might ever let go of her dad. It softened her heart to see the deep affection they held for each other. Their relationship had grown so easily and organically. Neither of them seemed to have been racked with self-doubt or had overthought the prospect of them getting romantically involved. They simply went with the flow, enjoying each other's company, seeing where the new and exciting journey took them. Was it because they were that little bit older? Abbey mused, and time was too precious for them to play games? Either way, it was lovely to see and Abbey had already decided to follow their lead in her relationship with Sam.

Once all the hugs and goodbyes were done, Bill, Abbey and Sam waved off the intrepid travellers as they went through the door to Departures. When they were beyond the closed doors, out of sight, Sam let out a big sigh of relief.

'Mission accomplished,' he said with a smile.

40

'You were so lovely with Lizzie today,' sighed Abbey, thinking what an all-round superhero Sam had been, rushing to Lizzie's rescue. 'You could see her mood visibly pick up when we arrived, and she seemed to settle down immediately knowing you were there.'

They were back at the cottage, having dropped off Bill at his home with a promise to pick him up later for a pub supper. In the meantime, they'd taken Lady for a long and leisurely walk over at Primrose Woods, and were now decompressing over tea and digestive biscuits.

'Ah, well, she's like a second mum to me. I have to make sure she's okay. She's always looked out for me well enough. This is a huge step for her. I feel incredibly proud of how far she's come.'

'Me too. Dad couldn't have found a lovelier person to fall in love with.'

Seeing Sam taking control and reassuring Lizzie had brought home to Abbey again what a lovely, genuine man he was, if she'd needed any further convincing. She'd obviously seen it in the way he treated her, with kindness and respect, but to witness it in the way he interacted with others, especially Lizzie, made her heart swell. She hated to make comparisons, but seeing how Sam treated the people around him only highlighted what a self-centred and selfish prig Jason had been. Why had she stuck with him for so long? She shook her head ruefully, a shiver running down her spine. Every time she thought of him, she was reminded of what a lucky escape she'd had.

'Do you think it's as serious as that already?' Sam asked.

'Yes, I think it is. I think it's pretty clear that they're utterly devoted to each other. I can imagine the pair of them growing old together.'

'Let's hope they do.' Sam fell quiet, lost in thought for a moment. 'Do you think it's possible to meet someone and to know, if not immediately, then pretty soon afterwards that you want to spend the rest of your life with that person that you've found, you know, the one?'

Sam's gaze locked on to hers and she felt her insides tumble. Her face tingled with anticipation as she pondered on his question. Avoiding his gaze, she reached for the bun on her head, pulling out the tie and allowing her red hair to tumble onto her shoulders.

'I'm not sure. I suppose it is. It happens all the times in the films,' she said lightly.

'Have you ever experienced it, though, personally?'

Still his gaze didn't falter and she felt her toes curl under his scrutiny. What could she say, without exposing her feelings and her vulnerability? Instead, she hesitated for a moment as she considered how to reply.

'I'm not sure. I'm hardly an expert when it comes to matters of the heart. What about you?' she asked casually, turning the question back on him.

'Yep, I think it's entirely possible.' He stood up from his chair and went across to where Abbey was sitting, reaching out a hand to lift her to her feet. His hand held her cheek as his gaze caressed her face, the space between them sizzling with electricity. 'I didn't think so before I met you, Abbey, but right from the start I felt a connection with you that I wouldn't have believed was possible with someone I barely knew. Does that sound crazy?'

She shook her head, smiling.

'My experience of relationships was that they were hard work, that you had to tiptoe around trying to discover whether you actually really liked the person, if they shared the same sense of humour and values as you, if you liked the same things, if you felt you could ever see a future together. Almost as though you needed to tick items off a checklist. There always seemed so much pressure to get it right. None of those thoughts came into my head when I met you. I just really liked you and knew that I wanted to see you again. I thought about you the whole time. I still do. We just seemed to click on a very instinctive natural level. Did I imagine that?'

She could hear the passion in his words and see the fire in his eyes as he delivered them. He was so close she could feel his breath on her face as he spoke.

'No, I felt exactly the same.' Abbey wasn't afraid to admit it. She'd been surprised by her strong and immediate attraction to Sam, and those feelings only intensified with every subsequent meeting. She'd worried that those intense emotions were a result of being on the rebound from Jason and that Sam might never reciprocate her feelings. It was wonderful and reassuring to learn he'd felt exactly the same way.

'Thank God,' said Sam, looking wholly relieved, his hands now resting on her waist. 'What I'm trying to say is that I always felt as though I was looking for something, but I had no idea what that was, and then when I met you everything fell into place. It was as though I'd found what I'd been looking for.'

'Really?' She gazed up into his dark, beguiling eyes, her whole body tingling with expectation. He was saying everything she'd dared hope for.

'It's the absolute truth. What I'm trying to say in my clumsy and awkward way – not the way they do it in the films at all – is that I've fallen for you, big time. And there's nothing I can do about that, even if I wanted to.'

She pressed her mouth against his, silencing his words, soaking in his scent, lost in the moment as his delicious, tender kisses greeted her. Her body felt as light as air, her head spun and for a moment she thought her legs might buckle beneath her. Sam pulled away, looking beseechingly into her eyes.

'I don't expect you to feel the same. Not yet anyway. You've just come out of a relationship and I appreciate how difficult that must have been. I don't want to put any pressure on you, but I'm hoping that... you know... we can have some kind of future together.'

She'd always been terrible at hiding her emotions. And she would have no idea how to play it cool or be elusive. What would be the point? If her relationship with Jason had taught her anything, it was that any future relationships would need to be based on absolute honesty and trust.

'It's what I want too, Sam, with every inch of my being,' she said breathlessly. 'When I first met you I wasn't sure if I could trust my emotions. I fancied you madly...'

'Well, you can hardly be blamed for that,' quipped Sam.

She shook her head at him indulgently. 'Yes, but I didn't know if was just lust or if those feelings were an indication of something much bigger and stronger. I quickly realised I was falling for you too and the strength of my feelings frightened me. Part of me wanted to run in the opposite direction. I knew I didn't want to be hurt again.'

'Hey, come here.' He pulled her close, hugging her to his chest, his hand running through her hair. 'I promise you, I'd never want to hurt you. I just want us to be together and see where this adventure takes us. The three of us.' He looked down at Lady, who was snoring melodiously, unaware of the heightened emotions in the room. 'I've never felt like this about anyone before. All I think about is you and the future we'll have together, whatever it might involve. I love you, Abbey.'

She closed her eyes, resting her head on his chest, his words caressing her in a golden glow.

'I love you too, Sam,' she said, unafraid to let her true feelings be known. It wasn't as if she could do anything about those emotions, even if she wanted to, which she absolutely didn't. She was simply revelling in the sensation of being in love with a wonderful man.

His kisses came more urgently now as his hands swept over her soft curves, her body alighting to his touch. Sam took her by the hand and led her towards the bottom of the stairs. She glanced at her watch, fanning the heat spreading through her body. She laughed, seeing her own desire mirrored in Sam's eyes, reading his mind perfectly.

'We can't. We're meeting Dad in less than half an hour. As much as I might love to,' she said, laughing, 'it will have to wait until later.' Although how Abbey mustered up the self-control in the face of Sam's attentive and not unwelcome advances, she had no idea.

'Nonsense,' said Sam, his eyes shining brightly. 'We don't always have to take our time. Although that's lovely too. Sometimes you need to seize the moment and this is definitely one of those times. Come on, quickly,' he said, chasing her up the stairs. 'We'll get to your dad's on time, I'll make sure of that.'

Seizing the moment? She didn't need any persuasion that it was absolutely the right thing to do.

EPILOGUE

'Honestly, why would you want to be trekking across Australia in the sunshine when you could be here in the pouring rain?' Sam had pulled Abbey into a doorway as they tried to find shelter from the sudden downpour. With his thumb, he wiped away the rivulets of rain streaming down Abbey's face, and she laughed, enjoying the exquisitely damp sensation, without a single care in the world.

'I can think of no other place in the universe I would rather be.'

'Well, that's just as well, then,' he said, laughing, touching his cold nose against hers. 'Because I'm not sure I could do a thing about this weather even if I wanted to.'

In fairness, it was the first time it had rained since they'd arrived on the Pembrokeshire Coast and they'd been lulled into a false sense of security by the unexpectedly warm weather. They'd spent their days waking up late, taking a leisurely breakfast in the fully glazed oak extension, which offered panoramic views of the bay, sitting companionably chatting or reading or doing the crossword, or sometimes just luxuriating in the wonderful scenery. They both commented on how they could simply sit there all day admiring the view, but Lady would allow no such thing. Before too long, she was running up and down towards the door, eager to get outside and gallop along the sandy path that led to the beach. Once there she would race to the shore, chasing the waves back and forth, never growing tired of the game. Now after a whole day of exploring, the bedraggled dog huddled close to Sam's side, shivering, trying to avoid the downpour.

'Come on,' said Sam, 'let's make a dash for it.'

They ran back to the cottage, laughing all the way. Back indoors, Abbey lit the wood-burning stove while Sam quickly rubbed Lady down with a towel, drying off her fur, before making mugs of warming hot chocolate, and settling down in the two cosy armchairs that overlooked the bay, with Lady stretched out on the shaggy rug between them. This had been a last-minute break away, booked on a whim, after several glasses of red wine late one evening. Both of them had managed to take some days off work either side of a weekend and they'd been lucky to find such a beautiful cottage in such a stunning location.

'Look,' said Abbey, passing her phone to Sam. 'Here are the latest photos from Rhi.'

They'd been coming thick and fast from across the seas. Rhi was clearly having a wonderful time on her adventure, sharing photos of magnificent sunsets, beautiful coastlines and of herself on the steps to the Sydney Opera House. In each of her shots, she was looking bronzed and lean, in shorts and strappy tops, sunglasses perched on her head, her radiance exuding from the camera.

'She's living her best life, which is wonderful to see. Jason will be nothing but a distant memory.' That was certainly the case for Abbey too. If Jason crept into her thoughts at all now, it was just as an annoying reminder of a time that she was pleased to have left behind. She had no reason to think about Jason, not when she had Sam in her life. 'I'm so pleased for her,' Abbey said, poring over the photos. 'I can't believe it's been almost three weeks since they left. Before we know it, Lizzie will be home again.'

Jason might have been a distant memory for Rhi, but Luke certainly wasn't. Rhi kept in regular contact with him, sending messages, photos and videos. If anything, she believed their friendship was deepening as a result of the enforced distance between them. Often, she wondered if he might be missing her. Not half as much as she was missing him, she suspected. When she returned home, Christmas would be on the horizon and there would be plenty of opportunities for festive celebrations and Christmas kisses under the mistletoe, a chance to take their relationship to the next level. She really couldn't wait.

There'd been plenty of photos sent from Lizzie as well. She looked so happy at the heart of her family, cuddling her little granddaughter, Rosie, walking hand in hand with her in the park, making up for lost time. She'd arranged her holiday dates perfectly because within a week of her arrival at Katy's, the new baby was born, a brother for Rosie, Pip James, who weighed a snuggly 6lb 3oz and had a full head of jet-black hair. Rosie was immediately taken with her little brother and spent her time gently stroking his head and offering him a selection of her soft toys. Lizzie took over the running of the house, keeping Katy and Brad supplied with endless cups of tea and preparing Katy's favourite meals, entertaining Rosie and providing another pair of helping hands with Pip when needed. Lizzie was in her element, finally able to properly fulfil her role as Nana for the first time. She was already dreading having to leave them to return home, but she was overjoyed in the knowledge that she'd been able to give her daughter the support she'd needed at such a vulnerable time. They were already making plans for the family's visit back to the UK next year. Lizzie couldn't wait to introduce them to Bill in person, although they had already met him over a noisy and chaotic video call.

In Lizzie's absence, Bill had been keeping busy catching up with some old friends, relationships he'd let slide after the death of his wife. He'd reached out and arranged a number of lunch dates with colleagues he used to work with and friends he played golf with. These days he had a renewed enthusiasm for life and he could only put that down to Lizzie. She'd given him a motivation and purpose in life that had been missing for far too long. Only another couple of weeks and he'd be getting ready to go and collect her from the airport. He couldn't wait to see her again and to hear all about the family and her new grandchild.

A couple of times Bill had met up with Luke and Sam in the pub after the two younger men had played badminton together. Their matches were always very competitive, but Luke was on a winning streak and Sam had yet to beat his younger and fitter opponent, but he certainly hadn't given up trying yet. Luke had told Sam he'd been offered a new job and was looking into a few other opportunities, before deciding the next step in his career path.

After their short romantic break away in the wilds of Wales, Sam and Abbey returned home, enjoying spending every possible moment together, with Sam, and Lady too, pretty much moving into the cottage. Abbey didn't worry that it might seem too good to be true. Nor did she dwell on those niggling doubts and hesitations that had so troubled her until recently. Sam had demonstrated what a thoroughly lovely and decent man he was, and that was enough for her. The fact that he was funny, intelligent and downright sexy too, with a culinary flair to rival a top chef, was simply an added bonus. These days Abbey was all about being spontaneous, carefree and embracing the moment and there was no one else in the world she would rather do that with than Sam.

It was funny to think that only a few months ago she'd been anxiously preparing for her wedding day, which was supposed to herald a whole new chapter in her life. It had certainly done that but not in a way she could ever have expected. The reality of her life after the big day had far exceeded all her expectations. She'd ditched her cheating ex and, at her lowest moment, when she'd least expected it, she'd met the man of her dreams. Who would have believed it? She'd allowed herself to let go and fall in love in a way that she hadn't even thought possible. With Sam at her side, she had become the best version of herself, confident, happy and positive, and she simply couldn't imagine a future without him now. Christmas was just around the corner, and she was excited to see what delights the festive season would have in store for them both, and for the Primrose Fancies too. Whatever it might be, she was certain that there would be plenty of love, laughter and good times ahead for them all.

ACKNOWLEDGMENTS

Goodness me, it's so lovely to be here! It's been a little while - too long really - since I've been waiting excitedly for the publication of a new novel, a new series in fact! It's great to be back in the writing groove.

Firstly, I have to thank my editor, Sarah Ritherdon, for giving me the opportunity to join Boldwood. I am so delighted and relieved to be back working with you! Your editorial insight, kindness and encouragement have helped immensely in bringing this story to publication and I feel very lucky to be in such a wonderfully safe pair of hands.

Thanks to Sue Lamprell and her team for your copy-editing and proof-reading expertise.

The whole Boldwood team have been wonderful in welcoming me aboard. I consider myself very fortunate to be part of such a young and dynamic publishing force and I'm excited to be working alongside you all. What a hugely talented and award winning group of people you are! Thank you all for your help behind the scenes. Thanks too to my lovely fellow Boldwood authors for your friendship and generosity.

As always, a big, big thanks to my lovely family, Nick, Tom and Ellie for your constant love and support. I couldn't do it without you!

And finally, a huge hug of appreciation to all those readers who have kept in touch asking when the next book would be out. Your messages of support really helped to keep me writing through those uncertain times. The book is finally here and I really hope you will love reading about these characters and their stories as much as I have enjoyed creating them.

MORE FROM JILL STEEPLES

We hope you enjoyed reading *Starting Over at Primrose Cottage*. If you did, please leave a review.

If you'd like to gift a copy, this book is also available as an ebook, digital audio download and audiobook CD.

Sign up to Jill Steeples' mailing list for news, competitions and updates on future books.

https://bit.ly/JillSteeplesNews

ABOUT THE AUTHOR

Jill Steeples is the author of many successful women's fiction titles – most recently the Dog and Duck series - all set in the close communities of picturesque English villages. She lives in Bedfordshire.

Visit Jill Steeples's website: https://www.jillsteeples.co.uk

Follow Jill on social media:

 twitter.com/jillesteeples
 facebook.com/jillsteepleswriter

ABOUT BOLDWOOD BOOKS

Boldwood Books is a fiction publishing company seeking out the best stories from around the world.

Find out more at www.boldwoodbooks.com

Sign up to the Book and Tonic newsletter for news, offers and competitions from Boldwood Books!

http://www.bit.ly/bookandtonic

We'd love to hear from you, follow us on social media:

facebook.com/BookandTonic

twitter.com/BoldwoodBooks

instagram.com/BookandTonic

Made in the USA
Monee, IL
18 May 2022

96658437R00157